House of Nightshade

G. L. Jones

Published by G. L. Jones, 2024.

HOUSE OF NIGHTSHADE

First edition. July 2, 2024.

Written by G. L. Jones.

For John

Preface

The floorboards creaked. Someone was coming. She crouched in the shadows of the room, realising instantly that she had blown her cover. Why would the lights be off in one of the loungerooms on a raging night at House of Nightshade? They'd know someone was hiding.

Damn it, now I'm done for.

If they had killed someone here once, they could do it again.

She held her breath as the walking slowed, furrowing her brow in an attempt to assume a face of confidence. She hoped someone downstairs saw her running and raised an alarm. If she screamed, surely the people down the hall would hear.

She looked down, reassured by the knife in her hand, its blade glinting in the dark. She could do this if it came down to it — couldn't she?

Chapter One

"But I don't want to go among mad people," Alice remarked.
"Oh, you can't help that," said the Cat: "we're all mad here." — Lewis
Carroll

D*ing-dong.*

It was an overcast spring day; the clouds had been on the cusp of weeping all morning. Addilyn waited apprehensively at the top of concrete stairs lined by gothic woven iron fences. The door in front of her was painted a shiny black, a decorative gold knocker perched in the centre.

This particular road seemed deserted. Addi was surprised by the quiet, being merely a couple of streets from the bustling, dirty main strip of the inner-city suburb with its small convenience stores, heaving cafes, and taxi drivers loitering opposite the train station in a bid for customers.

The smell of cigarettes wafted by with the lazy breeze. Addi tilted her head. A young woman with pin-up blonde curls and a heart-shaped face leant out an open window dressed in a scarlet bra. As if alerted by Addi's gaze she looked down, taking a drag and examining the newcomer nonchalantly.

Addi averted her eyes as she heard steps thudding towards her from inside the house, nervously twirling a strand of her brown, frizzy hair around her finger. She wished she had something better to wear — more suited to the venue — than her old, stripy T-shirt and faded jeans sitting baggily around her slight waist. Her foster parents had never bothered to buy her new clothes. They'd grumbled whenever she asked them for money, slapping spare coins in her hand despite Addi informing them that a decent top was at least forty dollars. As a result, she'd been forced to scavenge through racks at the local op-shop.

The door opened with a creak, revealing a tall silhouette in the doorway.

"Good afternoon." The voice was well-rehearsed faux velvet. "How can I help you?"

Tall, dark and handsome, was Addi's first impression. "Hi," she wiped her sweaty palms on her jeans. "Um, my name's Addilyn. I'm hoping to speak to the manager?"

"Speaking," came the slick reply. The man held himself with confidence and a plastered-on smile.

"Oh, great. I'm here because I saw the job post on Instagram. I'd love to be considered."

The man looked her up and down. Addi folded her scrawny arms uncomfortably.

"Well, Addilyn, this is indeed timely. My name's Freddy, pleasure to meet you." He held out his hand, revealing a tattoo on his forearm underneath the rolled light-blue shirt sleeve: two shaded circles drawn neatly atop one another. She shook it loosely, feeling his rough palm, and he invited her in. "Let's have a chat."

Addi stepped through the doorway onto a merlot runner that stretched the length of the hallway, the dark floorboards creaking with every step despite the thick carpet. More black doors with old-fashioned handles led off the dim hall, which was spotted with vintage tables holding antique candlesticks and elaborate flower arrangements. A tall mirror with a speckled frame leant on a table across the opposite wall.

Freddy put a hand on one of the doors, pushing it ajar. "Please." He gestured for her to enter.

The cold room was void of sunlight, a result of only one small window on the side wall looking directly at the brick wall of the terrace next door. Instead, yellow light emitted from a small chandelier hanging above. A chaise lounge stretched the entire right-hand side of the room, an empty fireplace to the left.

Side tables and plump armchairs scattered with pillows filled the remaining space. A couple of folded, ornate screens leant in the corner next to the most magnificent gramophone Addi had ever seen, a crate of records in peeling cases beside it.

Freddy recaptured her attention. "Would you like a coffee? Something else?"

"Oh, no, thank you." Addi refused out of politeness, awkwardly perching on a faded, upholstered chair.

Freddy sat on the lounge and reached into his pocket, pulling out a cigar and lighter. He stuck the cigar in his mouth, clicked the lighter and puffed, leaning back and crossing one foot over his knee and stretching an arm out casually over the top of the couch. "Do you know much about House of Nightshade?"

Addi recalled what she'd seen online. "Um... well that's the point, isn't it? It's supposed to be mysterious; a place to escape to. I mean, you're obviously a hospitality and performance venue," she added quickly, not wanting to sound like she didn't have a clue.

Freddy ran a hand through his hair, which was the shade of deep boot polish. "Exactly. My parents own it, they're currently in France — my mum adores the architecture there. They've been operating hospitality venues for over twenty years. My dad handles the operations side of it with me and my mum's the creative. She has an incredible mind." He smiled fondly.

Addie found the strong smell of his cigar distracting. "Wow, France."

Freddy continued. "House of Nightshade is a cabaret venue that combines performance, dining and hospitality. It's a place patrons come to forget about their mundane lives. We sell intrigue."

Addi leant forward. "How many people work here?"

Freddy sucked his cigar. "We have a large team of performers, exotic dancers, bar and wait staff, and a renowned chef. A House of Nightshade experience is one where guests don't want to leave; where they'll continue to buy tickets so they can chase the thrill of feeling like they've entered another world. That's the level of service we expect."

Addi slid her resume across the table along with a lie. "Well, I have experience waitressing, so you can pretty much slot me in wherever you need me."

Her face was red from painted-on confidence, but Freddy barely noticed as his eyes grazed over the resume fleetingly before letting it flutter back down onto the table between them. "Alright, let's do it. You're hired."

Addi couldn't believe it. After all her effort trying to invent a believable work experience stint, rehearsing lines for interview questions, and battling with nervousness so big she'd had to rush to the nearest public bathroom after getting off the bus, was this man seriously not even going to read a single line? Still, a smile crept onto her face as she felt excitement course through her. "Really?"

Smoke billowed from Freddy's lips. "Most staff live on premises and we have a room available if you're interested. Rent would be deducted from your weekly pay. Have you seen our rates?"

Addi tried to come across as composed, but her tell-tale expression gave her away. "Uh, yeah. I mean, yes. I actually do need somewhere to live so that would work."

"Great. Let's get you oriented." Freddy stood.

"Oh my god." It slipped out. Addi couldn't help it. Did she actually just get her first real job *and* have somewhere to stay that wasn't a foster home, for the first time ever? "Wow. Thank you so much!"

Freddy chuckled, the laugh lines on his face causing Addi to guess he was somewhere in his late thirties. "Don't thank me yet. You haven't met our head chef. Come." He gestured for her to follow. "This room used to be where our exotic dancers entertained clients one-on-one, by the way."

"Ah, right." Addi hoped the chair she'd sat on was clean.

"There are more on the first level." Freddy nodded at the half-open door across the hall as they strolled out. "My office is there. Guests have access to most of the House to explore."

As they passed different rooms, Addi noticed the place seemed to double as a gallery of collected antiques.

They reached a set of heavy double-doors at the end of the hallway. Freddy pushed them open and led Addi into a dingy bar lounge that looked like it belonged to an underground club. "Welcome to our main performance room."

Swanky jazz played in the background. The bar was to their right. Individual tables circled by mismatched chairs or upholstered armchairs littered the floor below a grand stage on which men and women in activewear were milling around, clearly in the middle of rehearsal. A grey-haired man with thick-rimmed glasses and a cigarette hanging from his mouth pointed around the stage, arguing with a voluptuous brunette Addi instantly recognised — she followed her online.

"We do table service, by the way," Freddy explained.

There was laughter from the stage, and Addi heard the grey-haired man shout, "From the top, people!"

The music restarted.

"This is the kitchen." Freddy shouldered through a set of swinging doors as Addi trailed him.

The steam hit her as soon as she walked in, along with a belligerent voice.

"...giant mess I tell ya! And it's me, all me, only me who bothers cleaning. Does anyone else notice? No! Does anyone else care? No! As usual, I do all the work." There was no one else in the room.

Addi peered through the billows at a stout silhouette upturning a colander of greens into an enormous pan. They hit the bottom with a sizzle.

Freddy announced them calmly. "Good afternoon, Ralph."

The chef started and turned, revealing a lined face with round eyes. His mouse-grey hair frizzed around his face, making him look like a mad scientist amidst the haze. He looked Addi up and down before turning back to the stove and shaking in some sauce. "You've got another one for me, Freddy? They're all the same. Let's see how she goes. She'll go. HA! None of them cope in this joint."

Freddy shot Addi a half-apologetic smirk. "This is Ralph, our chef. As you can see, years of heat and stress have not served him well. I will say this, though; he's committed." He talked to the back of the chef's head. "Ralph, this is Addilyn."

"Adelaide — what kind of a name is that?"

"No, Ad-di-lyn." Addi sounded it out slowly.

Ralph turned to look at her, as if surprised she'd talked back. "Ad-da-lin. Okay. We'll see, won't we? You know, I always say Freddy, don't I, I always say..." Freddy gestured for Addi to follow him again, and they started walking as Ralph continued, "how long will they last?' HA!"

"Dear Lord," Addi muttered as soon as they were out of the room. When Freddy let out a bark of laughter, she hastily amended. "Sorry. I just meant, he's interesting."

"He's certainly an acquired taste," Freddy agreed. "Don't worry, our cooks can hold a conversation, they'll help you in there. They start their shifts later."

Back in the main entertainment room, the jazz had been replaced with blaring cabaret music. Dancers flitted across the stage with giant feathers and other props. Ahead of them, the bespectacled director leant over the bar to reach for a spirit bottle and glass.

"Five o'clock already, is it?" Freddy commented wryly as they passed.

"It is somewhere in the world." The director eyed Addilyn as he poured himself a honey-coloured liquid. "Don't tell me you've got big dreams of being on Broadway, honey," he drawled, his mop of steel-grey hair flopping on his brow. He was stylishly dressed with a brightly-coloured scarf and vest.

Freddy introduced her. "Sawyer, this is our new waitress, Addilyn."

Addi was already forgetting everyone's names. "Hi." Addi managed a quick smile at Sawyer before rushing to keep up with Freddy, who'd strode back into the hallway and started ascending a rickety staircase.

He rattled off a reel of information as they climbed. "We're operational Wednesday to Sunday. Dinner and breakfast are provided. You'll be staying in our female dormitory – our living quarters are on the top two levels."

"So I'll have roommates?" Addi blurted.

"It's not exactly the Hilton but you'll get used to it." Freddy mistook her excitement for apprehension. "You'll have to buy your uniform: black dress pants with a white blouse. We'll give you suspenders and a bowtie." He swung around the bannister on the second level and continued up to a third.

Addi hated admitting to herself that buying her uniform would probably take the last of the cash she'd spent months pilfering from her foster parents' wallets. They mounted a fourth flight of stairs and travelled down the corridor at the top before Freddy stopped at the last door and turned the handle.

Addi took in the narrow room with ten single beds placed at regular intervals, chests of drawers and clothing racks between them, a beauty table and mirror at the far end. Wigs, eyeshadow palettes and colourful, sparkling clothes were strewn across the ground and beds, scarves thrown over lampshades and rugs covering the floorboards. Her eyes widened at the cigarette packs, women's magazines, wine bottles, lace G-strings and stray tampons left carelessly around the room. Some of the girls had strings of printed photos above their beds depicting blurry nightclub scenes and posed family shots. There were dying plants in empty liquor bottles on bedside tables, canvases with line drawings of naked women hanging on the wall and long necklaces dangling from bed posters. She breathed in a confusing mix of deodorants and perfumes. There were so many girly things in the one space; if she had ever wondered what it might be like to have sisters, this was it. A disorderly, dazzling disarray.

"You'll have to get used to the mess." Freddy mentioned condescendingly, "Our performance girls are apparently too important to clean. Now, let's see. We can give you Katie's old space."

Addi shadowed Freddy to a neatly-made bed and bare bedside table and dresser. "Bathrooms," he indicated a door at the end of the dormitory, half obscured by the drawers. "Laundry is down the hall. Meet me at the bar at, say, quarter to five, and I'll start your training."

As Addi nodded, the door opened with a *bang*. In walked the brunette, the one who'd been arguing with the director earlier. She fluttered her deep-brown eyes and sighed. "Stop perving in the girls' room, Freddy."

"Charming, Quinn. You can never resist making an impression, can you?" Freddy combated with a fake smile. "Quinn, this is Addilyn, our new waitress. Addilyn, meet our star performer. I'll leave you to settle in." With barely a glance at Quinn, he strode from the room.

Quinn studied Addi. "Just a warning now; don't even bother."

Addi stared at her blankly. "Sorry, with what?"

Quinn jerked her head at the door Freddy had just exited through. "I know he can put it on thick."

"Oh, no." Addi blushed. "He's not really... I mean, I didn't think of him like that."

Quinn's mocking eyes bore into her. "Okay, well, he normally likes fresh meat. If you wanna know what happened to the last occupant of your bed, she ran out of here crying after Freddy had his fun with her, then ditched her. Man, it's hot." She wiped her forehead, grabbed a bottle of water from her bedside table and took a swig.

Addi took her in, from the long, thick hair to the sporty crop-top and short, tight dance shorts. "You're Quinn Vandez," she said without thinking.

Quinn lowered the bottle from her lips, surveying Addi with an all-too-familiar expression — like she was that weird kid in school. "Uh, yeah...?"

Shit, Addi cursed in her head. Why couldn't she just introduce herself and start a conversation like a normal person? "I mean, I've been following you."

Quinn raised her perfectly waxed eyebrows.

"On Instagram!" Addi felt her face turning red. "That's actually how I found this job, from when you posted something about it. So thank you." She scrambled to make it light-hearted again.

"Oh, right." Quinn shrugged. "Have you been a waitress before?"

Addi avoided Quinn's scrutinising gaze. "Um, just a little bit."

Quinn raised her eyebrows again. "You don't seem very confident. Are you sure you're cut out for this place?"

Addi bristled. "It's not like I need a certificate to hand people their dinner."

Quinn laughed. "What was your name again?"

"Addilyn, but people normally just call me Addi."

"I like it," she said decisively. "Are you a dancer? I mean, are you starting as a waitress here because you want to get into the dancing side? It's fine, a few of the girls have done it that way."

Addi shook her head. "I can't dance. Besides, I don't think I quite have the... skills to dance at a place like this."

Quinn smirked. "You mean, to strip?"

Addi blushed again. "Well, yeah. I don't think I could ever be that seductive."

"That's a cop-out," Quinn said bluntly. "All women are sensual creatures. You're just scared."

Addi replied defensively. "Um, no, I'm just not interested."

"Right," Quinn said disbelievingly. "Well, at least I know you won't be coming after my job, then. I don't strip; the girls who work upstairs do that. I perform on the main stage." She gathered a wig and a bedazzled, short dress and threw them into her bag. "Let me guess. You're here because you're running away from some other situation, right?"

Addi grimaced. "Is it that obvious?"

Quinn popped some chewing gum into her mouth. "Most of us are running away from something. Enjoy your first night." With that, she swung her exercise bag onto her shoulder and left the room.

●

By the time Addi managed to jump on a train to the nearest shopping centre, buy her uniform and return, she was cutting it fine for her shift. She hurtled through the front door of House of Nightshade and took the stairs two at a time to have a one-minute shower and scrub up to the best of her ability.

"Damn pants." She grunted as she pulled and wiggled to get the tight trousers up her legs, then finally sealed the clasp and buttoned her blouse. She managed to twist her hair into some kind of bun before hurrying back downstairs to the main room.

Fittingly, frantic jazz played over the speakers when Addi walked in. Women twirled across the stage, their sparkling flapper dresses swinging around their thighs, so quickly it made Addi's head spin. Meanwhile, men in sequined vests tapped furiously to the upbeat tempo, following the migration of their female counterparts from one side of the platform to the other.

A man polished multicoloured tumblers behind the bar, turning from the dress rehearsal to eye-off Addi. He was wearing the prerequisite button-up shirt and black bowtie, his carefully gelled, spiked hair bleached so blonde it was almost white. Addi uneasily turned away to watch the performers .

"Kiss me, oh, kiss me!" She almost didn't recognise Quinn in a jet-black bob wig, eyes thickly winged and lined, belting out notes in a strong, sensual voice. The cabaret star spun into a fair-haired man in an open vest which revealed a toned torso before they joined the rest of the chorus, kicking, spinning, and swivelling their hips.

"Addilyn," came the smooth voice.

She started and turned to discover Freddy, holding another cigar lazily between two fingers.

He nodded at the dancers. "Dazzling, isn't it?"

The director, Sawyer, perched on a barstool as he followed all the beats, seeming much more pleased than he had been earlier. Two girls in corsets and silk robes loitered to his left, one leaning on the back of a chair, the second styling her hair, hairspray forming a halo-like cloud above her. Make-up and pins were scattered across the table.

"As soon as it hits five o'clock, girls..."

"We'll have it all cleaned up, Freddy." The girl who was styling smiled, flicking perfect blonde curls over her shoulder.

Freddy answered with a wink, before addressing Addi. "Alright, let's get you familiarised."

Addi inhaled the smell of cooking as they re-entered the kitchen. A teenage boy stood in the corner behind the stainless-steel sink, spraying plates with a tap and stacking them in trays next to a commercial dishwasher. Two junior cooks, male and female, had joined Ralph. Tattoos crawled up their necks and over their hands and fingers, and they each had multiple piercings in their ears and noses. The man waved at Freddy and Addi, knife in hand; the woman gave a shy smile before they both turned back to their meal prep.

"...whining and complaining. '*Can't you just look after the kid one weekend, Ralph?*'. I'm sick of it, I tell ya. I said, 'Jo, who's going to pay the bills then? Who's going to pay for her dresses and the roller-skating lessons, Jo? Not you, never lift a finger, Jo. No, I'll lift all the fingers and all I do is work...'"

"Ralph!" Freddy shattered the monologue. "He's divorced, by the way," he said as an aside to Addi.

Ralph looked around. "Ah, Freddy. Here's Adelaide, here she is. Showing her around, the young chap. Giving her the lay of the land, eh? Or as you'd probably prefer, just a lay-"

"Ralph!" Freddy shouted again, angrily. Addi blushed.

Ralph laughed loudly.

Freddy breezed on. "Her name is Addi*lyn*, remember? All of you, help her get her bearings. Addilyn, this is Logan and Danika." He indicated the tattooed cooks. "Twins. Come."

He showed Addi the fridge, freezer room and dry storeroom, explaining the set-up process. Addi nodded as he talked, trying to remember everything, knowing she'd forget. Freddy prattled on about the high-quality service and presentation, plus the temperament of the chef. Addi decided that her strategy was to spend as little time in the disaster zone that was the kitchen as possible.

Freddy then took her back to the bar. "You'll have to help run drink orders and keep everything clean and tidy. We're a full-range cocktail bar. You'll have to learn the menu."

They approached the blonde man with the gelled hair behind the bar, now polishing silver goblets. "This is our bar manager and my second-in-charge, Kyle. Kyle, this is Addilyn, our new waitress."

"Welcome to the crew." Kyle glanced down at her chest. "Addison, was it?"

"Addilyn," she corrected him.

Freddy's phone buzzed in his pocket. "Excuse me." He lifted it to his ear as he left. "Mum, what's wrong? Isn't it past midnight over there...?"

Without Freddy to lead the conversation, Addi smiled awkwardly at the barman.

Kyle spoke smarmily. "As long as you don't drink all my booze, and always give me first dibs on the food, we should get along just fine." He winked at her.

"Give it a break, Kyle," came a disapproving voice from behind.

It was the young man in the sequined vest who'd been dancing with Quinn, now wearing only the shiny, white pants, lean yet muscular torso on full display.

He leaned across the bar. "I'm parched. Could I get my coconut water?"

With a small huff, Kyle turned to the fridge and extracted a carton. "I think you'll find it's called 'polite conversation.'" He grumpily turned back to polishing goblets.

The two girls who'd been getting ready near Sawyer approached.

Kyle turned on a smile. "Ladies? Can I tempt you with a little poison before your shift?"

"Mmm, I don't know what's good," one said, playing with her hair.

Kyle leered at them. "Well, I came up with a little concoction you might like to try..."

"Now, ladies." Finished with his phone call, Freddy materialised next to the girls. "Let's not be getting *too* headless before work, shall we?"

Kyle simpered. "I'm sure they can handle it. They're good girls."

"Ugh." Addi groaned under her breath.

"That is the general consensus." The fair-haired dancer agreed, having overheard her. "I'm Leo, by the way."

She took his outstretched hand. "I'm Addilyn, but everyone calls me Addi."

"Addi it is. When did you get here?"

Addi fiddled with the lock of hair that was already falling out of its bun and curling around her face absent-mindedly. "Just today, actually."

"Cool. And don't worry, we're not all like that." He jerked his head at Kyle and Freddy, who were ogling the dancers together.

"Backstage everyone," Freddy called, puffing smoke next to the dancers. "Go on." His arms ghosted the girls' backs, gently guiding them.

They downed their drinks and followed the rest of the performers backstage.

"Gotta split," said Leo. "Good luck for your first shift." He gulped down his coconut water and disappeared through the velvet curtains.

"Alright, sweetheart." Freddy clapped Addi on the shoulder. "Showtime."

Chapter Two

"Ready? One, two, three."

Addi slung back the shot. The tequila burned her throat and she resisted the urge to spit it onto the table where she and Quinn were now sitting. She hurriedly sucked on a lime, her face pinched in dislike. "That is disgusting."

"Yep, I'm definitely a vodka raspberry kinda guy," Leo agreed with them from atop the now-sparkling-clean bar, swinging his legs over the counter

Quinn, having tossed back the spirit with ease, shook her head. "Pussies."

Leo shrugged breezily. "I'd rather be a pussy than drink that." He turned to Addi. "So, what do you think of this place? Wait, I'm gonna get juice." He disappeared momentarily behind the bar to retrieve a bottle from the fridge.

The performance room was like a ghost town compared to an hour ago. The guests had flocked in come nightfall, trading their tickets for a table. They'd drunk short tumblers of spirits, gulped down beers or sipped wine, sparkling or cocktails while the chef bellowed his ongoing monologue as he and the cooks churned out meal after meal. Addi had been lost in a flurry of bell *ding*s and lively burlesque music as she whirled in and out of the swinging kitchen doors, flailing in her attempt to learn the ropes.

Quinn and Leo were clearly the star performers, and Addi had caught them in glimpses between delivering martinis and serves of coq au vin. A drag queen had flitted onto the stage to entertain the crowd between acts in a flamboyant red, sparkling dress and brown, blown-out wig, seeming to be caked with more make-up than the entire cast combined. Addi wondered how on earth she managed to move herself so graciously in her towering, diamante-studded heels.

Other patrons had scattered throughout the house over the course of the night, enticed by the intoxicating offerings in the nooks and shrouded corners. Exotic dancers, including the two girls Addi had seen earlier, had perched themselves on the laps of various men. Late in the night, a drunk lady had decided to dredge up hazy memories of piano classes, pounding out notes on a timeworn piano with chipped keys in an adjacent room.

Now, Addi felt drained underneath her lingering buzz, her feet aching from the constant running around and heels red from rubbing against her new shoes. The alcohol definitely wasn't helping; she felt like she could fall asleep right there on the carpet. "It's amazing here. I mean, I feel like I'm in a zoo a little bit, but it's amazing."

Quinn snorted. "You're not wrong. Particularly with Freddy as our manager."

Leo returned with a bottle of orange juice, swigging before passing it to Addi, who reached for it gratefully. She decided she definitely wasn't a fan of tequila.

Leo explained. "He doesn't give a shit about this place. We don't know why he stays, to be honest."

Quinn rolled her eyes. "It's easier to get a comfy job from mummy and daddy than make it on your own."

"Who are his parents?" Addi asked.

"Emmerson and Emmeline." Quinn stumbled a little as she lifted herself from her chair and walked over to the wall, fetched one of the frames off its hook and passed it to Addi. "That's them." She tapped the glass with a French nail.

"Always watching." Leo gave a performative shudder.

It was as if the black-and-white photo had been taken from a fashion shoot. Addi could feel the elegance of the couple emanating through the glass. Emmerson, sporting a fitted jacket that hinted at designer and leaning on a walking stick, had the same mop of dark hair as Freddy and a stern gaze. Emmeline, dressed in a long, chiffon skirt and fashionable fur-trim coat reminiscent of the 70's, sat on a bench in front of him, curly hair piled atop her head.

"They look," Addi searched for the right word for a few seconds too long, "fabulous."

"Such a power couple," Quinn nodded. "Where are they now, Leo?"

"Le France," he answered with a French flair. "Eating croissants and sipping champagne."

Addi looked up, away from the photo, and felt her head spin. "Yeah, Freddy told me. Are they away often?"

Leo shrugged. "For the most part. That was their goal, I think. Create businesses that run without them so they can travel the world. Emmeline gave me the job here, and I haven't really seen her since."

Addi asked, intrigued, "Do you have to audition?"

"Pretty boy got poached," Quinn slurred, taking another swig of tequila.

Leo eyed her with good-natured concern. "Easy there, girl," then addressed Addi, miming quotation marks with his fingers. "Yes, I think I got 'talent spotted', as they say. I used to work at *Ezy Eggplant* further up the main road."

Addi fell into a fit of giggles.

"You little minx," Quinn snorted, lighting a cigarette. "Wanna drag?" she offered.

Leo shook his head, but Addi reached for it, feeling confident and adventurous from the alcohol, and took a puff. The smoke hit the back of her throat and she coughed it straight back out, scrambling for the juice.

Quinn thumped her back — the drinks had made her a lot warmer, Addi noticed. "Leo was one of the best performers in the area. I mean, still is. He had a rep."

"*Big reputation, big reputation*," Leo started, getting up and mocking a soloist, holding the juice bottle as his microphone. "*Ooh, you and me we got big reputations.*"

Quinn chucked a bottle cap at him.

Leo laughed. "Emmeline came in when I was working there one night. I still remember it, she looked so out of place and thoroughly unimpressed. Just think, I danced in front of Emmeline in my tighty whities."

"I'm sure she's seen worse," Addi motioned around her. "So, she'd come to see you?"

"Yeah. She approached me between clients and asked if I really wanted to work in a seedy dive for the rest of my life and to give her a call when I figured out I could do better."

"Classic." Quinn drawled.

Leo nodded. "Didn't take me long to figure out that I wanted to get my little tush outta there. I called her the next day."

"You literally got headhunted," Addi regarded him, impressed. "What about you, Quinn?"

Quinn poured tequila and juice into their cups, splashing liberal amounts of alcohol. "I used to have hopes. Dreams!" she bemoaned mockingly. "Instead I wound up here. Oops," she accidentally sloshed tequila. "I was studying psychology, got about halfway in and realised it wasn't what I wanted."

"Wow." Addi watched as Leo tossed a bar towel into their midst to stop the puddle of liquid crawling across the table. "You must've had great marks in school to get into that course."

Quinn shrugged messily. "I'd always done dancing, singing, cheerleading and stuff. I loved to perform. I wanted to be good at everything and put so much pressure on myself to achieve it all. Being at uni and hearing everyone talking about their career goals just made me realise how bored I was. It was like I'd created a five-year plan for myself based on societal and parental pressures; not what *I* actually wanted."

Leo passed around the cups. "School isn't for everyone."

Quinn continued drunkenly. "Anyway, I started partying and getting messed up all the time, dropped out of the uni my parents were paying for and tried to join the circus. *Cirque Du Soleil*, you know? No one tells you how bloody hard this industry is. I totally failed; didn't even make it through the first round of auditions."

Addi's eyes widened. "Your parents paid for you to go to a university and you just left?" She couldn't imagine what it must feel like to have parents pay for a whole life.

Quinn rolled her eyes. "I should never have wasted my time going in the first place."

Leo repositioned his hair. "Personally, I'm glad I never bothered with the whole uni thing. I honestly don't know how people sit still for eight hours straight. How about you?"

The alcohol made Addi gush. "You can't tell anyone else, but I'm actually seventeen."

Leo laughed. "Don't worry, it's so corrupt here that they wouldn't care."

"Yeah, there's a rumour that Freddy's parents buy the police off," Quinn chimed in. "They pay them a monthly sum to look the other way, to give us more licence flex."

Addi's head felt fuzzy. "What does that mean?"

Quinn answered, "We can stay open longer, we don't get any drug raids. Basically avoiding shit we'd get shut down for. It's great."

"They won't ask you for paperwork so you'll be fine." Leo assured her.

Addi justified herself. "And I'll turn eighteen this year anyway so it's not like, a big deal."

Quinn gathered her hair and flicked it over one shoulder. "So you legit ran away from home?"

"Yep." Addi took another sip. "I really can't believe it, actually. My head's still spinning that I'm here."

Quinn passed a tumbler to Leo. "That's the alcohol. You'll get used to it."

"I, for one, won't tell anyone your dastardly secret." Leo winked. "Finally someone younger than me in this place!" He raised his glass.

Addi clinked hers against his. "How old are you?"

"Nineteen," Leo replied. "I've been the baby in this place the whole time."

"The Golden Child," Quinn rolled her eyes. "Don't even ask me how old I am, I'm due for my quarter life crisis any day now. Anyway, back to you. Why did you run away?"

"I'm a foster kid." Addi realised her half-sucked cigarette had gone out. She picked up Quinn's lighter and flicked it clumsily until the flame appeared and relit it. "I've been shipped from one family to the next my whole life. My last one, the dad was a drunk – they were just in it for the money. One night when he was flying off the handle and yelling at me, I thought, screw this, and I left."

Quinn exhaled smoke. "Will they come looking?"

"Probably not, if they're still getting payments." Addi tapped the cigarette to get rid of the ash, just like she'd seen Quinn do, and took another drag. "I'm no use to them after my eighteenth birthday, they were gonna kick me out then anyway."

"I didn't make it to my eighteenth birthday at home either." Leo sipped from his glass and screwed up his face. "I don't know how you guys are drinking this. I'm going to get something else."

"Why did Leo leave home early?" Addi whispered to Quinn as Leo darted behind the bar and searched through the bottles.

"Religious parents." Quinn explained under her breath. "They kicked him out on the spot when he came out to them. His dad said he never wanted to see him again."

"Alright ladies, stop talking about me," Leo announced his return, vodka in hand. "No more talk of our history. Histories?" he self-corrected sloppily. "We're here now in another messed up family, but at least it's one we've chosen." He pointed the clear glass bottle at Addi. "As Buddha would say, 'live in the now', or something."

Addi grinned. "Cheers to that."

Leo added, "And if we'd like to kick this party up a notch, ladies, I've got a teensy stash of party favours in my room..."

A high-pitched giggle suddenly sounded from the other side of the door. Their heads snapped up.

Addi whispered, "Are we allowed to be here?"

"Um..." Leo pretended to ponder for a moment, while Addi and Quinn tittered, before gesturing at the bottles scattered around them. "I'm not sure they'll approve of this bar tab."

The giggle sounded again, louder this time, and Quinn swore under her breath. They grabbed the spirits and rushed everything back to the bar, jamming bottles back in their original places.

"Over there," Leo waved frantically at a large, velvet couch behind a low table on the side of the room. The three hurried over to squeeze into the tight space between the couch and wall, ducking down to the carpet as the doors opened. Addi felt her heart thumping as another shrill laugh sounded.

The scent of cigar smoke filtered into the space as two people approached. "Just one second, sweetheart. Can I get you something?"

"Surprise me," a girl responded.

There was a clink as Freddy chose a substance from the bar. "Shall we take this upstairs?"

Pressing up against Addi in the shadows, Quinn pretended to gag.

Addi heard the pair retreat and the door close.

Everything was still. The trio waited with bated breath for several seconds, before emerging into the gloomy room.

"Another one lost," Leo commented wryly. "We could make a reality show about Freddy's sexual partners. *No-Fidelity Freddy*," Leo lifted his arms as if signalling an 'up in lights' title. "Ooh, I like that."

Quinn wrinkled her nose. "Ugh, I don't."

Leo guffawed. "How could I forget? Rest in peace, past Quinn."

"What are you talking about?" Addi glanced at Quinn, who shook her head.

"Quinn once moonlighted as one of Freddy's girls," Leo tried to maintain composure. "It was a phase, and my client here prefers not to speak about it."

Addi widened her eyes at Quinn. "You slept with Freddy?"

"Multiple times." Leo inserted unhelpfully. "On purpose."

Quinn closed her eyes as if to block out the memory. "Don't remind me."

Leo filled Addi in. "In fact, if I recall, they were an item, to be precise."

Quinn groaned. "I was young and dazzled by his charisma and didn't know any better, okay? I was drunk for the entire period of our..." she searched for the right word, "...mating."

Addi and Leo snorted.

Addi asked naively, "Did you like him?"

Quinn attempted to block the question. "Hardly."

"Yes," Leo clarified, "he liked her and she was into him."

Quinn held up her hands. "For like, two seconds, I'd like to clarify. Didn't take me long to realise he's a piece of shit."

"I'm hungry, let's go to the kitchen." Leo motioned for them to follow him.

"What ended up happening?" Addi asked Quinn as the party of three staggered through the empty tables, Leo accidentally knocking a chair over.

Quinn tossed her head. "Well, Freddy can stay committed for about as long as he can stay away from those damned cigars. Whatever. You live and you learn." Her eyes landed on Addi with sudden intensity. "I'm not just one of those idiot floozies he brings to his room every other night."

"Nobody's perfect, Quinn. Not even you." Leo winked as he pushed open the kitchen doors. "People suck sometimes. Besides, girl, don't even get me started on the trash I've slept with."

"Men," Quinn commented sagely.

They both looked to Addi, as if expecting her to pile on.

"Oh." Addi quickly overcompensated to shield the fact that none of the boys from school had ever shown the slightest amount of interest in her. "Yeah, totally, that's why I haven't really had anything serious with a guy. Yet, I mean. I don't wanna deal with their stupidity."

Quinn raised an eyebrow. "Right."

Leo surveyed Addi knowingly too but didn't say anything. He located a loaf of bread, sliced off an oversized chunk with one of the huge silver blades on the wall, and put it in the toaster.

"Got enough bread there, mate?" Quinn playfully poked him in the ribs visible under his thin singlet top.

Addi lounged on one of the silver benches that smelled strongly of cleaning chemicals as Leo withdrew a tub of butter from a fridge.

She felt a new contentment with the world; whether it was from the alcohol, she couldn't be sure.

Leo's toast popped and Addi heard the rasping sounds of him spreading the butter on. She felt the grin spread across her face.

Leo's voice, thick with toast, pulled her back into the kitchen. "Right. Bedtime, children?"

They filed out, Addi feeling like she was wobbling as she followed the star performers up the sweeping staircase leading to the dorms above. She'd never drunk this much before in her life — she'd never been invited to parties, she guessed because she'd never stayed in one school long enough to make proper friends.

A door was cracked on the third floor, letting a sliver of yellow light out onto the hallway runner and eighties tunes playing softly. Addi peered in as they crept past.

Sitting in a chair in front of the mirror, clothes strewn over deep red bed covers, with a made up face, fake eyelashes and nylon wig cap, was the director. A pair of diamante-studded heels lay on the floor.

Addi whispered, "Wait, he's the drag queen as well?"

Leo continued thumping up the stairs, two at a time. "Sawyer's a man of many talents. Anyway, hope you enjoyed the welcome wagon, Addi. See you in the morning." He headed for the boys' dorm, leaving Addi and Quinn to meander to their beds.

●

Sunlight streamed through the window. Addi squinted, taking a few seconds to remember where she was. The craziness of the night before hit her at the same time as a throbbing over the top of her head. Everything felt like a movie; a life that wasn't hers. Had she really gone from the suburbs where nothing ever happened to being part of a mysterious and otherworldly venue in the bustling city?

She sat up groggily, rubbing her eyes and trying to ignore the nausea that was creeping into her stomach. She could see the mop of Quinn's brown hair across the room, the rest of her wrapped up under a leopard-print bedcover.

Around them, girls were waking up with matted hair and smudged mascara, pushing arms through robes and shuffling feet into slippers. One girl fiddled with the lock on the window before managing to open it with a slow screech. She lit a cigarette, whacked an ashtray on the windowsill and puffed out the window.

Addi pulled on her jeans, trying not to draw any attention to herself as she changed. In comparison, the other girls made their morning commute to the bathroom in their underwear or totally nude.

Addi threw on her T-shirt and followed some of the girls downstairs to the breakfast buffet in the main performance hall. A long table was pushed against one wall, housing silver trays of eggs, toast and bacon amidst cereals and fresh fruit. People had pulled tables together to eat with one another.

Leo was seated at one of the smaller round tables wearing square-rimmed glasses, flicking through a newspaper and sipping orange juice. He waved to her to catch her attention. Addi fetched a piece of plain toast, grabbed an apple and pulled out the chair next to him.

"Morning." She slid gratefully into the seat, her stomach and head now severely protesting. "Feeling okay?"

"Just peachy." Leo smiled serenely. "I've learnt how to take my liquor in this job. The toast always does the trick. Yourself?"

"Ah, yeah, I really don't know if eating something will make me throw up or not."

Leo raised his orange juice to his lips. "Honestly, hon, hangovers are like bad sex. It's best to just get it over with or it'll drag on and you'll still feel terrible."

Kyle sauntered by wearing grey tracksuit pants and an old T-shirt. "Morning, Addilyn. How did the old house treat you for your first night?"

"Good, thanks," Addi responded.

"That's the way. You'll get used to it. In the meantime, I'm more than happy to help you learn the ropes." He seemed to Addi like a proud private school boy as he puffed his chest. "Us hospitality folk know a little more about what really goes on in this place than the dancing girls." He threw a dirty look at Leo.

Leo rolled his eyes. "Ah, calling a gay man a girl; how original. Have you been watching 90's sitcoms again?"

"Um, thanks Kyle," Addi replied, "but Leo's already showing me around."

"Right." Kyle's lip curled slightly. He turned abruptly and left to pour himself coffee.

"Wow," Addi remarked.

Leo nodded, unsurprised. "That's Kyle."

Quinn entered the room, looking effortlessly cool in tights and a midriff tee sitting off one shoulder, revealing the strap of a lacy crop top underneath, her hair tied back into a braid. Addi made a mental note to find out where she shopped.

The dancer stacked pancakes on a plate and joined Leo and Addi. "Morning."

The smell of the fluffy, buttery pancakes that Quinn was coating in maple syrup and peanut butter made Addi's stomach churn. "You shouldn't have to put up with that, Leo."

Quinn chewed loudly. "What are we talking about?"

"Kyle," Addi told her.

"Ugh. The whole of society shouldn't have to put up with Kyle. We must've pissed someone off in a past life to be living under the same roof as that asshole."

"He's always been a homophobe, so you could say we started off on the wrong foot," Leo explained to Addi.

"Also," Quinn added, "Kyle's jealous of Leo because he gets along with everyone and always makes friends with the new people. Kyle, not so much."

"Ah, I see." Addi said, "Maybe he could do with a friend?"

"That's on him." Quinn stabbed another piece of pancake and shoved it in her mouth. "I think it's a good thing they stick him behind the bar. Everyone finds him insufferable."

They watched as Kyle loaded a plate, sticking one more slice of toast between his teeth for good measure, and moved to pull up a chair at Freddy's table. On Freddy's other side were a handful of girls, who were all laughing and flicking their hair until Kyle butted in and began talking Freddy's ear off. Freddy stared ahead, smoking his cigar, the expression on his face indicating it was the last place he wanted to be.

"Ew. We shouldn't have to watch someone try and suck ass at breakfast," Leo said under his breath.

Quinn laughed loudly and Kyle looked up, shooting another unfriendly look at Leo before leaning closer to Freddy and muttering.

Quinn asked Addi, "Aren't you gonna eat your food?"

Addi pushed her plate away queasily. "Nah, I'm not feeling so great actually."

Quinn laughed. "Can't handle your drink, huh, kid? Don't worry, it just takes practice..."

"Dear Lord," Leo whistled. "Look what the cat dragged in."

Addi and Quinn followed Leo's gaze. He was staring over the top of his newspaper at two figures who'd just walked through the door frame.

"Is that...?" Addi scrutinised the older of the two men, who was wearing a lilac shirt and holding a fancy walking stick.

"It is." Quinn sounded perplexed. "I didn't know Emmerson was coming back. Did you?"

"Nope. And where's Emmeline?" Leo added.

"And who's *that*?" Addi nodded at the dark-haired young man with high cheekbones beside Emmerson.

Quinn shrugged. "Never seen him before in my life."

The whole room had fallen silent.

Freddy pushed back his chair with a scrape and walked up to greet his father, cocking his head . "To what do we owe this unexpected pleasure?"

"Son," Emmerson clapped Freddy on the shoulder. "I have a little business here to take care of. I've also found someone to fill the waitstaff position. Everybody," he raised his voice, commanding the staff's attention, "this is Grayson."

Chapter Three

"I had always known the sky was full of mysteries—but not until now had I realised how full of them the earth was." — *Ransom Riggs*

Whispers swirled around the room like leaves across pavement. Everyone gawked at Emmerson, Freddy and the new arrival. Addi thought Emmerson looked the same as he did in the picture she'd seen, only with more lines on his face. He shrugged out of his long, navy coat and folded it over his forearm.

"Can I speak with you in private?" Freddy requested.

"Of course. Grayson," Emmerson turned to the younger man, "how about you get something to eat and meet some of the team?"

Freddy's expression was unreadable as he followed his father from the room.

Grayson was dressed in black skinny jeans and a faded, black band T-shirt with a blue denim jacket and black boots. His dark hair flopped to one side over his pale face as he meandered unenthusiastically to the breakfast buffet.

"It was nice knowing you, Addi," Leo grinned. "I hope you enjoyed your twelve hours as a House of Nightshade employee."

Addi pressed her lips together, uncertain. "Maybe they need more than one new person?"

The whole room was staring at Grayson.

Kyle had sprung from his seat and was across the floor like a lightning bolt, introducing himself to Grayson with a shake of his hand. "Hi, I'm Kyle. I work in the bar with Freddy."

"Grayson," was all Grayson responded, shaking his hand carelessly before dropping it and taking in the room.

"Right." Kyle seemed a little taken aback by Grayson's lack of interest. "Did you just arrive to the city or...?"

Grayson shrugged nonchalantly. "Pretty much."

"Excellent. And what will you be bringing to our group of rascals?"

"Not sure yet." Grayson could not have looked more unbothered.

Quinn snorted under her breath to Addi and Leo. "This is painful."

The door opened again and they all looked up expectantly, but it was just Sawyer, without the make-up and wig cap from the night before. He was dressed for the day in trousers, a light-pink, paisley shirt and suspenders. He poured himself a cup of coffee and pulled up a chair at their table while some of the dancers filed out of the room.

"Another one already?" Sawyer nodded at Grayson as he brought the cup to his lips. "You newbies are piling up faster than Freddy's girls. Who's this one?"

Quinn filled him in. "His name's Grayson. He arrived just now with Emmerson."

They all peered over their shoulders, watching Grayson pick out some toast.

"Odd." Sawyer frowned. "Did Emmerson say why he's back all of a sudden? I thought he was supposed to be gallivanting around Spain."

"France, " Leo corrected him. "So did we."

Sawyer pursed his lips. "I'll eat my wig if he's not up to something."

"Why do you say that?" Addi asked.

Leo warned, "Before you get completely pulled in by Sawyer's stories, just know it's all speculation. Although I will admit, because Sawyer's a dinosaur, he's seen and heard some stuff about the family during his time."

"Ouch," Sawyer playfully pretended to be offended. "The next person to remind me how long I've been here gets evicted from our island." The table laughed. "Must've been something important to bring Emmerson back from collecting passport stamps with his wife while I'm buying half of your costumes from deceased estate sales."

"Freddy's weird about money too," Quinn commented. "He never talks about how the business is doing."

Sawyer remarked, "I honestly didn't expect Freddy to last this long."

"Why is he here, then?" Addi asked. "I mean, he could just get another job away from his family, right?"

Sawyer's eyes glinted with gossip. "Of course; the man's a hospitality master. He's very loyal to his mother, and maybe he's also had years of parental pressure to take over. Who knows. Then again, a guaranteed inheritance is hard to resist."

Leo annotated, "Freddy's here for the free booze and girls."

"That sounds like a sweet deal." Breakfast plate in hand, Grayson had paused by their table on his way to sit.

"How long have you been eavesdropping?" Quinn demanded.

Grayson smirked at her rudeness. "It's hard not to when your voice is that loud."

Addi couldn't help but stare as he ran his spare hand through his mop of hair coolly, ruffling it so it fell messily to one side.

"Well, why don't you join us?" Leo offered. "Pull up a chair."

Grayson set his plate on the table and dragged a chair next to Addi. She futilely tried to pat her wild curls down, suddenly self-conscious about her old clothes again. She wondered how the conversation between Emmerson and Freddy was playing out. Was this new arrival going to replace her?

Grayson mistook her stare. "I can sit somewhere else."

"Oh, no, of course not," Addi felt blush blooming on her cheeks. "I just... this is kind of awkward but I actually got the waiter role yesterday, so..." Her brain was working too slowly so she let the sentence fizzle. "My name's Addilyn by the way, but everyone calls me Addi."

"Nice name. Maybe we can be newbies together."

Up close, Addi noticed his high cheekbones, the gentle smirk playing on his mouth, and the dark hair framing his face. Perhaps it wouldn't be a bad thing at all to work together with this new boy, she thought, now feeling the blush lingering on her cheeks for a different reason.

Quinn interjected. "I don't think so. Like she said, you're a bit late."

Grayson shrugged, unphased. "What's that saying about two pairs of hands being better than one?"

Quinn retorted. "If they needed two people they would have asked for two people."

"Quinn," Addi warned, "it's not his fault. Besides, I'm sure they could always use the extra help."

Grayson smirked at Quinn again. "Sounds like there's room for everyone, princess."

Quinn gaped, affronted. "What did you just call me?"

Leo swept in before the situation worsened. "How do you know Emmerson?"

Grayson surveyed the dark walls and fading mauve carpet. "He and my mum went to school together. Boss man owes me so I thought I'd hit him up for a job."

Addi was intrigued. "Where did you move from?"

"Sh," Sawyer interrupted. "Listen."

Muffled arguing sounded from down the hallway.

"Do Emmerson and his son not get along or something?" Grayson asked.

"Of course they do." Sawyer waved it off. "That's family business for you, though." He raised his eyebrows and took a sip of coffee.

The room was zapped of conversation as the sound of one door slamming and another being wrenched open cut through the noise.

"Freddy, don't you walk away from me!" Addi heard Emmerson bark.

Another huge thud sounded, which could only be the front door. Moments later, Emmerson marched haughtily back into the performance hall. Everyone snapped back to their food or struck up conversations again so it wasn't evident they'd been listening.

"Grayson." Emmerson looked down his beak-like nose at the table with furrowed eyebrows. "I'll show you to your room. You," he turned carelessly to Addi, whose palms started to sweat. "No need to worry, you still have your job."

Addi breathed out a sigh of relief as Emmerson swanned away without a second glance. She grinned at Quinn while Leo gave her a congratulatory pat on the arm.

"See? Room for everyone," Grayson told Quinn, which caused her to cross her arms in a huff. "Catch you around," he farewelled Addi, ignoring the others, then followed Emmerson out of the room.

"See you later." Addi gazed after his retreating back.

Leo grinned slyly at Addi. "Don't tell me you have a thing for mysterious boys."

"Shut up." Addi shook her head.

Quinn folded her arms. "I don't like him."

Leo chuckled. "Oh, really? Couldn't tell."

"I didn't get a good vibe. I mean, who does he think he is? He just got here and he's acting like we're all beneath him," Quinn grumbled. "You can't say you disagree," she looked pointedly at Leo, who just shrugged in response. "I'm going for a cigarette." She pushed her chair back with a scrape and exited the hall.

"I'm going to finalise some choreography," Sawyer announced. "Welcome to the nuthouse, honey." He patted Addi on the hand before leaving too.

•

"Addilyn?" Kyle called, talking at her breasts. "Run these drinks for me. That new guy's even slower than you."

"My eyes are up here, Kyle." Addi scowled, dumping a pile of plates next to the sink.

Apparently, she was supposed to be running at lightning speed and know the job like the back of her hand after only two shifts. Kyle had been annoyed at her all night for making mistakes, which only caused her to grow increasingly frazzled. Added to the lingering headache and lack of sleep, she felt like she just wanted to curl up in bed right then. The other waitresses bustled around her, the pile of dishes stacking high next to the kitchen hand.

"Don't worry, he did that to me too when I was new," one of them sympathised as she passed by.

Addi wiped her hands on her apron and clutched a tray tightly, the drinks already wobbling slightly as she walked. She wondered how long it was going to take to get a hang of the art of balancing glasses.

The music was blaring, Quinn and Leo leading an old-time jazz sequence wearing bowler hats and bowties. Addi spotted Grayson near the middle of the cluster of tables, attempting to stack empty tumblers on his tray. She smiled to herself, thankful that not only did she still have her job but she now wasn't alone in her newbie struggles.

Kyle and Freddy darted around the bar, looking like they were also performing choreographed movements, dodging one another and pouring spirits into glasses with flair, lining up elaborate cocktails on the counter.

Addi took a tray with several orders and made her way clumsily around the tables, delivering drink orders to the finely-dressed patrons and praying she'd got them right.

She glanced up as she placed some champagne in front of a lady and caught Grayson's eye as he walked through the tables with his stacked tray. He winked at her. Addi couldn't help but giggle. The lady she was serving turned to look at her sternly.

"Excuse me." Addi pretended to cough.

The final note of the performance sounded out and the audience clapped hard as the curtains drew. Addi rushed back to the bar.

"Staff meals, sweetheart." Freddy materialised behind her, setting down the bottle of spirits he was holding.

He'd barely said a word to anyone all evening after storming out of the House earlier, returning just in time for the doors to open. The suave smile he usually donned was absent.

"Sure." Addi tailed Freddy into the kitchen, glad for an excuse to leave Kyle, who was looking stressed as the demand for drinks started increasing. She grabbed the steaming hot meals that Ralph was lining up under the heat light, slapping chicken breasts on individual mounds of rice and muttering all the while

"Oh, they need this gluten-free. Gluten-free! Ten years ago we didn't have any of this nonsense. Now every second meal I make is no gluten, no dairy, no meat, no this, no that, no freaking flavour. Ha! As if they're royalty! Am I right?" Ralph searched for acknowledgement from the other cooks, who chorused an unenthusiastic 'yes, chef'.

Addi grabbed three meals, her fingers still adapting to the wide, thick-rimmed plates, and skirted around the performance hall to take the dinners to the dancers.

Backstage was small and cramped. It looked like the inside of a dress-up box, bursting with sequins and velvet in bedazzling colours. In the corner stood a hatstand with Quinn's various wigs hanging on it. It had made Addi jump in fright the first time she'd been in the room, thinking it was a person. Mirrors leaned against walls, propped up on dressing-tables strewn with make-up, fake eyelashes, hairspray and pins. The floor was faded black, open gym bags laid everywhere and empty tubes of cosmetics and hair products had been left carelessly under the tables.

The performance crew filed in and the air became thick with all the bodies, clouds of hairspray and men's deodorant hanging in the air.

"Everyone, dinner!" Addi hollered.

"You've gotten much better at that already." Leo took a plate straight out of her hand, referring to the first time she had come backstage with meals and announced herself as meekly as a mouse. "Adapt or die, huh?"

Freddy came in behind her, showing off managing four plates. Addi dashed back to get more, until all the dancers had their meals and she was able to sit with Quinn and Leo to eat hers.

"How's it going in waitstaff-land?" Leo asked as he chopped his chicken and shovelled a huge bite into his mouth.

"I have to run everywhere just to keep up," Addi whined. "I don't know how they all do it. Kyle's been so horrible to me, he puts me down literally any chance he can get."

Leo held out a hand, motioning them to wait while he swallowed his mouthful. "Ignore Kyle. It's not worth getting your panties in a twist over him. He just wants a rise from people. Don't cave."

"I know, I know." *Easy to say when he's not standing over you all night*, Addi thought. "But he's the only one in the bar who's teaching me. It's hard to put up with for hours on end. Freddy hasn't shown me how to do anything."

Quinn munched on her broccoli. "Get used to it."

Addi continued to complain. "Freddy's been in a bad mood all night, so he's barely been talking, either. And my head *still* hurts."

"What about that Grayson kid, is he messing things up?" Quinn enquired in a hopeful tone.

"I don't know, I haven't really had the time to watch him," Addi replied shortly, ticked off at her friends' lack of sympathy. "But hey, at least I'm not the only learner now."

Leo dished, raising his eyebrows. "He's been given his own room down the other end of the boys' hall, you know."

"That is so unfair." Quinn stabbed another vegetable. "You and me basically hold up this whole shebang and we don't even get our own rooms."

"I guess he's better than us plebs." Leo feigned a sigh.

Addi scooped the last of her gravy. "I better get going. No doubt Kyle needs to get me in trouble for something that isn't my fault."

"Chin up, hon." Leo gave her an empathetic look. "No one's dying. It's just a hospo job."

Maybe for everyone else, Addi thought. Her whole new life depended on it.

She exited the backstage area, navigating the hubbub of the main space where guests were chatting, moving around and ordering more drinks while they waited for the next performance to start. Jazz music issued from a record player in the interim.

She reached the kitchen, where Ralph was knocking pots and pans around as usual. Freddy threw plates down on the stainless steel bench in a frenzy for the dish-hand to wash.

"Addilyn, you need to be out taking orders now that people aren't watching the performance," he snapped as she dropped her stack on the bench, barely looking at her.

"Yep," she responded shortly, turning on her heel and heading back out the way she came, quietly seething. Apparently, she wasn't even allowed to take five minutes for her dinner.

Addi scurried between clusters of customers, scribbling meal orders. One of the patrons, a young woman dressed in a pencil skirt, blouse and blazer waved her down. "Excuse me, our gluten-free meal replacements still haven't arrived," she motioned to herself and a man next to her who donned an expensive-looking suit and tie.

"I'll check that with the kitchen, won't be a minute," Addi ducked back through the kitchen door and pinned the orders one after the other for the cooks. "Um, Ralph?" she raised her voice tentatively.

Ralph turned around from the stove, tongs in hand. "Yes, young Adelaide?"

"How long do you think until those gluten-free meals will be ready?"

"Those meals?" Ralph stared at her blankly. "They're done. They're out. I did them."

Addi couldn't tell if he was trying to pull her leg or not. "Ah..."

"Don't you believe me? Don't you believe me, young Adelaide? You took them out! I saw you, you took them out ten minutes ago. They already have them."

"I didn't..." Addi began to protest, but then she had a sinking feeling in her stomach. "The chicken and rice?"

"That very one," Ralph turned his attention back to the meat on the griddle.

"I... um, I accidentally thought that was for the staff," Addi admitted quietly.

"Hm?"

"I said, I accidentally thought they were staff meals," Addi repeated a little louder, her face blushing. Logan looked up from chopping herbs on the stainless steel bench with a smirk before looking down again.

"Well, that sounds like your problem, doesn't it?" Ralph shook his head, turning back around to look at her threateningly. "You're going to have to go out there and tell them you ate their dinner, then, aren't you?"

"I'm sorry, I didn't realise, Freddy told me to take out those meals to staff."

"Trying to blame it on Freddy, now, are we? It's not Freddy's fault, young one, that you took the wrong thing."

Addi fought back tears. "I said I'm sorry. Are we please able to just make two more?"

"Oh ho. She wants more now! She wants more," Ralph chortled, prodding the meat cooking on the hotplate with his tongs and turning it over. "That was it. I don't have any gluten-free meals left."

Addi stood blinking back the dampness that was threatening to leak down her face. She felt like she was back in one of her foster homes again, Ralph reminding her of her old foster dad, always picking on her for something. Logan was still sneering, his knife making staccato sounds as he chopped herbs. She shrunk in on herself.

"What's going on?" The floor manager, Ivy, walked in. She was a few years older than Addi with straight, brown hair smoothed into a perfect ponytail that was as no-nonsense as her personality.

"I accidentally messed up the meals," Addi explained. "I'm really sorry..."

"Stop whinging," Ralph dropped his tongs on the bench with an aggressive clatter, "I'll get you your meal." He walked in front of Addi and Ivy and out the door to the fridge and freezer outside.

"The gluten-free couple?" Ivy asked, and Addi nodded. "I'll handle this. Can you help Grayson clear glassware?"

Glad to leave, Addi bolted out the kitchen swinging doors, grabbed a tray and started circulating the room. First Kyle, now Ralph. Why were they treating her like this? She was trying her best to learn everything but she was bound to mess up. She stared embarrassedly at her feet as she marched around. Was it because she was a young woman, or new, or both?

Addi walked full circle around the performance hall without clearing anyone's tables, so consumed with her own frustrations. She felt the tears welling up in her eyes, and as she tried to wipe them away she didn't see Grayson turn around near her with a tray of empty glassware. Her head snapped up as she collided with him. His tray of glass hit the floor with a resounding shatter, melted ice and the last dregs of beer running into the carpet.

"Oh, dear," Addi heard a lady nearby exclaim.

Luckily, the blaring music and performance was still going, which was enough to distract the other guests.

Addi ducked down, her face growing hot. "Oh my god, I'm so, so sorry," she gushed.

Grayson knelt down beside her. "Hey, who cares? It's not a big deal. Besides, I was bound to break something at some point tonight," he consoled her with a sideways grin.

Another waiter arrived with a glass sweeper and some napkins. Addi was grateful it wasn't Kyle.

"Damn carpet," Grayson muttered as he swept up as many tiny fragments as he could while Addi dabbed it with a crisp, white napkin. "Be careful, there's lots of shards stuck in there."

Their heads were close together as they cleaned the carpet, and Addi could smell the strong and intoxicating scent of his deodorant. Looking up, they caught each other's eyes for a few seconds.

Grayson frowned slightly. "Are you alright?"

"Oh, yeah," Addi dabbed at her moist eyes, embarrassed. "I've been having a bit of a bad night to be honest."

"Bad how?"

Addi shrugged. "Everyone seems to be having a go at me right now for stupid little things. Ralph made fun of me in front of everyone because I accidentally messed up the gluten-free meals-"

"Whoa, hold up," Grayson said sardonically. "How dare you."

Addi chuckled. "I know, right? And Kyle's been awful to me pretty much ever since I got here."

"What, really? For no reason? What a prick."

Addi smiled; finally someone who understood. "That's exactly what I was thinking. I've been telling people about it, too, but no one seems to care around here. I think that's probably all we can do for now," Addi stood up with the tray and napkin, giving up on damp patches. "Let's just get out of the way. I'll vacuum the rest up later."

They made their way back to the kitchen.

"Thanks so much for helping me clean, I'm really sorry," Addi apologised again. "I should have been paying more attention."

"Hey, I told you, don't worry about it. If anyone asks, it was my fault. Pretty sure no one was expecting much of me tonight anyway." He flicked his hair slightly as he pushed the swinging door to the kitchen open, carrying the sweeper in one hand. "And you know what..."

Just exactly what, Addi didn't get to find out.

"Addilyn!"

Kyle was waiting in the kitchen, face pink with anger, feet apart and arms crossed in a power pose.

Addi's stomach dropped. For yet another time that night, she was about to be in trouble; she was beginning to lose count. "Yes?"

"Do you care to explain what happened out there?"

"Ah, we dropped a tray and the glass smashed and we cleaned it up," Addi said. All she wanted to do was give up and go to bed.

"And *why* did that happen?" Kyle prodded.

"Why do you need me to tell you? You obviously know." Addi was surprised as she heard herself snap in frustration.

Trying to ignore Kyle, Addi walked to throw the napkin in the bag of dirty cloths and empty the glass shards into the bin. Waiters buzzed in and out of the swinging kitchen doors with stacks of empty plates and orders scribbled down on notepads. The waiter who had handed them the glass sweeper before gave her a sympathetic look as he rushed past with a tiramisu in each hand.

"Because you weren't watching where you were going," Kyle continued loudly over the bustle of the kitchen. "Why am I not surprised? You've been lazy and sloppy all night. This job isn't *hard*. People ask for food or drinks and you give it to them — very simple."

"Then why do you make it so difficult?" Addi muttered angrily, not looking at him as she shook the last shards of glass off the tray.

"Don't talk back to me!" Kyle yelled.

Everyone in the kitchen stopped and looked up at Kyle.

"Ooh, Adelaide is not having a good night, oh no. How did those meals go, young one?" Ralph called to her snidely.

Addi gritted her teeth and exchanged a look with Grayson, who frowned at the chef.

Kyle smirked with Ralph and turned to return to the bar. "Just concentrate on learning how to walk without destroying the place. Can you manage that?"

"Hey!" Grayson stepped towards Kyle, arching up. "Where do you get off, mate? She's only been here for two days, give her a break. You were new once — did someone stand there and yell at you the whole time? I believe it's the supervisors and the managers who are responsible for training their employees to do a good job and create an environment conducive to learning, but you just stand there and bully people instead."

Addi's mouth fell open slightly as she stared at Grayson. Had he really just stood up for her like that?

Kyle took a deep breath, puffing his chest out even more. He looked like he was about to kick something. Grayson faced him coolly, a slight smile playing around his lips as if he thought the whole thing was amusing. Addi tried to get his attention to show her appreciation for him sticking up for her, but he just stared at Kyle calmly.

"I'm just doing my job as a supervisor," Kyle raised his hands as if he was innocent. "And that involves having difficult conversations..."

"Yelling in someone's face isn't a conversation, dude," Grayson cut him off.

"I wouldn't be so disrespectful and rude if I were you, boy. How dare you just waltz in here with your blatant disregard for authority..."

"Authority? Pfft. You keep telling yourself that," Grayson scorned. He strode right past Kyle and back into the bar without a single glance back.

Ralph's face was gleeful, revelling in the drama. "*That's* how you put on a show, ladies and gentlemen," he hooted. "You got told, Mr. Bartender. Don't mess with that young one, that young one with the cool hair," Ralph mimicked running a hand through hair. "How does that medicine taste, eh? Don't know what all those people are doing, sitting out there. *That's* the show we all came here to see tonight!"

Kyle slammed his palm on a stainless steel bench nearby. "Everyone get back to work!"

He stomped away, red-faced.

"Ooh-hoo! That young one better watch out," Ralph continued to gloat. "He's gonna pay for that, you mark my words."

Chapter Four

"Everyone is a moon, and has a dark side which he never shows to anybody." — *Mark Twain*

The dining hall was tensely quiet. Addi could hear her eggshell crack as she tapped away at it in its cup with a teaspoon, revealing a perfectly gooey centre. Around the table, Leo read the daily headlines while Quinn scrolled on her phone and Sawyer jotted down performance ideas, the wrinkles across his forehead growing more pronounced as he occasionally frowned at what he'd written.

Feeling a pair of eyes on her, Addi glanced up to see Kyle staring her down from across the room. He narrowed his eyes before looking away.

"Geez, what's his issue?" Leo noticed as he steeped his teabag.

"He went off at me properly after dinner last night," Addi yawned widely. She didn't think she had ever been more grateful to go to bed as she had been the previous night, but sleep hadn't come easily; she had laid awake staring at the dark ceiling as the girls snored softly around her, replaying the night's events over and over. "I accidentally bumped into Grayson and he dropped his tray. Glass smashed everywhere, it was so embarrassing."

Quinn laughed, fiddling with her hair to try and make it look messy-chic and moving her neck various angles as she took a selfie for Instagram. "That sucks."

"Yeah, well, apparently it was the end of the world," Addi continued. "Kyle yelled at me, of course, but then Grayson told him to stop taking it out on me and basically called him a bad supervisor and a bully straight to his face. It was... pretty impressive."

Leo's eyes sparkled. "Someone's made an impression, huh?"

"Shut up," Addi rolled her eyes. "It was more standing up to Kyle than standing up for me, I think. I just don't understand why Kyle doesn't like me."

"Well, so?" Quinn shrugged, mindlessly scrolling. "You don't like him."

Addi bristled. "That's the thing, though. I'm sure he'd be bearable if he tried to be nice to me. Why can't he be a decent human?"

Quinn sipped her coffee. "Do you really care?"

Addi was stumped at first. "Well, I don't want anyone to not like me unless I've given them a particular reason not to, I guess."

"Ha," Quinn scoffed. "You're gonna need thicker skin to survive around here."

"I wouldn't take it personally, Addi," Leo reassured her. "He just doesn't like the fact that you're hanging out with us. He doesn't like us, therefore he doesn't like the fact that you chose to hang out with us instead of him. Simple mathematics."

"By the way, you picked right," Quinn added. "We're much better than Kyle."

"I'd noticed," Addi replied. "Man, it's tough being the new one here. I need a manual."

Leo put on his glasses and opened his newspaper again.

"Ah, the sweet sound of no one arguing at breakfast," Sawyer chimed in, changing the topic. "I notice neither son nor father have shown their faces at this morning's meal."

"Do they fight much?" Addi asked.

"Oh yes, that family can fight," Sawyer nodded. "As you'd expect, I suppose, it being a family business and all. Honest to God, you could not pay me to go into business with my family."

"Why?" Addi inquired.

Sawyer raised an eyebrow as if to suggest it should be obvious. "My proclivities, dear. Far too deviant for my traditionalist, corporate, golfing father to bear, or even comprehend. When my cover story of being a personal trainer at some testosterone-filled gym unravelled, we stopped speaking."

Addi's eyes widened awkwardly. "Oh. I'm sorry."

Sawyer waved it off. "Distant memories now."

"I may be wrong," Quinn lowered her voice, "but I reckon their fight had something to do with a certain someone." She jerked her head to Grayson, who was sitting alone and being thrown wary looks by the surrounding tables. "It's like he's enjoying this."

Addi consulted Grayson's uninterested face as he mindlessly pushed cereal around his bowl with a spoon. "Doesn't seem like he's enjoying anything. Besides, why would Freddy and Emmerson be fighting about him?"

"Why would Freddy be mad that his father came back? The thing that's different is Grayson, and they've both been weird ever since he got here," Quinn flicked her hair back as if it was obvious.

"Yes, but also it could be for a completely different reason. Emmerson's back all of a sudden, but there's no sign of Emmeline?" Sawyer pointed out. "Maybe there's something going on there. Anyway, it appears everyone has forgotten we have a rehearsal in about ten minutes. Quick sticks, everyone." He stood and called to the performers in the room to get ready.

"Well, whatever," Quinn shrugged as she rose. "The new kid may be your knight in shining armour now, Addi, but I still think he's dodgy. I'm going to get ready for rehearsals."

Leo waved cheerfully, abandoning his newspaper on the table and following Quinn.

"See you later." Addi pulled her plate and cutlery together to take to the sink in the kitchen.

"May I?" came a voice behind her.

Addi started and turned around to see Grayson, standing still against the backdrop of staff bustling out of the room. He was gesturing to the newspaper.

"Oh, of course," Addi pushed it towards him. "By the way, thanks for last night. I know you didn't just do that for me, but I still really appreciated it."

"Honestly, any time," Grayson replied. "People like that need to be confronted every once in a while. Does them good. He seems like he's far too used to being a shithead around here."

"Yeah. It just wasn't a good night though, and your first shift and everything. It was really bad timing for me to knock your tray."

The corner of Grayson's lips curled. "Bad timing seems to be my special talent."

Addi laughed. "You and me both."

"Are you feeling better today?" Grayson asked.

Addi nodded. "You have no idea how relieved I was when we finished work last night. So, where did you move here from?"

Grayson's dark eyes darted around the room. "Oh, just some small town on the north coast."

Addi thought he looked like the opposite of someone who lived by the ocean, with his pale skin and moody demeanour. "Were you living with family?"

"Yep, just me and my mum. My dad basically got her pregnant and then pissed off. What about your family?"

"That really sucks. I know how you feel, actually. I was a foster kid."

"Ah, another one with abandonment issues. I thought I recognised you from the meetings," Grayson smirked.

Addi laughed, enjoying how easy it was to be around Grayson. "It's so nice not to receive that 'Aw, honey' look for once. Normally when I tell people I'm a foster kid they look at me with pity and quickly change the subject."

"People always try and avoid what's uncomfortable."

"They do. You're good at that."

Grayson gave a short chuckle. "What, making people uncomfortable? Why thank you, it's a special skill."

"No, no..." Addi blushed. "I meant to say, you're good at summing things up about people in a way that makes sense." She gave an affirming nod.

"Oh, thanks. Also, the uncomfortable thing," Grayson winked. "Did you have more than one foster family?"

"Yeah, a few actually," Addi said. "I only have vague memories from when I was younger. My families were never great, though. Then the last one... it didn't end well. I mean obviously, I ran away and came here. I got sick and tired of being treated like I didn't mean anything. I was never really anyone's proper family, you know? I always felt like an outsider."

"Yeah, understandably when you're just being ferried around from one to the other."

"Exactly. I don't know what it will take for social services to realise that some of these foster families are as messed up as our original ones that leave us behind," Addi muttered. "I don't know if I can fully put this into words, but I always found the same look in my foster mums. I could see in their eyes that they were trying to connect with me and understand me like they would if I was their real daughter, but we always came up short. I don't know how the brain works but there's something there with the whole 'carrying your child around for nine months and pushing it out' thing. I just always felt like an outsider. Sorry, that got a bit deep."

"Don't apologise. It's good to be deep — people don't have enough real conversations anymore," Grayson told her. "You know, you've been apologising a lot these past twenty-four hours for things that aren't your fault."

"True. You kind of get used to that, though. Apologising, I mean."

"That's what society teaches us," Grayson mused. "Apologise for speaking about hard things, keep your troubles to yourself. What a way to deal with things. And they wonder why people turn out the way they do."

Addi didn't really know what to say to that except to agree. She wanted to sound interesting, so she diverted the conversation back to Grayson. "Anyway, you said your mum went to school with Emmerson?"

"Oh, yeah, they know each other from way back. Both went to some old, pretentious selective school. How did you come to be here?"

"I responded to their job ad. I'd been following Quinn on Instagram and saw her post about it. I saw that they got to live here and decided to take my chance to get out of my foster home and start living my life."

"Quinn... is she the bitchy one with the long hair?"

"Uh..."

Grayson raised his eyebrows. "Oh, come on, you can't actually like her."

"She's not that bad. I think she's just stressed, that's why she can be a bit... short."

"That's a nice way of saying that someone's an asshole," Grayson gave her a piercing stare.

"No, I wasn't..."

Grayson shook his head. "You're too nice for this place."

Addi fidgeted with her cutlery. "You don't know that."

"I feel like I do," Grayson said simply. "To be honest, most of the people I've met here so far seem like the types who would just screw you over."

"Are you just assuming that they're going to screw me over?"

"I didn't mean it as in *you* particularly. Just that... I don't know," Grayson sighed. "You seem way more genuine than anyone else I've met here so far. Do you really want to hang around in a place where people like Kyle yell at you every night for stuff that's not even important?"

Dancers began milling back into the room, ready for rehearsal in exercise shorts, leotards and tights. Addi spotted Leo making his way down the stairs in the throng.

"Well, I don't actually feel like it's all bad," Addi lowered her voice, "especially now you're here."

Straight away she regretted saying it.

Grayson's expression turned hard. "You deserve a better friend than me." He turned swiftly, striding away from the table and sinking into a lounge chair on the other side of the room.

Addi frowned as Leo pulled up a chair beside her.

"Oh no, what happened?" he noticed her facial expression.

"Nothing." Addi was immediately defensive.

Leo raised his eyebrows. "Romeo didn't look happy."

"Don't call him that," Addi blushed. "We were just talking and then all of a sudden he told me that I deserved a better friend than him."

"You do, Addi," Leo sighed, exasperated. "He doesn't seem that nice."

The twenty or so bodies that made up the dance troupe clambered onto the stage and began to stretch and warm up. Quinn flounced through the maze of chairs and tables, high ponytail swinging, ditched her exercise bag and pushed herself gracefully up onto the platform.

"Move," she blasted a few girls who had gathered at the centre point.

They glowered at her as they shuffled obediently out of the way.

"The stage is for everybody, Quinn. You can't just claim the middle..." a girl with black hair pulled back into a neat bun began to retort.

Quinn kicked one leg back and forth in a warm-up sequence. "Speak to me when you're a lead performer, Chorus Girl Number Three."

"My name is Jen, in case your self-centred brain has forgotten."

Quinn turned and began the motion with her opposite leg. "I don't care, and as long as I'm around, which will be longer than you I daresay, you're Chorus Girl Whatever."

"Why couldn't you just have done us a favour and stayed in the circus? Oh wait, you tried and you didn't make it past round one of auditions." Jen made a mock sad face.

Quinn's lip curled. "Oh, you mean just like how you tried out for lead but I'm the one who got it instead? At least *I'm* the best somewhere. You're not the best anywhere."

Jen pouted and turned on her heel. As the dancers moved to the outskirts of the stage to stretch and bitch, Addi noticed Grayson saunter around the furniture towards the door. He paused with a hand on the door-knob and glanced around the room; Addi hurriedly looked away for a moment so he wouldn't spot her watching him. When she looked back, he was gone.

She got up and followed him out of the performance hall. Voices floated out of the cracked door of one of the rooms off the deserted front hallway.

"You will keep me updated, won't you?" It was Grayson.

"Obviously," Freddy responded tersely.

"It might just take us some time." Addi recognised Emmerson's voice.

Grayson deepened his voice. "The longer I'm kept waiting, the worse it will be for you."

Freddy started to say something else. Barely able to hear him, Addi took a step forward. The old floorboard groaned underneath the pressure of her foot.

Addi cursed inwardly. She only had one option. She strode purposefully down the hall and, without looking into the room where the three men were, opened the front door and walked down the steps, letting it close behind her.

She'd have to stay out for some time to make it believable that she had gone out on purpose. She turned left and started down the road lined with old terrace houses behind spike-topped fences, leaves and litter blowing across the concrete pathway as cars and buses drove by, breathing in the mix of second-hand smoke and garbage. The conversation Addi had overheard nagged at her brain as she traipsed the city streets. Had Grayson really been threatening Emmerson and Freddy?

●

Over the following days, Addi felt as if she graduated from being a stranger at House of Nightshade to a warm acquaintance. She definitely wasn't in the suburbs anymore. She had catapulted from a world of bleak school classrooms and lonely, tense nights being yelled at by a father figure while the television flickered in the background to a realm where people lived for the night, slept until noon and got paid for hosting one of the most sought-after experiences in the city.

What was a drab, dingy club in the light of day transformed into a display of glamour and seduction of the senses as the sun went down and the rooms filled with patrons dressed to the nines. Addi felt as if she was part of some dizzying production, each staff member assuming their role night after night to carry out what the local paper dubbed "an adult candy land of entertainment to indulge and delight bored housewives, overworked office slaves and critics alike."

Among the irregularities of life at House of Nightshade, Addi began to familiarise herself with her new reality. For one, she was slowly adjusting to the exposure of human flesh on a daily basis. The lack of walls in the girls dormitory meant there was no privacy from one another. Exotic dancers, so accustomed to taking off their clothes for work that full nudity seemed borderline boring, walked around underwear-less with zero qualms. One afternoon when Addi walked in to get ready for her shift, a dancer was lying back on her bed with her knees bent as her friend delicately applied wax strips for a full Brazilian.

During her first few mornings at House of Nightshade, Addi faced the wall to change out of her pyjamas to minimise the chances of someone spotting her exposed body. What followed was a skilled and overly-complicated procedure of slipping on her outfit for the day over her sleepwear and squirming around like a caterpillar to retrieve her undergarments out of her overgarments.

A few days in, upon witnessing this coordination of 'right-arm-through-that-sleeve-then-this-sleeve-out-of-that-opening', Quinn gave a derisive snort. "Are you twelve years old? Trust me, no one here will even notice those itty bitties." The star performer pranced away to the shower in her G-string, chest bouncing as if to add more insult to injury.

Addi blushed and shrunk in on herself. The next morning, she pulled together her resolve and faced the rest of the room to pull her top off.

Like a scientist studying the wilderness, Addi quickly realised that quiet observation of this strange environment was the best survival tactic in learning the ropes of her new life. While the outside world may have viewed House of Nightshade as unpredictable and exciting, truth be told, Addi's newfound counterparts were creatures of habit like everyone else.

For instance, Leo opened his newspaper every morning at the breakfast table, and it was imperative that he was given at least ten minutes of quiet reading time somewhere in that window to be cooperative for the rest of the day. She also learnt that after consuming a certain amount of scotches (Addi hadn't yet been able to decipher what the magic number was), Sawyer took to perching on the piano stool in full drag and pounding out showtunes and ballads from "back in his day" across the ivory keys when there was a performance break, losing focus for anything else that had been consuming him that evening. This was a known intervention tactic used by the performance troupe on nights when Sawyer was being insufferably irate or obsessing over tiny mistakes and details.

Then, of course, there was the vulgar courting routine carried out by Freddy, Kyle following suit like a parrot, on dancers, performers, waitresses and young female guests alike. This played on loop night after night, consisting of Kyle striking out miserably early on and concluding with Freddy escorting a different long-legged lady up to his room at the end of the night (often coincidentally skipping clean-up).

"Another one bites the dust," Sawyer would lament as they witnessed this procession.

As she fell more into step with its reprehensible charm and eclectic inhabitants, there seemed to be one person who was less than enamoured with life at House of Nightshade.

Grayson was the whisper of the breakfast tables, skulking around the halls with his hands shoved into his pockets when he wasn't avoiding everyone —which seemed to be his activity of choice. When he did emerge for meals, he opted to sit alone and had taken to purposefully staring people down for an unnerving amount of seconds if they dared steal a glance at him, knowing they were talking about him. Addi couldn't help but peer over at him when Leo and Quinn weren't looking while she sipped her tea, the conversation she'd overheard between him, Emmerson and Freddy playing through her mind, and wondering over and over what they had been talking about. The fact that his sinister tone that day didn't match up with the way he'd been so understanding that first night was bugging her more than she wanted it to. She felt like she knew him less than she did before.

"Oh look, it's House of Nightshade's favourite cockroach," Quinn declared when she passed him in the hall.

Addi hung her head, avoiding his eyes as she trailed behind Quinn and Leo. Aside from their interactions about customers and tasks while working, she hadn't had another one-on-one conversation since she'd put her foot in her mouth.

Tension between Grayson and Kyle continued to boil like one of Ralph's pots on the stove. If she had any notions before about Grayson having confronted Kyle to stand up for her, Addi was now confident that Grayson's defiance had absolutely nothing to do with her.

Snubs and snarks were supplied at every opportunity by both parties. The ping-pong back and forth was too much to keep track of, but a standard night might play out like this: Grayson rolling his eyes whenever Kyle said anything in his vicinity, Kyle pretending Grayson didn't exist, Grayson ignoring any direction given, Kyle using his physical stature to literally stand over him, Grayson picking up a glass in the bar, holding it out at arm's length and purposefully staring Kyle down as he dropped it to the ground, letting it smash, Kyle turning pink in his attempt to refrain from yelling (as that would acknowledge Grayson's existence) and Grayson sauntering away with a satisfied smirk, having secured the point for that round.

"Addison, clean up your boyfriend's mess," Kyle barked.

Addi clenched her jaw. If Grayson could do it, she could. "You know what, Kyle? Ivy actually needs me to stay in the kitchen — strict instructions." She turned and departed, smiling giddily to herself at her own audacity.

Ivy, meanwhile, was not impressed to say the least, glaring at Grayson across the room. "I don't know what you think this is, but as part of your job you are actually required to *work*, not stand around smashing things. I know you're trying to piss Kyle off, but I'm a supervisor too, and we both take the fall if we've wasted too much money on inventory because our staff keep breaking items. You're distracting everyone, deliberately causing trouble and not pulling your weight, making the rest of us run around after you instead. If it was up to me I'd get rid of you. I don't know why they're keeping you here."

Grayson gave a careless roll of his eyes. "Geez, someone needs to loosen her ponytail a bit."

A few of the other waiters giggled. Ivy frowned at them sternly and they scurried off.

At the conclusion of her first week as a House of Nightshade employee, Addi entered the performance hall for breakfast to see Freddy had monopolised an entire table on which he was separating notes into piles. Cigar almost falling out of his mouth in his concentration, he frowned, licked his finger to shuffle through money and finished compiling notes with a tick off a long paper list.

Addi had almost finished her coffee (feeling like a proper grown-up; her last foster parents had never let her have caffeine) when Freddy appeared by her side. "For you, Miss Addilyn." He handed her a yellow envelope with a swish of his tattooed wrist.

Addi felt the wad of thick notes in her hands and grinned to herself. She had never earned money before. She peered inside — there were at least a few fifty dollar notes in there. What would she even do with this amount of cash every week? Possibilities started running through her mind faster than she could keep up. She could go out and shout food and drinks for herself, Leo and Quinn, or finally buy herself some new clothes at those fancy shopping centres in the middle of the city.

As if in knowing, the blisters that had formed on the back of her ankles from all the time she was spending on her feet twinged. "Good point," Addi spoke down to her socked feet. She mentally committed to buying a sensible pair of work shoes.

"Who are you talking to?" Eyebrows raised, Quinn stood behind her with a few pieces of toast in her hand, already dressed for a day of practice in tight workout shorts over ballet stockings she'd cut to three quarters, layered singlet tops and leg warmers.

Addi fiddled with one of her curls. "Um, no one."

Quinn scoffed. "You're so weird."

Addi gestured to Quinn's choice of sustenance. "Do you want to sit here to eat?"

"Nah, Sawyer's calling rehearsal extra early today. Honestly, it's slave labour. Just because Grandpa's up at the crack of dawn doesn't mean the rest of us don't need our beauty sleep. Gotta go."

Sawyer had barely slept a wink over the past few days, garnering snide remarks from his troupe about working himself into a not-so-early coffin. When he wasn't overseeing the performance and emceeing in drag each night he could be found madly scribbling in his notebook in a dim corner during the day, slinging back alternating espressos and whiskey and dragging sharply on cigarettes. Routinely throughout this creative process he would stand, block out a few moves and snap his fingers in satisfaction, returning to his sheet and jotting it down. Helpfully, one of the waiters had attempted to offer Sawyer some food, only to be barked at by the frenzied director to leave him alone.

While on a ten-minute break one afternoon, Leo explained to Addi that Sawyer had huge critics coming to view his performance the following Saturday night.

Addi pretended to wipe the table so she and Leo could converse. "Ah, the nervous bubble makes a lot more sense now."

"He's already had a preliminary meeting with them, and they're quite interested apparently. This is Sawyer's chance to finally get the hell out of here and into a company, where he belongs."

Sawyer flicked his floral tie over his shoulder and hollered through the room. "Where are my star performers? Quinn, Leo, we need to keep going over your final duet for Saturday until you can do it perfectly in your little dormitory beds. This is going to be the biggest night of the year."

Chapter Five

"And there are never really endings, happy or otherwise. Things keep going on, they overlap and blur, your story is part of your sister's story is part of many other stories, and there is no telling where any of them may lead." — Erin Morgenstern

Saxophone melodies filled the air with their happy, swing-time jazz. Addi stayed in the corner of the bar to wash glassware in the sink, looking out at the backs of heads in chairs and Quinn and Leo performing onstage. They were portraying an old-timey, boy-pursues-girl scene which mostly involved Quinn pretending she couldn't see her adoring pursuer as she flitted around the stage, while Leo used various props and impressive moves in a bid for her attention. The crowd laughed as Leo pretended to trip over his character's briefcase as he tried to approach the leggy burlesque dancer.

A haze hung in the air between tables and lounges as patrons in suits, silk dresses and glistening jewels smoked, tapping their cigarettes on crystal ashtrays. The venue held a blatant disregard for the 'no smoking inside' rule that applied everywhere else; the result was a lounge that felt like it was out of the 1950's.

Addi was still amazed at how lavishly all the guests would dress for their night at the performance house. There were women with furs draped over their shoulders seated at one table, a lady under a black-lace veil that covered her face sitting in a booth and a man in a long, velvet coat and leopard-print vest waiting for his drink at the bar. The patrons took seriously the dress code Addi had spotted stamped on every single House of Nightshade ticket when Freddy had showed her — 'Dress: To the Nines.'

The critics were huddled together at a small table near the front of the stage, scrutinising the show with unreadable expressions. Addi could see Sawyer perched on the piano stool, dressed lavishly in a glittering silver dress and a wig of tight curls, tearing his eyes away from monitoring the performance to throw nervous glances to their table every few seconds.

Freddy approached the bar with a tray crammed with empty wine goblets and tumblers. Addi bowed her head, occupying herself with rinsing and stacking the glasses in the dishwasher. She could feel Freddy's gaze as he deliberately lingered.

"How are you going, sweetheart?" he asked slickly.

She glanced up. "Pretty good."

Freddy surveyed her for a reaction. She could tell by the small, fake smile and the slight smugness of his eyes that he thought he could figure her out.

"Enjoying being behind the bar? It's a nice break from the floor, isn't it?"

She could barely remember Freddy striking up a conversation with her since she first showed up on the doorstep. The only words he'd spoken to her since had been short, barked instructions.

"I enjoy watching them from here," she nodded to Quinn and Leo dancing underneath the warm, yellow lights. "It's a free show every night."

Leo's character had finally achieved an audience with Quinn's, and they were spinning around the stage together in a courting dance.

"They do put on an alluring performance, don't they?" Freddy pulled a cigar from his pocket and lit it.

Watching Quinn, Addi could tell why Freddy had been attracted to her. She had an ownership of the stage that kept the audiences coming back each night.; an unwavering confidence in front of a crowd.

"Do you want to try it up there?" Freddy noticed her watching Quinn.

"I can see the appeal," Addi responded, "although I'm not sure I'd even last a full day."

Freddy cocked his head quizzically.

"Two left feet," she explained.

Freddy puffed out smoke. "Ah. I'm sure you'd be better than you'd expect."

I'm sure you're trying to butter me up, Addi thought. "Who knows. Did you always want to work in hospitality?"

Freddy gave a bark of laughter. "I'm not sure if 'want' is the right word."

"But it's the family business, so you had to?"

"I mean, I grew up here." He looked around the dimly lit room, people scattered across the jumble of mismatched chairs and tables, flames flickering atop their wicks in small candle-holders and staff weaving expertly amongst the tables. "I was helping set tables as soon as I learnt how to walk," he shook his messy crop of chestnut hair. "I'm not sure I ever had a choice in the matter."

Addi pulled a tray out of the dishwasher and began to dry glasses with a towel. "So you've only ever worked here, then?"

"Oh, no. I'd be as mad as Ralph if that was the case. Thankfully I did go out in the world for a while there, worked odd jobs in hospitality overseas for quite a few years. Those were the best years of my life. That's actually when I got this tattoo." Freddy tapped the colon daubed in black ink on the inside of his wrist. "A punctuation mark that keeps a sentence going. A reminder that you have the power to add more to the story — and knowing when it's right to do so. I could have easily stayed here but it's important to get out and experience something different."

"Exactly." Addi remembered what it had taken for her to build up the courage to leave her foster family.

Kyle made his way out of the maze of squished tables and chairs, balancing a double-stacked tray while attempting to hold on to three jugs in the other hand. The result was a rush towards the bar to offload the slipping glassware.

Addi sighed and rolled her eyes as one of the cups tumbled off its precarious placement and smashed on the bench in front of her. "Jesus, Kyle. You can go back more than once, you know."

Freddy caught her eye and grinned, looking away.

"Well, someone has to be working out on the floor," Kyle retorted.

"And someone has to clean the glassware," Addi rebutted. "I can talk and clean at the same time."

Freddy puffed his cigar while Kyle swept up the broken shards. The audience clapped and the lights went down momentarily as the rest of the chorus traipsed onstage to join Quinn and Leo for the last act before intermission. The saxophone started up again as Freddy picked up a tea towel and started drying glassware alongside Addi.

"Why did you come back after all that time away?" Addi asked.

In all the discussion about himself, Freddy seemed to have forgotten that he had been enquiring after Addi when he had struck up the conversation with her in the first place.

"Ah, I wasn't doing so well with my mental health," he frowned, stacking the glasses back on their shelves. "Crazy work hours and stuff. You can fly across the world but you'll never outrun your problems apparently. Family business is...complicated."

With the lights up for intermission and the entertainment on hold, the audience idled towards the bar. Sawyer shot up immediately and accosted the critics with a toothy smile planted on his face. Kyle zigzagged hurriedly through the throng to start pouring everyone's orders again. Freddy chucked the tea towel over his shoulder and switched on his smile as he faced the first customer. "Sir, what can I get for you?"

"Excuse me, madam, excuse me!" Sawyer pushed his way to the front of the bar waiting line. "Kyle, I need one Whiskey Sour, an Old Fashioned and a glass of Pinot Noir stat for the critics table. I don't want to see their glasses empty at all tonight, you understand?"

As Addi reached for a bottle on the messy, crowded counter, Kyle shot his hand out and cut in front of her rudely. Addi glared at him. Freddy, who was waiting patiently behind the two of them while they used the liquor he needed, raised his eyebrows at Addi.

When intermission ended, the crowd dispersed back to their seats and Freddy zipped out to dim the lights. The music started playing again.

"I'm going to check on food," Addi announced quickly, darting out behind Freddy to escape being alone with Kyle. She now figured anger was actually just his permanent mood, and she wasn't about to expose herself to another run-in if she could help it.

In the kitchen, Ralph didn't provide any more of a supportive environment. Addi was still wary after she'd mixed up the meals the previous night and avoided his gaze. Once again, she couldn't wait for the evening to be over.

Kyle pushed open the door from the bar to the kitchen, large bag of ice in hand, while Addi and the other waitstaff waited for meals to run.

"Bloody ice not crushed," he grunted as he stomped around the bench and reached to the wall of utensils, pulling a meat mallet from the jumble and beginning to smash the bag of ice with it against the floor. "Can one of you go and clean upstairs?" he demanded, face pink from the activity, "There's mess everywhere, it looks terrible."

"Alright, sire, whatever you command, what-eeever you command," Ralph goaded, shaking his head at Kyle attacking the ice on the floor near him as he arranged asparagus in a large dish.

The cooks smirked as they poured jus over racks of lamb. The rest of the waitstaff were already loaded up with plates.

Addi rolled her eyes. "Yep, I suppose I'll do it, and you can help these guys run out meals then because they're going to need it," she said faux sweetly.

Kyle didn't give thanks, rising clunkily and kicking the door open to take the now-crushed ice back into the bar. It swung forcefully in his wake.

"The bar can't do it, oh no, that would be too much for them. Let's steal the waitstaff to clean up our mess because Freddy's too busy smoking his cigar, can't lift a finger. It's not like we have anything to do in the kitchen here, oh no," Ralph prattled on as he wiped excess sauce from the edges of the plate with his tea towel. "Ready to go!" he slapped the stainless steel table.

"Thanks Addi," Ivy called as she rushed out with meals.

The mahogany stairs creaked as Addi ascended, tray tucked underneath one arm. Her feet throbbed, still getting used to the long shifts spent traipsing around the house on a consistent loop in and out of the kitchen. The loud, vigorous music became muffled as she climbed, transitioning into quieter, vintage melodies floating out of old vinyl players and gramophones. Warm, yellow light spilled out of rooms onto the deep-red hall runner. Candlesticks with pools of hardened wax gathered at the bottom adorned side tables and cabinets next to mismatched vases weeping with roses. People had abandoned empty glasses on the cabinet; Addi began carefully removing them from amongst flowers, doilies, mirrors and delicate china teacups.

She followed the sound of tinkling of cups and jovial chatter into the nearest room, pushing the already-ajar door open and slowly twirling in. A woman crooned from the 1920's record player in the corner:

Care a little, care a lot.

Let me love you, let me not.

Pale-green wallpaper was peeling from the topmost corners, the bottom half of the wall covered in dark wood panelling. A younger couple were sitting back on a pastel pink, squishy lounge in the corner, being entertained by a voluptuous red-head who was wearing a black-lace teddy and stockings that went just over the knee. Her abandoned silk slip dress was draped over the lounge arm and she was perched on the man's lap, legs draped over his companion. She reached over to a fruit platter on the circular coffee table in front of them, plucked out a strawberry and fed it to the man, who was dressed in a deep grey suit.

The woman beside him had one lace-enclosed arm spread over the back of the lounge as she perused their young entertainer with eyes that sparkled with curiosity. She reached forwards, cleavage grazing the girl's legs, to grab her crystal goblet of champagne. The exotic dancer opportunely snatched another strawberry and lobbed it into the sparkling drink before the woman could bring it to her lips. Giggling, the red-head swung her legs around and began grinding on the man, while his partner sipped champagne and watched.

Addi moved quietly around the room to collect abandoned flutes and tumblers. In another corner, half hidden behind a hanging tapestry, a middle-aged man with an unkempt beard and a stain on his business shirt was thoroughly enjoying his personal performance from a beautiful, dark-skinned dancer. She whipped her tight curls around as she spun and danced, and defined abs were visible between her gold crop-style top and high-waisted underwear. Addi was mesmerised by the way she moved, as fluidly as water, this upstairs wonderland of sensuality a result of the House's philosophy to celebrate it rather than hide it away.

The woman turned to shimmy and the man instantly cupped her behind. She looked up and saw Addi staring — Addi flushed and gave a small smile. The woman winked back before flicking her hair majestically and twirling around to place her hands on the man's chest, sticking her toned backside out. Addi stared for a few seconds at her soft curves before remembering what she was there for and moving on.

Each of the upstairs rooms were slightly different. Some were cleverly divided by antique separators, wall hangers and sheets of gauze in various shades, creating little tepees with patrons inside lying back on multi-coloured cushions while they were treated to private shows. One room paid homage to the vibrant colours of India with furnishings and decorations in bright pink, orange and red, the girls bumping their hips sensually to exotic Indian music adorned in hip-hugging silk skirts and golden jewels.

Addi's tray was almost full as she entered a room that looked like it had come straight out of the roaring twenties. In the corner, girls wearing short flapper dresses were draped over a man in a black suit, surrounded by a haze of smoke, flutes of champagne and a dusting of white powder on the table in front of them. As Addi passed, the man turned to face one of the girls he had his arm draped around, cigar hanging out of his mouth. She did a double-take — at first glance she thought it was Freddy, but the lined face and silver hair revealed it to be Emmerson. Addi pictured Emmeline sitting in an apartment with the Eiffel Tower in the distance, no idea that her husband was currently sitting underneath a handful of young women.

Arm now gently aching under the weight of her full tray, Addi started to head back.

"Hey."

The voice caused Addi to pause and double back.

The beautiful woman who had winked at her was no longer with her customer and was standing just inside the door. "New girl, we haven't had a chance to talk." She gave a dazzling, straight-toothed smile.

Addi wondered if she had had braces when she was younger and absent-mindedly twisted a curl around her finger with her spare hand. "Yeah, I haven't really seen you around in the dorm."

"I prefer other people's beds," the girl responded coyly. "I saw you looking before."

"Oh, sorry, I didn't mean to stare," Addi fumbled slightly over her words. "It's just the first time that I've really seen... you know."

"I can show you more, if you like."

Addi hovered. On the one hand, she was supposed to be working. What if Emmerson spotted her sitting down up here? On the other hand, she felt the tug to see more of what occurred upstairs. Besides, Emmerson was in a different room and had seemed rather preoccupied with pin-ups and powder. "I guess I could spare five minutes."

"Come, sit," the girl instructed, closing her hand around Addi's wrist and leading her into the room.

Addi felt a thrilling flutter in her stomach; she had never done anything like this before. She abandoned her tray on one of the side-tables, and the girl led her to a couch and sat her down.

"I'm Jayda, it's so lovely to meet you," the exotic dancer took Addi's hand in both of hers and batted her eyelashes. Addi felt the fluttering within herself move down below her stomach at Jayda's touch.

"My name is actually Summer— just don't call me that up here," Jayda-slash-Summer winked, scrunching up her head of curls as she sensually lifted her arms in the air. "We all make up alter egos. Our stories need to be believable, but not too ordinary or realistic. Just kind of always out of reach. There's a very fine balance."

"Is it easy to make up your alter ego?" Addi asked.

Summer placed her hands either side of Addi on the back of the couch and leant forward, swaying her hips side to side behind her. "Surprisingly so."

Addi felt her face, now close to Summer's throat and clavicle, growing warmer, beginning to sweat under her long-sleeved, button work shirt. She took in Summer's musky scent, thinking she smelled quite amazing for someone who had been dancing all night.

Summer slid her fingers up Addi's arms. "You know when you were a kid and you would play pretend and there was always that girl character you'd make up in your head that you wanted to be?"

Addi nodded, willing the blush on her face to cool off.

"That's kind of what it is. The best part is that you can choose to be whatever you want."

"I always wanted that as a kid — to be someone else," Addi said, trying to look anywhere but the girl's cleavage. "Do you always talk this much with your clients?

Summer turned and slid down to the floor against Addi's legs. "Much more, actually. The longer they talk, the more they tip, the more drinks they pay for and the more likely they'll be to keep coming back." She shimmied back up again.

Addi took a deep breath. "I'm sure you'd have no problem keeping people coming back for more."

"Don't stop on my account."

Addi and Summer turned their heads simultaneously to the newcomer.

Grayson lounged in the doorway.

"Grayson!" Addi groaned inwardly. "I, um...what are you doing here?"

A smirk played on Grayson's lips. "No wonder it took you so long to, ah, 'clean up' here."

Addi shot up from the couch like a rocket. "I was just a bit tired, and then Summer was showing me–"

Grayson held up a hand. "I really don't care what you do. Kyle was asking about you, that's all, so I figured I'd try and help you avoid trouble."

He left.

"Crap." Addi snatched up her tray. "See you around, I guess," she farewelled Summer awkwardly.

"I would say sorry to get you caught out, but I'm not really." Summer grinned mischievously before floating away to greet a couple of men that had just entered.

Addi left the land of boudoir and carried her lot back down the stairs to the bar unenthusiastically, showtunes increasing in volume as she descended. Between Kyle, Ralph and whatever was going on between her and Grayson now, she was half-tempted to become a dancer like Summer so she wouldn't have to work downstairs ever again.

Kyle was the first to greet her as she arrived back in the kitchen. He was finishing off dishing soup into three separate bowls with a large, industrial-sized ladle. "Barely on time, as usual. You and Grayson will need to eat quickly here in about five minutes, you've both run out of time to have a break tonight — you can thank yourselves for that. Then you can get back out on the floor. I'm going to have my dinner now."

Kyle dropped one soup bowl in front of where Grayson was leaning on the bench, then handed a second to Addi before grabbing the third dish and stomping past her out into the courtyard.

Addi moved out of the kitchen chaos to the benches in the corner where Grayson was, avoiding his eyes, their conversation at breakfast the other morning replaying through her head.

"Enjoy your lap dance?" Grayson asked softly.

Addi slurped her soup. "What's it to you?"

Grayson shrugged. "Nothing, I guess." A beat. "So, you're into girls?"

Addi paused, spoon halfway to her mouth. "I don't know. It was just a bit of fun. Why are you talking to me, anyway? I thought you said we shouldn't be friends."

Grayson swallowed his mouthful. "I said you *deserve* a better friend, not that we shouldn't be."

Addi raised her eyebrows. "Oh, excuse my confusion. That's not mixed messaging in the slightest."

She was once again surprised to hear herself speaking so directly — she normally had zero assurance when it came to boys. However, something about her lap dance with Summer had left a lingering spark of confidence.

"Exactly." Grayson gave a small grin despite himself.

Addi rolled her eyes performatively. The thrill that she had felt earlier with Summer was re-entering her stomach. "Thanks, then, for coming to get me earlier and saving me from the wrath."

Grayson gulped more soup. "It was nothing."

"Still think I'm too nice for this place?" Addi grinned coyly.

Grayson chortled. "Okay, maybe you're a bit more naughty than nice now."

Addi blushed and looked away. She was in uncharted territory now with this exchange and silently wished she'd had at least a little experience with boys in high school. She wanted to ask him about his conversation with Emmerson and Freddy, but couldn't let on that she had been eavesdropping. "How are you settling in?"

"Fine. I've never met people who are so over-the-top, though. It's weird. Kind of like being back in school again."

"Have you spoken to Emmerson much since you got here?" Addi prompted.

Grayson dabbed at the corner of his mouth with a cloth napkin. "Not really, aside from the welcome basics."

Addi studied him for a few seconds. He hadn't even paused in the slightest before his lie.

"Have you been out in the city much?" Grayson asked.

Addi shook her head. "By the time we finish pretty much every other venue is closed, too."

"We don't finish too late. There'd still be some places open. Want to go and see what's out there in the real world after we pack up?"

Addi quickly tried to hide her smile. "You mean tonight?"

"Yeah, but if you don't feel like it that's fine."

"No, no," Addi answered quickly. "That would be cool." She tried to play it casual, not wanting to let on to the fact that this was the first time someone had actually asked her out to a bar. She bit her lip; she would probably need to show ID to get into most places, which she didn't have. She didn't want Grayson to think she was too young and naïve, but at the same time she felt confident he wouldn't judge her for being slightly underage. "Maybe we can go to some smaller bars without a guard out the front because actually-"

"Kyle?" Freddy popped his head through the kitchen door, cutting her off. "Anyone seen Kyle?"

"His Royal Mightiness is eating," Grayson responded sardonically.

"Right. You then, Grayson. I need help moving some props on stage during the next song, we have to be quick. Let's go."

Grayson trailed after Freddy.

For the thousandth time, Addi pondered the tiny snippet of conversation she had overheard between Grayson, Freddy and Emmerson. What was Grayson waiting for from Emmerson and Freddy? What did he mean that it would be worse for them? That didn't sound good on the face of it, but then, Addi reasoned, she had only heard a few seconds of conversation with no idea of the context. Was she overthinking what she had heard, like she always did? *Come to think of it*, she thought, *they could have just been talking about his new job.* That made a lot more sense. It was probably something boring, like taxes.

At that moment, a thud and a wail sounded from the performance hall. Addi heard the collective gasp of the crowd, and the music halted abruptly. She ran out of the kitchen. On the stage, performers were crowded around someone who was lying on the floor. Addi could just make out the brown hair styled into vintage curls — it was Quinn.

Other waitstaff abandoned their tasks and made their way towards the stage to see what the fuss was about.

Ivy was straight into action. "You, get some ice in a tea towel," she barked to a waiter. "Addi, fetch the first-aid kit from the kitchen. Everyone else, what are you milling around here for? Service hasn't stopped — get back to work!"

Addi obliged.

"What happened to the music?" Ralph called as she headed out of the kitchen once again. She ignored him.

The curtains were drawn and the lights flicked back on, signalling another intermission. Kyle recruited the bar staff to pour more cocktails in the interim to keep the guests happy. Addi rushed up the stairs on the side of the stage and pushed through the performers to Quinn.

"I've got the first-aid kit if you need it," she called as she battled through the crowd.

Quinn had managed to prop herself up on her elbow. Tears spilt out of her eyes, making her thick, black mascara and eye shadow run down her cheeks. Freddy was holding the ice on her now-swollen ankle. Grayson hovered awkwardly nearby, looking confused.

"Ah, thank you," Freddy said to Addi. "Hold this for me." Addi held the ice as Freddy rummaged in the kit and started patching up Quinn's bleeding knee. "We're going to have to get her to the hospital; that ankle might be fractured."

Leo came through the curtains with a glass of water and knelt beside Quinn, stroking her hair. Sawyer followed, dressed fully in drag, tapping people on the shoulder so they'd part for him.

"What happened?" Addi asked, glancing at Grayson and having a growing feeling that she already knew the answer.

"Old mate was trying to move furniture, went the wrong way and tripped up Quinn," Leo confirmed sourly, nodding at Grayson as Quinn stared ahead, wincing as Freddy pressed the ice around her injured ankle.

"Look, I'm sorry," Grayson interjected. "I don't know what happened, honestly. Those hot lights are getting to me..."

"Oh please!" Quinn glared up at him. "You bloody did this on purpose because you know I don't like you."

Grayson pressed his fingers to his temples as if he had a headache. "I said it was an accident. Why would I intentionally hurt you?"

"Liar!" Quinn blasted.

Sawyer stabbed a shaking finger in the direction of the curtain. "Do you know who is sitting out in that audience right now, boy? No? Only the best damn critics in the country, here to see my choreography which *you* have just turned into a right hot mess!"

Grayson spluttered. "I...I didn't know, how could I have known that? You all seriously think I did this on purpose? It's not a big deal–"

Sawyer inflated like a bullfrog. "Not a big deal? Not a big deal?!" he repeated. "How many chances do you think critics give you? I'll tell you: it's one. You get one shot, and you've just blown mine."

Grayson held out an arm as if balancing himself. "Oh come off it, surely they'll understand it was a mistake. These things happen."

Sawyer barely regarded him. "You're right, mistakes do happen. You being here at all is one. Just go. I don't want to see your face again tonight."

Grayson glowered but did as he was told, turning on his heel and marching off.

"Sawyer, what can we do for the rest of the show?" Freddy looked up at him from his position crouched on the floor. "Is the understudy ready?"

"Yes, of course." Sawyer spun around, his long dress swirling around his high-heeled boots, and stared pointedly at a slender dancer. "It's your lucky day. You have two minutes to get dressed."

"No," Quinn almost growled through tears. She made a feeble attempt to get up but only managed as far as her elbows. Freddy pushed back down on her shoulder gently.

The girl couldn't help but smile visibly before rushing off to get changed.

"Troupe," Sawyer clapped his hands. "Be ready to begin the next dance. Over here!" He seemed to sweep up the rest of the performers as he walked to the other side of the stage, herding them like sheep.

"Come on, let's get you up." Leo and Freddy both helped Quinn to her feet, Freddy holding Quinn's weight as she kept her injured ankle hovering above the ground.

"Hopefully it's just bruised and I'll be back onstage soon." It was the first time Addi had heard a complete lack of confidence in Quinn's voice. "You should get ready for the next act," she told Leo.

"I don't want to leave you but Sawyer will eat my head if I don't go over there right now. Keep me updated." Leo galloped back to the rest of the group.

"Cover me in the bar, Addilyn," Freddy instructed as he took Quinn to the dressing room and through the back way to avoid the audience.

Addi shot Quinn a sympathetic look — underneath her tear-stained face, Quinn looked very put out having to lean on Freddy. "I'll check up on you later, Quinn," she promised before resuming service.

A nearby, elegantly-dressed older woman tutted to her companion. "Poor girl. What a disaster."

•

Leo and Quinn's understudy managed to save the night with a fantastic performance. Multiple cocktails and a very messy bar later the patrons appeared to have all but forgotten about Quinn's fall. Freddy hadn't resurfaced since taking Quinn away. Addi was relieved to see the guests amble out of the House at the end of the night, giggling and leaning on one another as they stumbled into taxis out the front. In contrast, the critics filed out looking disenchanted, Sawyer shaking each one of their hands and apologising profusely. After the door snapped shut on them Sawyer pummelled it with his fist, screamed out an unidentifiable sound of rage then stormed up the stairs.

By the time her shift was over, well past midnight, Addi was exhausted. She traipsed to the dressing room backstage, where performers were removing their make-up and swapping tap shoes for furry slippers. She scanned the room twice — no sign of Leo. Perhaps he was already checking on Quinn.

She walked back out to check the performance hall again. Without the blaring music she could hear muffled yelling from the hallway. Curiosity piqued, she moved closer. A group of performers and waitstaff were gathered by the door that led into the front hallway, peering ahead. The shouting had grown louder. It sounded like a hysterical woman. She spotted Ivy.

"What's going on?" Addi whispered.

"Screaming match," Ivy murmured back. "Freddy versus Quinn."

"Oh, man," Addi sighed. "How long have you guys been here?"

"Just a few minutes. If they wanted the conversation to be private, they shouldn't be yelling," Ivy shrugged.

"Fair point," Addi conceded, joining the huddle. "Have you seen Leo?"

"Not recently. He sped off right after the show ended," Ivy responded.

"That's weird," Addi frowned.

"Everything okay?"

"Oh, yeah, it's just that he normally hangs around," she explained. "I would have thought he'd be with Quinn."

"For Christ's sake!" Their heads snapped up as Quinn shouted. "Do you care about any of us at all? It wouldn't kill you to at least fake some decency!"

Addi turned her ear towards the hall, but she couldn't make out what Freddy was saying back.

"He tripped me up in front of the *entire room*," Quinn continued. "It's going to be in the show reviews tomorrow, he completely humiliated me!"

Freddy raised his voice. "Don't be such a drama queen, Quinn."

"That's kind of my job, Freddy!" Quinn yelled back.

Addi thought that was an extremely valid point, now Quinn mentioned it.

"You know, not everything is about you," Freddy said loudly.

"Well, not everything is about that weird Grayson kid, but for some reason you're defending him when he's only been here for what, a few days? Just man up and fire him. Then again, I'm barely surprised. Manning up and taking responsibility has never really been your strong suit, has it?"

"Ooh," one of the performance girls near Addi breathed, looking excited.

"What is that supposed to mean?" Freddy responded testily.

"Oh, don't pretend. You love being difficult to get to know, always trying to be so mysterious and suave, tricking people into thinking you're a good person. You're not, though. You're just some fake, two-faced..."

"Oh, so it's turned into an attack on me now, has it?"

"Because you can't even do this one thing for me!" Quinn blew up. "You've completely screwed me over once before. Even as my manager you *still* can't do anything to show that you actually give a damn about my wellbeing. There is absolutely no reason to keep Grayson here other than the fact that you can't say no to your daddy. You're a coward!"

A well-delivered slap rang out clearly from behind the door.

Everyone around Addi inhaled sharply.

"Quinn!" Addi jostled her way through the group. She knocked twice on the door and started to push it open. "Quinn, are you okay?"

A sliver of yellow light fell out of the room and splashed onto the hallway floor. She could see Quinn sitting on the edge of a chaise lounge with her head in her hands.

"It's fine, Addi, please just go," Quinn mumbled through her fingers.

Addi could make out Freddy's figure hovering on the other side behind the door. "Okaaay," she began uneasily, not wanting to leave any woman with someone who would hurt her. There was a finality in Quinn's voice, however, that told Addi to drop it for the moment. "See you upstairs." She retreated to the huddle.

Ivy clapped her hands briskly. "Okay, show's over, guys. Come on, Addi. If she doesn't want help right now, I don't think there's anything we can do."

They climbed the stairs and reached the floor of the boys' dormitory.

"I'm just gonna... I'll be up there later," Addi told Ivy, peeling off abruptly.

A boy walked out the door of the bathroom with a towel wrapped around his waist, a bottle of shower gel in his hand. It was the waiter who had brought the glass sweeper to her and Grayson the night before.

"Hey," Addi stopped him, waving awkwardly to catch his attention. "Do you know which room Grayson's staying in?"

The waiter blinked at her in the shadowy hall light. "Weren't you just there?"

"No," Addi replied slowly.

"Oh. It's that one." He pointed to a door with a golden hook on the front with a yawn and ambled off to bed.

"Thanks." Addi knocked on the door. "Grayson?"

She waited. No reply came. There was a small knock of something from the other side of the door, signalling that he was inside.

"It's me, Addi. I know you're in there, but that's fine, you don't have to open the door. You probably don't feel like going out anymore, hey?" She waited — nothing. "I'm pretty tired anyway, so that's fine. I know people are kind of mad at you after what happened with Quinn tonight, but if you need to talk, I'm around. Maybe we can go out some other time."

Silence.

"See you in the morning, then."

She left dejectedly. Just as she was going to spend time with Grayson alone, outside of work, he was now ignoring her. Again.

"Addi?"

Addi jumped. "Quinn!" she exclaimed. "Are you okay? What did they say about your ankle?"

Quinn was leaning on the staircase bannister. "I'm feeling bloody terrific, aren't I?" she snapped. "It's freaking sprained. I don't know how long I'll be out of action. I've been trying to hop up these stairs to bed and it's taken me, like, twenty minutes to get this far."

"Let me help you." Addi hurried over, put Quinn's arm around her shoulder and helped carry her weight up the stairs. She bit her lip, unsure whether she should ask Quinn about the slap or not mention it.

In the low light, Addi could make out mascara tracks imprinted on Quinn's cheeks. As if reading Addi's mind, she said, "Let's just talk about this in the morning, okay? I'm too tired right now."

"Of course," Addi nodded fervently.

"What were you doing in the boys' hall, anyway?"

Addi avoided her eyes. "Oh, you know, just trying to find Leo."

"Yeah, he didn't come to help me or anything after the performance. A bit rude don't you think, in this, my hour of need?"

They had reached Quinn's bed in the dormitory. Addi helped lower her onto it while the other girls changed into pyjamas and began getting into their own beds.

"Do you need anything else?"

"Some painkillers would be good, actually." Quinn started changing out of her dancing outfit.

"Sure, I'll be back in a minute."

Downstairs was eerie when it was empty, the ghosts of colourful guests who had now gone home dancing against the walls as shadows. She reached the kitchen, flicked on the light and rummaged through the first-aid kit, finding the painkillers quickly. She made her way back to the dormitory with the silver and green box clutched in her hand, flicking the light off again on her way out.

She was almost at the other end of the dark performance hall when she heard one of the doors from the hallway open and two pairs of feet tread clunkily down the hallway.

"Don't worry, I told you, it's fine," Addi heard Kyle blustering.

"What do you think that will look like?" Freddy snapped back.

"I-I just wanted to take care of it for you," Kyle's voice faltered slightly.

Addi's ears detected a groan from Freddy as the footsteps faded. Her tired mind felt too fuzzy to process their conversation. She departed the shadowy room.

Addi yawned as she handed the painkillers to Quinn then pulled on her pyjamas sleepily. As she plonked her head down on the pillow, turned off her bedside lamp and settled into a comfortable position, she was glad that the night was over. Staring through the gaps in the curtain at the hazy night sky cloaking the city, pollution blocking the stars, Addi comforted herself with the hope that it might be a calmer day when she woke up. She fell asleep within minutes.

Unfortunately, she couldn't have been more wrong.

Everyone was jolted awake the next morning by a harrowing, high-pitched scream that reverberated through House of Nightshade. Something was terribly wrong.

Chapter Six

"You never think it will happen to you. You think about what it would be like. You go through it over and over in your mind, changing the scenario slightly each time, but deep down, you don't really believe it would ever happen, because it's something that happens to someone else, not to you." — *Tonya Hurley*

ouse of Horrors: Dead body found inside esteemed cabaret venue.

A man has been found dead at prominent entertainment venue House of Nightshade.

The body has been identified as 18-year-old Grayson Reid. It was discovered in his room at 6:30am this morning by the venue's cleaner.

House of Nightshade is a well-known and revered entertainment venue specialising in cabaret performances, food and cocktails. It is owned by esteemed hospitality professionals and power couple Emmerson and Emmeline Halloway, whose son, Frederick, is the Manager.

Police are currently taking evidence for testing and questioning staff members. The body will undergo an autopsy, but it is suspected that the time of death was not long after midnight.

Leading the investigation, Detective Inspector Paul White said the Homicide Squad has launched a full-scale investigation. "There was a wound on the back of his head, suspected to be from a metal object with a rounded or curved edge. House of Nightshade is a unique venue in which all the staff members live on premises — they sleep in rooms upstairs. There's no shortage of suspects here."

Quinn Vandez, Instagram personality and leading performer at House of Nightshade, said, "He generally kept to himself. No one really knew him that well at all."

Ivy Adams, Supervisor of Food and Beverage, says, "The only thing we knew about Grayson was that he was family friends with the Halloway's or something. That's how he got the job here."

The venue has released a statement via their website stating that all staff will be cooperating fully with police and that they hope to get to the bottom of this investigation as quickly as possible.

●

Click. Addi could hear the cameras from the open door of the room upstairs.

"How would you describe your relationship to the victim?"

Click. Addi blinked, rubbing her eyes.

"Pardon?"

"I said, how would you describe your relationship to the victim?"

Click, click. This sound came from right next to her. The police officer was pushing the top of his pen over again as he interviewed her from across the table in a corner of the performance hall.

"Aah... unusual?" Addi stared in front of her at the mass of pyjama-dressed staff milling around the room like confused farm animals, unsure of what to do with themselves.

A few of the others, including Jen and Ivy, were also being questioned by police at separate tables. People made tea and passed cups around. Police officers and forensic scientists dressed in what Addi thought looked like moon suits swarmed the place. The front door of the House was opened for access to emergency personnel. Addi could see the police tape on the pathway, blocking off the staircase.

The officer in front of her made a note on his pad. *Shit*, Addi thought. *That's so not what you're supposed to say.*

"I mean, I only just recently started working here. I didn't really know him that well," she added. "He's...he *was*...an unusual person, is what I meant to say." She trailed off, wishing the interview would be over.

"Unusual how?" the officer prompted.

"He was just different from everybody else," Addi said slowly. Her brain felt foggy. "You didn't really know what he was thinking, either. He was edgy."

"Edgy?"

"Um, cagey. Kind of closed off, you know?"

"Mmm, aha," the officer pursed his lips as he scribbled. "So not really a likeable character?"

"I didn't say that."

"Okay. But you wouldn't describe him as warm or personable?"

"He usually was with me, but I suppose less so with others while he was here," she replied honestly.

"Which was for...?"

"About a week," Addi replied faintly. It was hard to believe that less than twelve hours ago she had been excited at the prospect of going out in the city with Grayson, and now those plans had been robbed from her forever.

"Let's talk about that, shall we?" The officer didn't give her time to respond. "Approximately how long have you been working at House of Nightshade?"

"I got here a day before he did."

"Okay." The officer wrote that down. "Do you have any other information about the victim?"

"He said his mum was friends with Emmerson."

"That would be Freddy's father, the co-owner of this venue?"

"Yes."

"Did the victim have a prior relationship with anyone else here?"

"Not that I know of."

Addi glanced through the throng of staff and spotted Leo's blonde hair. He was gesturing to the stage as he was questioned by another officer. He had dark shadows under his eyes.

"Right. Did you know the victim before you began your employment at House of Nightshade?"

"No," Addi responded.

"You had no connection to him at all before he showed up?"

"No," Addi repeated. "We — I mean, the staff— had no idea who he was."

"So you know for a fact that none of the staff, except for Emmerson, knew who Grayson was when he started working here?"

"Well, I mean I'm ninety-nine per cent sure..."

"Mmm," the officer made a note.

Addi sighed, frustrated. "Okay, well, to my knowledge none of the staff knew who he was."

"What was the general reaction when the victim showed up that morning to the House?"

"Um... probably the normal reaction to a new person starting at a workplace?"

"Was there anything else? Suspicion? Irritation, perhaps?"

"No irritation," Addi shook her head. "Why would anyone be annoyed at someone they didn't know?"

"Aha, okay. Did you get to know the victim in the, ah, brief time he was here?"

"A little, yes," Addi said carefully.

"What did you talk about?"

"Um..." Addi shifted uncomfortably in her chair. She didn't want to tell him about her crush on Grayson or the fact that they had flirted and had planned to hang out together — that was her private business. She wanted to finish this interview as quickly as possible. "Just general stuff, I guess. As I said, he was pretty quiet."

"Where did he say he had been before his employment here?"

"Um," Addi closed her eyes, trying to recall. "North."

"North?" the officer asked in an *'Are you sure?'* tone, like a school teacher who knew she was wrong and was trying to give her another chance to answer.

"Yeah, that's what he told me," she shrugged.

"No other details?"

"It was a small beach town, he said."

The officer frowned slightly. "Thank you, Miss," he flipped his notebook closed. "If you think of anything else, please get in touch." He took a card out of his pocket and scrawled his name and phone line on it before handing it to Addi.

"Thank you," Addi breathed a sigh of relief as the officer moved off to speak to someone else, glad that the questioning was finished for the time being.

She shuffled off to the big silver urn that sat on the table of breakfast food and poured herself a tea. She thought she might be sick if she tried to eat anything.

"How did you go?" Leo suddenly appeared next to her, reaching for a cup.

"I'm not sure," she whispered, looking around. "The officer was a bit annoying, actually."

"You forget it's just another work day for them," Leo pointed out astutely. "They have to get all the information though while it's fresh in people's minds, I guess."

"I feel too tired to be thinking about it all right now," Addi twirled her teabag in the boiling water, watching the brown swirl through the clear liquid and deepen its colour. "My brain just wants to switch off. Do you know where Quinn is?"

Leo looked over his shoulder then turned back to Addi with a grim expression. "She's being interviewed in a room somewhere."

"Shit, on her own?"

"Yup."

"We weren't taken into a room."

"I know. I think it's because they would have found out about Grayson running into her and tripping her up last night. Those performance bimbos probably couldn't wait to tell the officers all the drama of the past week," Leo rolled his eyes and shook his head.

"Exactly. I guess with how much they disliked each other they're now trying to build a case," Addi reasoned. "Anyway, did you hear what happened last night? Wait... where even *were* you last night? I tried to find you after pack-up."

Leo faltered for just a second too long, glancing to the side. "Oh, I met some friends out for a drink. I, ah, lost track of time. We were out until closing."

"Oh, gee. Did you... I mean, what time did you get back? Did you see...?"

"Shh," Leo whispered, touching her arm in warning.

Addi raised her eyebrows.

"I just mean, you know what people are like around here," he continued. "I was a little intoxicated, but I definitely didn't come across anything out of the ordinary."

A few of the performance girls were huddled nearby, comforting each other with red, teary eyes.

"I hate this," Addi said. "I just want to get out of here."

"This place has officially turned into a horror house," Leo nodded.

"Oh look," Addi nudged him. "Here comes Quinn."

Quinn had certainly seen better days. She limped across the floor, followed by the officers. Her hair was dishevelled and knotted, falling out of its hairspray from the night before. Remnants of her thick, black eyeliner and glittering eyeshadow were smudged around her eyes. She joined Leo and Addi, throwing the officers a dark look as they continued past. Addi searched her face — she couldn't see any red mark that alluded to the slap she had heard the night before.

"How'd you go?" Leo squeezed Quinn's arm gently.

"Swimmingly," Quinn's voice dripped with sarcasm. "They completely interrogated me. They just want to frame someone so they can say they've done their job."

"You're not... I mean, they don't still think you're suspicious, do they?" Addi whispered.

"They kept asking me about last night. The bloody chorus girls dobbed me in for not liking him," Quinn glanced up the stairs to the police tape blocking off the area where Grayson's room was located.

"Oh, Jesus," Leo rolled his eyes. "Of course they did. That's so unfair! We only knew the guy for like, five minutes."

"I know right, and I certainly wasn't the only one. He didn't make a good impression on anyone," Quinn added.

Leo's eyes flitted to Addi for a brief second.

Addi looked down into her cup. "How is your ankle, Quinn?" Addi asked.

"Not much different from what I can tell — still sore and swollen," Quinn replied.

"Sit down," Leo instructed like a parent, pulling out a chair nearby.

Quinn didn't argue, leaning on a table to help her balance. Addi and Leo pulled up chairs around the table as well. Quinn glanced up at Addi for a moment and the pair exchanged a look. Addi knew they were both thinking of what had gone on in Freddy's room the night before. Quinn looked away, obviously not wanting to talk about it, and Addi didn't want to bring it up on top of everything else.

Sawyer walked past them to the urn. Addi thought he looked like the rich owner of an old manor dressed in a regal, navy silk gown. He heaped coffee grinds into a mug, filled it up with boiling water and swanned over to their table.

"Well, I've had better wake-up calls." Sawyer took a loud slurp of coffee. "Jesus, that's hot," he touched his lip as if he'd forgotten he had poured it just seconds ago.

"Did you get the third degree from the police, too?" Quinn asked.

Sawyer nodded. "Grilled me like a sausage at a pool party. Definitely left a bad taste in my mouth." He pursed his lips and looked a passing officer up and down with disdain. "They're trying to typecast the caster, for heaven's sake."

Quinn snorted. "They tried to paint me as the jealous diva, out for revenge." She said, gathering her hair at the back of her neck and flicked it over one shoulder. "How original of them."

"Oh, no," Leo suddenly exclaimed, covering his mouth with a hand.

Addi, Quinn and Sawyer followed his gaze up the stairs. Everyone around them stared, transfixed, as the body wrapped in black body bag was carefully moved down the stairs on a trolley, then rolled out the front door. It was hard to believe that Grayson was under there, frozen and cold, his life snuffed out like a flame.

It struck Addi how close they all were to the body — so close that they could almost have walked over there and lifted the plastic off him. She couldn't help her mind drifting to the thought of what he would look like under there.

The front door was pushed open as widely as possible to let the trolley through. Addi saw a huddle of reporters gathered outside, a collection of cameras and microphones bobbing over a sea of heads. Their cries for answers faded as a police officer pulled the door firmly closed behind him. Just like that, Grayson was gone.

Addi felt a wave of nausea roll through her. She propped her elbows on her knees, holding her face in her hands.

"You okay?" Leo patted her back.

"I feel a bit sick," Addi mumbled. She could feel how clammy her forehead had become. *Stop being weak*, she scolded herself. She hated how horrible situations affected her body. *Pull yourself together*.

She took a deep breath through her nose and pulled herself back up to a normal seated position. The room was much emptier now, the officers rolling up their tape and packing up. The staff all hovered around, unsure of what to do.

"Don't rush back," Sawyer farewelled them under his breath as the last of the police cleared out.

Quinn mock waved after them. "I don't think they could possibly have anything left to ask me."

Freddy closed the door behind the last of the police and swivelled to face the staff. Emmerson put a hand on his son's shoulder, just like he had the day that he'd brought Grayson to House of Nightshade, and stepped forward. He removed his hat as he did so, holding it over his chest.

"Staff," his voice rang through the deep quiet, "what happened overnight was a complete tragedy. We are extremely shaken that this happened under our roof, a roof that should be a safe haven for all of you."

Behind him, Freddy was looking everywhere but their table. Addi glanced at Quinn. She sat with her arms folded, glowering at him purposefully.

"We did not know Grayson for long," Emmerson continued stoically, "nor did we have the chance to truly welcome him into the House of Nightshade family…"

"What a load of rubbish. *Family,*" Sawyer surveyed his boss with narrowed eyes. "Look at him, trying to play the part."

Addi's gaze wandered around the room as Emmerson drawled on. Most of the staff's expressions reflected how she felt — tired and dazed. She spotted the blonde head of Kyle, who was focusing intently on Emmerson's speech. Logan and Danika, the twins who worked in the kitchen, sat side by side near the back corner looking bored. Nearby, Ralph was leaning against the wall watching Emmerson, eyebrows seemingly permanently raised and hair swept up and back, making him look like a madman. Addi realised it was the only time she had ever seen Ralph outside of the kitchen.

Could it really be true that someone inside this very room had killed Grayson?

The sudden absence of Emmerson's voice pulled her attention back to the front. Freddy looked around the room wearily. Addi could see the lines in-between his brows and crease marks on his forehead as he frowned.

In a most un-Freddy-like fashion he let out a sigh, rested his forehead briefly on his fingers then looked around at everyone and said, "Let's just get out of here, shall we? We can all go and get some breakfast or something."

Everyone stood at once, the scraping of chairs filling the room.

"Oops, sorry," Ivy apologised, accidentally bumping into Quinn on her way.

"Careful, Ivy. You don't want to be next," the dancer, Jen, commented snidely. Addi recognised her voice — it was the girl who had walked into the bar with Freddy when she, Leo and Quinn had been hanging out there after her first shift.

"What the hell did you just say?" Quinn blew up immediately.

Leo stood shoulder-to-shoulder with Quinn. "Wow, Jen, that's low."

"You heard me," Jen said stubbornly. People around them fell quiet again, eyes fixed on Quinn and Jen. "We all heard your fight with Freddy last night, demanding that someone get rid of Grayson."

"Get rid of...?" Quinn repeated with a shocked laugh. "I meant *fired*, you moron! See, this is why you're Performance Girl Number Five — they keep idiots in the back row."

"Jen, this is ridiculous," Leo shook his head.

"Is this about Freddy or something?" Quinn posed. "Hon, I know better now and I couldn't even be jealous if I tried. Sleep with him as much as you like, far be it from me to stop you from continuing to embarrass yourself."

"That's rich coming from you," Jen narrowed her eyes. "I seem to remember you pathetically swooning over him..."

Quinn moved forward. Addi and Leo both grabbed Quinn's arm and held her back.

"Quinn!" Jen reactively flinched away. "You all see this, right?" She garnered support from the room. "She's aggressive!"

Addi searched for Freddy, expecting him to intervene, but he merely leant against a wall as he observed the fight. *Some manager,* Addi thought.

"Let's just go, Quinn," Leo said loudly. "You're better than anyone who believes this rubbish."

"We're all asking who here has the potential to murder someone, but I think we can clearly see who among us would have it in them," Jen called. "When the cops ask me who I think did it, I'll tell them that they should be watching Quinn Vandez."

●

<u>A Performance to Die For?</u>

Plot thickens in House of Nightshade murder.

N.B. The performer's name and gender has been omitted for anonymity.

An anonymous source has confirmed that alleged murder victim, Grayson Reid, was involved in a heated argument the night he died.

A source has revealed that Mr. Reid had been accused of deliberately sabotaging one of the venue's star performers.

"[The performer] performed the night before Grayson... well, you know. Grayson was helping on-stage moving some props during the performance to make way for the rest of us to come out and do our part on stage. As he was moving a piece of furniture or something he accidentally blocked off [the performer] and tripped [them] up. [They] fell down in front of everyone, it was awfully embarrassing. [They're] a strong personality, you know. [They were] furious at the poor guy."

The witness confirmed that the performer in question suffered a twisted ankle.

"Then, later, we all heard a loud argument between [the performer] and management. It was about Grayson. [They] wanted them to get rid of him. It got pretty heated and out of control."

The question on everyone's mind — is it hot enough to kill?

"[The performer] never liked Grayson at all. [They] also don't take any kind of embarrassment well, and was absolutely humiliated when Grayson made them fall over in front of that whole crowd of people. The fight with management about Grayson didn't go their way either. As the main performer, [they're] used to getting what they want. Then the very next morning Grayson turns up dead. I mean, what does that look like to you? I'm just telling you the facts."

Police are still gathering evidence and conducting interviews with the staff of House of Nightshade.

"What we do know for sure is that someone who lives in House of Nightshade knows something about who did this, or did it themselves," says Officer Paul White, who is working on the case.

Could it really be true that one of House of Nightshade's leading performers is the murderer responsible for this tragedy? Only time will tell.

The venue's manager has refused to comment.

●

"I. Am going. To kill that bitch."

A small table of girls nearby turned and looked up from their coffee, eyeing Quinn off and whispering to each other.

"Bite me!" Quinn snapped at them.

"Quinn, don't you think in light of what's happened you shouldn't be saying that you're going to kill someone in the middle of a crowded room?" Addi suggested as lightly as possible.

"What? I'm just talking like the murderer I am," Quinn quipped loudly, the newspaper she was holding flapping as she waved her hands dramatically.

People stopped spreading butter on their toast and turned, watching her warily.

"Where are my freakin' cigarettes?" Quinn patted the pockets of her grey tracksuit pants, flopping grumpily onto a chair at their breakfast table.

"We must be cautious of our actions and words during these tempestuous times," Leo commented daintily, tapping his boiled egg with an antique silver spoon.

Addi giggled at his intentionally silly fanciness.

"Have you read this?" Quinn blustered on, ignoring them both. She opened the newspaper on their table, covering Leo's plate of toast cut carefully into soldiers. Her hair was falling out of its messy top knot, and it looked as if she still hadn't removed her make-up from two nights ago.

"Oh, Quinn, that newspaper is garbage," Leo retrieved his toast from underneath its pages and removed the lid of his egg. "Anyway, since when do you care what people say about you?"

"You wouldn't be so calm if this was happening to you. They're calling me a *murderer*. Freakin' Janice," Quinn grumbled.

"Jen," Leo corrected.

Quinn ignored him again. "It's not enough that she called me a murderer in front of everyone I live with. She had to go and tell some idiot reporter who's now published it to thousands of people across the city! I had to suspend all my social media accounts because I'm receiving hate messages from complete randoms because of this stupid article."

Two girls who were walking by their table stared wide-eyed at Quinn before hurrying to the other side of the room with their bowls of yoghurt and fruit.

"That's right, hurry along before I stab you with this butter knife!" Quinn shrieked at them. She dug into the pockets of the black hoodie she was wearing, pulled out a packet of cigarettes and lit one up at the table.

"Lovely," Leo pursed his lips, flapping the smoke away from his breakfast with one hand.

Quinn pulled her hood further down over her face.

"That Jen girl is just trying to get as much attention as she can," Addi started.

"I don't see anyone else being accused," Quinn butted in.

"I'm sure it'll blow over in a few days and everyone will forget what she said."

"And you know this because you've been in my situation before, have you?" Quinn blew smoke out, narrowing her eyes at Addi.

"Well, no, but…"

"Yeah, look, I don't take life advice from kids," Quinn fired at her.

"Come on, Quinn, she's just trying to help," Leo reasoned.

"She should stop trying."

"Um, I'm right here," Addi interjected, annoyed.

"Okay, so we can't change what's happened," Leo folded the newspaper so the article was no longer staring out at them, "but we can plan how to respond from here. What do you want to do about this?"

"I want to take that bitch down, and everyone else in this bloody place. They all need to learn a lesson," Quinn muttered gruffly.

Leo patted her hand supportively while Addi worried about just what a vengeful Quinn might be capable of.

Jen walked by their table, having just filled up a cup of tea. "Morning, Quinn. Ooh, you're a pretty sight," she smirked as she surveyed her. "Did you read my interview?" Her smug smile disappeared into her teacup as she raised it to her lips.

Quinn gritted her teeth, not looking at Jen. "Trashy newspaper for a trashy person. Fitting."

"Are you glad you've got your five minutes of fame, now?" Leo posed.

"I wouldn't be so smug if I were you, Leo," Jen said snidely. "Or haven't you told your BFF the news?"

Quinn's eyes flickered between Leo and Jen. "What news? What's she talking about, Leo?"

Jen's smile widened. "My days of being your back-up are over. *I'm* the new female lead."

Quinn snorted. "You can't be serious."

"Leo?" Jen prompted.

Leo fiddled with his hair. "Yeah, ah, Sawyer decided yesterday that Jen will be subbing for you while your ankle heals."

Quinn blinked profusely. "What... how did this happen?" Her voice was shrill again. "She can't just waltz in and take my part! She's not even good enough, I mean, there's a reason she was dumped in the chorus. Where's Sawyer? What about my understudy? He can't allow this!"

Addi sank lower into her chair. She thought she was doing well by making friends and already being in a group at House of Nightshade, and now they were becoming the most hated group of people there. Not to mention that the boy she was starting to like had died. Just her luck, she thought to herself.

Jen gave a fake sigh and turned to walk away. "Too late. You're really just upset that nobody is worshiping you anymore. Isn't it funny how things turn out? I hooked up with Freddy, *and* I've taken your place as lead performer. I don't think many people will pay to come and watch a murderer sing and dance. How the mighty fall."

"You'll regret this, you fake bitch!" Quinn yelled after her. Jen didn't look back.

"Excuse me, Quinn."

Quinn gave a start.

Freddy's form towered over their breakfast table. "If you wish to shout could you please take it outside and direct it at a brick wall or something instead? Your co-workers are trying to enjoy their breakfast. Save making a scene for the stage, yeah?" He walked away swiftly.

"As opposed to the hundred times you and your family have made a scene here?" Leo called after him.

Quinn scrunched her face as she watched Freddy go. "I bet it was him. That lying asshole," she seethed. "He's just angry because I slapped–" Quinn stopped herself as Addi and Leo looked up at her. "Excuse me."

She scrunched up the newspaper article and threw it on the ground before limping out of the hall.

"Oh, gee. It's going to be one of *those* days," Leo sipped his tea, then caught a glimpse of Addi. "I know Quinn can be a lot."

"Yeah, I'd noticed," Addi couldn't help but roll her eyes. "I was only trying to be helpful and she bit my head off."

"Just give her space, she'll sort it out."

"What happened with Quinn and Freddy in the end?" Addi asked Leo. "They really seem to resent each other."

"Yes, they do. For good reason too on Quinn's part. What was that about slapping someone?" Leo frowned.

"Last night Quinn and Freddy were having an argument after our shift finished. Pretty much everyone heard it. Quinn was furious about the Grayson thing and wanted Freddy to fire him. Then we heard one of them slap the other but didn't really know who it was — until now."

Leo sighed. "That's what happens whenever they interact for more than one sentence; it completely boils over. Freddy can never admit that he might have done anything wrong. It's infuriating for Quinn. Look, I trust you Addi, and I think you should know what Freddy's really like, but you can't let on that you know to Quinn, okay? She's way too proud to tell anyone this story."

"Of course," Addi agreed quickly.

"You know they were seeing each other a bit. They were hooking up, and it wasn't just sex. There was something more. Quinn never admitted that, but I could tell. That's the thing with Freddy — it's better not to get involved at all because he just takes people on this completely fucked-up ride. One minute he's looking at Quinn like love is right on the tip of his tongue. Next second, she barely existed. All the girls he cycles through are like cocaine addicts or something, junkies addicted to his messed up way of liking them. I hated watching Quinn go through it; I never got a good feeling about Freddy from the get-go. There was always something two-faced about him. I tried to warn her, but you know Quinn, she doesn't like being told what to do and I just had to let her do her thing and discover for herself."

"Sometimes that's the only way," Addi nodded.

"It kills me though, because I know I'm right about these people. I have a great bullshit detector," Leo tapped his head, "but people don't want to know the truth, Addi." He dipped the last of his soldiers into the soft, bright orange yolk of his egg and munched the end off.

Addi thought about her small crush on Grayson and inwardly cringed. Meanwhile, Sawyer tinkled around on the black, glossy piano in the back corner under the stage, providing a soothing background to the breakfast chatter.

"So, no one listens to you and that's why we all make stupid mistakes," Addi summarised. Both of them grinned. "What happened next?"

Leo continued. "It got pretty exclusive between them. Everyone knew about it and it looked like they might have had a shot at having an actual relationship. On the outside, it did seem as if he really cared about her. It was only me that knew what was actually going on. They'd be getting along and flirting at work one minute, she'd spend the night in his room, and then the next thing you know he wouldn't even say a word to her at all and be smarming it up with other girls. Quinn always made excuses for him. She said that he'd told her some really deep things, about how he suffered with his mental health and stuff from his past."

"He started talking to me about that, too," Addi nodded.

"I bet he did," Leo pursed his lips. "Quinn would pass it off, saying that he was just really complex and that was his nature. I said, we're all complex — that's not an excuse for someone's behaviour. Anyway, one day, Freddy told her a friend who he'd met while he was living overseas was coming to visit, someone who used to work with him. He needed to get to the airport. She offered him a lift and drove with him there. They were waiting at the arrival gate together and, in Quinn's words, this beautiful Japanese woman with the silkiest hair she'd ever seen came swanning off the flight and lit up when she saw Freddy. She walked over to them and kissed Freddy on the mouth... and he kissed her back. Right there in front of Quinn."

"Oh my god," Addi gaped.

"Mmhmm," Leo nodded in agreeance with her reaction. "Apparently he put an arm around this new girl and introduced Quinn to her as his 'friend'. Quinn then had to drive him and his freaking international *girlfriend* back home."

"Oh... my *god*," Addi repeated. "What an asshole!"

"Makes sense now, doesn't it?"

"Who even does that?" Addi thought of Freddy and wanted to go and slap him, too

"Messed up, hey? Like, he could have just caught a train there. He actually *wanted* Quinn to see that. She learned a pretty tough lesson that day. You give away your trust and look what happens."

"Jeesh, no wonder she's bitter," Addi observed.

"That's where the rivalry began. Around here, you're either on team Freddy or team Quinn. Speak of the devil."

Quinn hobbled back through the door, limped over and sat sideways on a chair at their table, launching into conversation as if she'd never left. "You know what? I think Chorus Girl Number Eight needs to be taken down a rung or two and know what it feels like to be humiliated in front of everyone. I can't do much with this ankle, so I'm going to need you guys to help me. To start, I'm thinking we get water or something and pour it on the stage tonight so she slips and falls during performance — she can see how she likes it."

"Ah, do you really think that revenge is the way to go about this...?" Addi began.

"Oh, this is just the beginning, don't you worry."

Addi gave Leo a sideways glance. "I just don't think you should sink to their level if you want to prove a point."

Quinn pierced Addi with a stare. "I cannot believe that you've witnessed what they've done to me and you're going to sit there and judge *me*."

"I'm not judging you, Quinn, I just don't agree..."

"So you won't help me?" Quinn demanded.

Addi stood her ground. She was still too new to be taking sides, and she certainly didn't want any enemies. "No, I don't want to do that," she responded quietly, avoiding Quinn's piercing stare.

Quinn studied Addi for a second. "You're just a scared kid. You know, technically you wouldn't even be here if it weren't for me."

"Don't be harsh," Leo reasoned. "Addi's new. She doesn't know Jen enough to go marching off into battle with her."

"Right, okay, stick up for your new little friend," Quinn grumbled.

"Don't be ridiculous, Quinn. You just need to cool off for a couple of days…"

At that moment, the doors from the kitchen opened and Emmerson strode grandly in, his cane unnecessarily tapping the ground in front of him irregularly as he did so. Logan and Danika sauntered into the performance hall, followed by Ralph. The twins sat in the corner, eyes flitting around the room, seemingly uncomfortable outside of their usual kitchen habitat.

"Here we go," Leo sighed apprehensively.

Sawyer's piano song cut out midway and he spun around on his stool. Ralph chose a spot near him and leaned back against the stage, observing the scene in front of him with childlike anticipation.

"We thought we would have a short, impromptu meeting," Emmerson began. "We appreciate your patience with us as we have dealt with the repercussions of this tragedy."

Kyle's blonde head was visible sitting near Emmerson, staring up at him like a keen schoolboy.

"Whilst I'm sure we all have hundreds of questions racing through our heads, it is crucial that we let the police do their work and get to the bottom of this as soon as possible."

Freddy stood. In contrast to his father, his light blue button-up was visibly crinkly, stubble dotting his chin and neck. He had dark purple shadows under his eyes. "The police will be coming back to the House periodically to further question us." His voice sounded tired and dejected. "It is important that we all comply and answer questions as requested. I know we didn't exactly, ah, *know* Grayson all too well, so do not feel bad for saying so to the police. We can only do as much as we can." He stepped back, apparently finished with his part, and pulled a cigar out of his front pocket, lighting it and taking a drag.

"Right," Emmerson clapped his hands together and rubbed them. "We would also like to announce that, in the interest of maintaining normalcy, we will be resuming rehearsals immediately and continuing operations as normal."

A murmur swept around the room. Addi heard Ralph give a bark of laughter before turning to say something indistinguishable to Sawyer, who nodded and rolled his eyes in response.

"Needless to say," Emmerson raised his voice over the hubbub, "for the time being we still have costs to cover, which includes having a place for all of you to live."

That shut everyone up.

"The media remain camped outside our premises. We will present a united front and uphold the reputation of House of Nightshade."

"What reputation? In case you forgot, someone just got murdered here a few days ago," Leo said loudly.

"Ohh, shit," Quinn laughed, impressed.

Emmerson shot Leo a stern look. "I understand you're upset," he said testily. "This is going to be a very trying and emotional time for us all..."

"Is he pulling this stuff straight out of his ass?" Leo muttered. Addi snorted.

"...However, we think it is of utmost importance to help you all get back to a normal routine, which means back to work. Not to mention that, as you can tell from the constant barrage of our media friends outside," Emmerson continued with subtle derision, "this story has, naturally, been all over the press. We are therefore expecting an influx of guests due to this incident."

"Ugh, people are messed up," Quinn muttered.

"Why would you want to go somewhere where someone's *died*?" Addi wondered aloud.

"To be a part of the mystery," Leo shrugged. "People probably want to see where it happened for themselves so they can tell everyone about it."

"I would remind you all, however," Emmerson raised his voice, "that maintaining optimal performance during this time is also in your best interest for the future of your employment here at House of Nightshade."

The girls near Addi bowed their heads as if being told off.

"Is that a *threat*?" Leo asked distrustfully.

"No, it's a fact." Kyle had turned around and decided to chime in.

"Oh, fabulous, cue the lackey," Leo rolled his eyes.

"Emmerson is right," Kyle continued. "Performing well at this time is good all round — good for business and good for our image in the media."

"What, are you their secretary or something?" Leo jerked his head in the direction of Emmerson and Freddy.

Kyle's eyes turned to slits. "No," he blustered, starting to turn pink in the face, "I'm just not as ignorant as you. Let's look at the positives here."

"Someone just died and you want to focus on the positives?" Leo asked. "Do you even think about what's coming out of your mouth?"

"Well," Kyle searched for words, "what would you rather do, sit around all day doing nothing?"

"I know that's the preferred strategy of our current manager," Leo slighted.

The room all sucked in a breath collectively.

"Oh ho!" Ralph clapped his knee, looking gleeful.

"Young man," Emmerson began as Freddy slowly slinked back further, "if you have a problem with the way things are run around here, I would urge you to come and express your concerns to us rather than letting your emotions get the better of you."

"Funny you should say that, because whenever anyone has anything to say to the man you've left in charge he always seems to find some excuse to avoid the conversation."

"Leo, you should not let personal biases cloud your judgment..." Freddy began.

"Oh for Christ's sake, a staff member was killed and we've barely heard from you," Leo pointed out.

"Nice performance you're putting on there," Kyle piped up.

"Excuse you?" Quinn reacted before Leo could.

"I just find it odd that Leo suddenly seems to care that Grayson is dead, however I don't recall you being his biggest fan when he was alive."

"Kyle, do you really want to go there right now?" Addi tried to interject. He ignored her.

"What, like you were, Kyle? We could almost hear you from the stage, yelling at him every night," Quinn snapped back.

"Don't pretend that this hasn't turned out just the way you wanted. You didn't like him and suddenly he's dead?"

No one spoke. Freddy's head swivelled from Kyle to Leo. Emmerson's brow was furrowed.

"In fact," Kyle belligerently forged on, "I don't remember seeing Leo around much that night at all."

The staff all looked uneasily to Leo. Ralph chortled from his spot near the back, and a girl near Addi turned her head to give him a disapproving look. Quinn gaped at Kyle. Freddy frowned, staring at his shoes. Sawyer shifted uncomfortably.

"Are you seriously accusing me?" Leo asked slowly.

Kyle held his hands up as if to excuse himself. "I mean, I'm just stating facts here. Maybe you were helping your best friend Quinn, I don't know."

Quinn threw her hands up in the air. "What is wrong with everyone in this place?"

"Okay, then, tell us where you were," Kyle directed at Leo.

"Are you the police?" Leo raised his eyebrows.

"It's not a hard question," Kyle prodded. "Where were you when Grayson was killed?"

"I went out for drinks," Leo replied tensely.

"Oh, that's convenient," Kyle said. "Can anyone confirm that story?"

Leo paused. "Yeah, Addi saw me when I was leaving to go out."

Addi glanced at Leo for a second before looking away. He knew that she knew that was an outright lie. What was he hiding?

"But Addi was asking where you were," Ivy piped up. "When Quinn and Freddy were screaming at each other, I ran into you, remember, Addi? You said you hadn't seen Leo all night."

Kyle looked as if Christmas had arrived early. "Very interesting, Leo, how you seem to be lying about what you were doing on this pinnacle occasion and no one can confirm where you were. What have you and Quinn been up to?"

"Oh dear Christ, nothing!" Quinn started shouting again. "How dare you accuse us, you psychos are all victimising us and you're lucky you have a spineless weasel as a manager who's just sitting over there letting you concoct this absurd story because *you*," she pointed at Kyle, "have always been jealous of Leo and *you*," she jabbed a finger at Jen, "have always been jealous of me because we're the stars of this whole freakin' show!"

"Why so angry? Are you on your period or something?" Kyle sneered at Quinn.

"How would you know? You've never even seen a vagina," Quinn shot back.

"You..." Kyle spluttered. He gave up on a retort and turned to Addi instead. "Let's ask Addilyn, then."

Addi fought the urge to run away.

"Did you see Leo, or not?"

Addi's hands fidgeted in her lap as thoughts scrambled through her brain. Leo was pretty much her only friend in this place so far, but she couldn't lie; Ivy had already pointed out the truth. She didn't want to make herself look guilty, too. "What Ivy said was true."

Quinn audibly scoffed at her. Addi couldn't even look at Leo. She didn't want him or Quinn to be accused of this, but what else was she supposed to do?

"There you go," Kyle gestured triumphantly.

Freddy puffed his cigar, appearing partially amused by the scene playing out in front of him.

"Okay, okay, settle down," Quinn seemed to have regained some calm. "I think we're all missing one crucial point here. Who was the last person to see Grayson? Who actually spent time with him that night? Yes, he was working, then he tripped me up and was told to leave, presumably to his room. When I was walking back up the stairs to go to bed that night, I saw Addi in the boys' hallway."

Addi stared in disbelief at Quinn. Was she seriously trying to throw her under the bus now? Yes, she had knocked on Grayson's door, but she hadn't actually *seen* him. She racked her brains quickly. Should she say that, or should she keep quiet? "I...I was looking for Leo. I told you that I was looking for Leo."

"Mmm, I don't think you were, though. You were acting weird about it when I saw you there, and you were the only one that ever really talked to Grayson."

"Quinn, this is ridiculous," Addi sputtered.

Emmerson shook his head and, apparently bored with the back-and-forth, gestured to Sawyer, Ralph and Freddy to talk business.

Addi continued to desperately try and defend herself. "Grayson and I were friendly, but I didn't really know him any better than anyone else here," she lied.

"And why would we believe a word you say?" Quinn asked the room at large. "You haven't even told the truth about your own age. She's not an adult yet, you know? Technically she's working here ill-"

"*Quinn*!" Leo flashed his eyes over at the management huddle as the staff began to chatter at Quinn's reveal. It appeared the three older gentlemen had tuned out of the conversation, however Freddy turned his head back to their huddle just a little too late.

Yet again, Addi started to feel sick alongside the rage now boiling inside her. She couldn't believe it. Not only was Quinn, someone she had thought was becoming her friend, trying to paint her as capable of murder, she had also carelessly put Addi's future on the line. If Freddy and Emmerson did indeed investigate her age, she was well and truly screwed. If she was fired, she had nowhere to go.

Addi clenched her fists. "I don't know what you're talking about, Quinn. And I didn't see Grayson at all after he tripped you." *Technically true*, she reminded herself. "I already told you, I was in the boy's hall looking for Leo." *Very untrue.*

"I saw her outside Grayson's room."

Addi felt like her heart had dropped into her stomach. Everyone's heads whipped around to the waiter sitting near the back; the waiter who had helped Addi and Grayson clean up the tray that Grayson had dropped the other night. The same waiter Addi had bumped into when she was near the boys' dormitory, who had told her where Grayson's room was.

The boy's eyes flicked uneasily around the room, seeming unsure under the sudden attention. "Uh, yeah, she was hanging around the boy's floor after the show had ended. She asked me which one Grayson's room was."

Addi gulped as everyone turned to stare at her. Quinn's eyes flashed with malice.

So this is how it feels, Addi thought. In less than one minute, she had become the latest suspect in the murder case.

Chapter Seven

"Man is not what he thinks he is, he is what he hides." — André Malraux

Interview with Frederick Halloway

Officer: How long have you worked at House of Nightshade?

Freddy: Technically, my whole life. It's owned by my parents, I've been folding napkins from about as soon as I learnt how to walk. My parents used to send me out onto the floor in my nappy. In a proper salaried capacity, however, I came back to manage the venue a few years ago.

Officer: Came back from where?

Freddy: Puerto Rico. I worked in management for a hotel franchise and lived over there for the job.

Officer: That's quite the change, from exotic beaches back to the place you grew up. Why did you decide to trade that life for your old one?

Freddy: Yes, yes it was. Well, my family needed me. The stress of owning and managing the House was beginning to take its toll on my parents. They've been in the industry ever since they started working, and after a couple of decades it's just become too much for them. They were under a lot of pressure and didn't know what to do — they were thinking of selling the place, but they didn't know what they would do for money. Add to that the, ah, incident with my mum hiring a private investigator on my dad... well, there was a piling up of things putting a lot of stress on their marriage. To be fair to my mum, she did think he was seeing someone else, but things were never the same after that. I had experience in management and, you know, I'd left the country for years, so I felt like it was my turn to step up for them.

Officer: That's very honourable of you. It must have been difficult to adjust. Did you ever hold any resentment for having to come back and fulfil this familial duty?

Freddy: I mean, of course there are days I wish I was back living in some tropical location, but don't we all have those days? I made my choice and I wouldn't have chosen to come back if I didn't want to.

Officer: Of course. And have you always managed teams of people?

Freddy: Mostly. I started working here — at House of Nightshade — as a waiter when I was a teenager, but progressed to supervisor for a few years and then worked in operations management in hotels when I went overseas.

Officer: How would your staff describe you as a manager?

Freddy: [clears throat] I think generally peaceful and laid back. Unlike other types of managers I don't hover, you know... let them take the reins. It's what people need to develop professionally.

Officer: Have you ever had any run-ins, incidents or arguments with your staff members?

Freddy: No, no. I stay out of any squabbles. Arguments, gossip, none of that is really my thing.

Officer: Outside of work, do you ever spend time with any staff members? Have deeper friendships or bonds that go beyond the usual employee-manager relationship?

Freddy: Of course not. That would be unprofessional.

Officer: And you manage that, even though you live with your staff 24/7?

Freddy: I prefer to keep to myself.

Officer: How well did you know the victim?

Freddy: I didn't. My dad was friends with his dad, but I never met the boy until he came here.

Officer: Right. And how long have you been on antidepressant medication?

Freddy: You really have done your homework.

Officer: Just doing our job.

Freddy: Naturally. Probably about eight years, on and off.

Officer: Currently on?

Freddy: Currently on. Although the goal is not to be.

Officer: How do they affect your mood?

Freddy: It's just...numbing. Not up, not down. You just flatline. It stops the bad emotions, but it also prevents the good. You're kind of getting through life. I presume you don't need to take my full medical history, though, and we don't need to continue talking about the state of my mental health?

Officer: I think that's all for now. You may go.

●

The performance hall and kitchen were in a flurry. Ivy rushed past Addi at top speed in the opposite direction, a huge armful of velvet and lace tablecloths almost tumbling out of her arms. Sawyer studied a flat-laid notebook of scrawled writing and diagrams of the stage filled with spots and arrows. One of the little alcoves of couches was now host to a plethora of tulle, feathers and various fabrics piled up high. A handful of performance girls sorted through the collection, laying out outfits and holding items up on one another to see if they fit. Wigs were draped over chair arms or lay on the floor, splayed out like a cat lying flat on a rug. Quinn was perched on the arm of the large, navy couch, grumpily fixing a garment with a long thread. Having been moaning and complaining about having to rest her ankle, Sawyer had instructed her to zip her trap shut and do something useful instead.

More waitresses traipsed in and out of the kitchen doors carrying trays loaded with freshly polished, mismatched antique cutlery.

A girl whizzed by clutching candles. "Addi, can you light?" She chucked a box of matches to her as she went by. Addi could hardly believe the girl didn't drop everything she was holding in the process of doing so.

Addi agreed as quickly as she could, but the waitress had already sped by and was plonking candlesticks and small, crystal candle holders on every available surface. Addi tried to follow her trail, obediently striking matches and watching the flames flicker to life. There was a drone as Kyle turned on a vacuum and began steering it across the floor, adding to the raucous rhythm of upbeat jazz blaring out of speakers.

"Honey, don't you dare light these pages on fire," Sawyer warned as she approached his table with the matches in her hand, grinning slyly.

Addi felt a little lighter as she smiled back. In the fall-out of Quinn's accusation, barely anyone else in the House was being nice to her. "Can't promise anything. There's only about a thousand candlesticks in this place."

"Tell me about it." Sawyer rolled his eyes. "Emmeline loves collecting the entire contents of antique shops, that's why we can hardly walk in here without knocking one over." He surveyed the staff buzzing around the room. "God, this is a madhouse," he muttered, before calling out to the dancers on stage, "Right! I think you four need to spin to the other side instead for those last eight counts..."

Addi glanced up at the rehearsals on stage where Leo and Jen were practicing their sequence with each other, awkwardly fumbling as Leo tried to get used to lifting his new partner. She turned away quickly, feeling sad that things were now awkward between them because of what had happened at breakfast that morning. She felt so angry at herself for trusting Quinn enough when she was drunk to confide her real age in her. It had been so nice to feel like she was making real friends that she had got caught up in the moment and wanted to share her secret — of course, the alcohol had played a part in that too. She wished she had never seen Quinn's post and knocked on this door. She couldn't run away now, though; that would look even more suspicious. Besides, she'd spent her paycheque on new work shoes and didn't have any money to afford somewhere else to live.

Addi was glad to have the distraction of busily setting everything up for the night ahead. Emmerson had been right; ticket sales for a night at House of Nightshade had skyrocketed with all the publicity the venue was receiving. At least the music and Kyle's vacuuming was loud enough to drown out the noise of the press outside, knocking on the door every ten minutes and waiting to pounce like seagulls on staff coming or leaving.

Nearby, Ivy sighed in frustration, shaking and flapping one of the large velvet tablecloths out in front of her in an attempt to smooth it out evenly over the table.

"Need some help with that?" Addi asked tentatively, unsure how her supervisor felt about her now she was clued into the fact Addi had lied to get her job.

"Thanks."

Addi left her candle-lighting duties and picked up a corner of the mauve velvet cloth. It drooped heavily in the middle as she and Ivy began to stretch it out between them.

"Have the place all set up in twenty minutes, Ivy," Ivy mimicked, "Yeah, no dramas, boss. You know why he thinks we can do that? Because he can't even remember the last time he's done actual work in this place."

"I'm sure he didn't really expect us to get this all done in twenty minutes," Addi tried to assure her.

Ivy gave a small chuckle as they moved the cloth and draped it over a circular table crowded with too many chairs.

"What?"

"I forget you're still so new," Ivy shifted the cloth slightly, pulling it further towards her, before nodding, apparently satisfied. "Hey, I know what I said after breakfast put you in a tough spot. I wasn't trying make Leo look suspicious on purpose, but I feel like telling the truth is the best thing to do in this situation."

Addi waved a hand awkwardly. *Count on Ivy to address any slight tension head-on*, she thought. "You're right. Someone's obviously not telling the truth as it is, we don't need even more lies on top of that."

Ivy raised her eyebrows at Addi in a way that told her she was thinking about exactly what Addi thought she was.

"Um," Addi started sheepishly, starting to blush. Having lied to Ivy suddenly felt much worse than lying to her actual managers. "Yeah, I guess I need some practice at that too. Look, I didn't want to lie about my age to work here but I just had to get out of my home. I'm almost 18, and it's not like I'm working behind the bar very often anyway..."

Ivy gave an excusing smile at Addi's verbal dump. "Not that I condone lying, but I've been working here long enough to know that being a few months off the legal age of serving alcohol is probably on the lighter side of the slips of the law that have gone on here. Personally, I like to give everyone the benefit of the doubt when they're new so I'll pretend I didn't hear what Quinn said. Far be it from me to judge you if Freddy failed to do his due diligence when making hires," she shrugged pragmatically. "Let's be real, I need as much help as I can get around here."

Addi twisted a strand of hair, a little taken aback at Ivy's quick acceptance. "Thanks, Ivy."

"I know they're getting to you right now, but try not to let them. Otherwise you'll just wind up bitter like the rest of us." Ivy grimaced, picked up her pile and continued dutifully to the next table.

Addi had returned to lighting candles when Emmerson flitted through the entrance. She watched him look around, unnoticed by anyone else amongst all the kerfuffle and noise, grab his hat from the stand near the door, skirt around the edge of the performance hall and — in contrast to how he usually walked, tapping his stick in front of him without caring about drawing attention to himself — slink through the doors of the kitchen.

It was definitely suspicious. She hovered, the conversation she'd overheard between Grayson, Emmerson and Freddy running through her head, followed by her own words from a moment ago: *Someone's obviously not telling the truth.*

Leo and Jen were in serious conversation with Sawyer on the stage, nodding in understanding as he pointed and gestured around. Quinn appeared to be having some issues with her new task and was bent over, fixated on stabbing the garment with the silver needle. Kyle pushed chairs disruptively as he manoeuvred the vacuum. Everyone else was speed-walking across the floor to set tables. No one was paying attention to Addi, being the latest social outcast of the workplace. Had it been someone other than Emmerson, perhaps she wouldn't have followed them. However, past experience was giving her the strong sense that this father figure wasn't to be trusted and, as she had done before, it looked like it was up to her to do something about it.

She turned and marched purposefully towards the kitchen, through the swing door and right through the door out the back, closing it quietly behind her.

The back of the House was a small courtyard squeezed between brick walls of the adjoining terraces. With limited space in the city, the raised garden beds overflowed with myriad herbs amongst thick bunches of green, leafy vegetables. A rusting bird bath stood, forgotten, on the uneven red brick. She let Emmerson walk down the constricted path between the garden beds and disappear out the wrought iron gate before slinking out behind him onto the street.

Litter tumbled across the ground past her feet in the wind. She scrunched her nose as she walked through tendrils of second-hand smoke emanating from a man wearing a leopard-print jacket. Emmerson didn't stop to look back as he strode purposefully through the crowds ambling down the walkway. For the first time in a long while Addi was grateful for her slight, flatter frame as she squeezed between office workers, laughing and strolling slowly on their way to get coffee or late lunch, to keep up with Emmerson. She followed him around a corner, passing a large pub on a street corner with a few people sitting out on the deck, throwing back beers. Cars honked as they streamed in from the city centre and pedestrian crossings sounded alongside the *whooshes* of wind.

Addi rounded a corner, passing hole-in-the-wall coffee shops with steamers screeching and milk gurgling, their window displays nearly empty as they were almost closed. She caught whiffs of cooking food mixed in with the pungent smell of rubbish and cigarette smoke from the streets. Even though it wouldn't make a difference with the amount of people and traffic noise around, she tried her best to walk quietly as she trailed a fair distance behind Emmerson. She felt a strange excitement come over her — she had run away from homes before, but she had never trailed someone. She felt as if she was in a movie. Would she get to jump in a taxi and yell, "Follow that car!"?

Emmerson came to a halt after crossing the street. Still on the other side, Addi hung back, taking a seat on one of the two chairs at a tiny table outside a drab takeaway chicken shop. She tried to pull her hair down in front of her face (a fruitless task as it was determined to spring back up immediately) and watched as Emmerson waited for something. The kitchen inside the shop crackled and popped as the cook loaded slivers of pale, frozen potato into the frying basket and submerged it into the boiling oil.

A taxi slowed in the street with a small screech, brake lights glowing red. Emmerson turned to greet a woman who emerged from the car. Her long, straight black hair fell down her back over a brown fur coat. They pecked each other on the cheek, Emmerson briefly grazing the woman's waist with his hands. She slunk back down into the backseat of the taxi, disappearing behind the door. Emmerson looked around himself. Addi put her head down briefly, pretending she was reading something on the table in front of her. When she looked up, Emmerson was already closing the door of the taxi on the other side. She watched as it glided down the street, turned a corner and disappeared.

Whatever Emmerson was up to, she was going to keep watching him. In fact, she vowed as she trod her way back to the House that she was going to keep watch on all of them. If no one was going to believe that she didn't have anything to do with Grayson's murder, she would just have to prove it and make sure herself that her name was cleared.

Leo was unconvinced when Addi hurried to tell him between songs as soon as she got back. "I mean, it could have been anyone. They tend to set up business meetings when they come back to Sydney."

"He snuck out the back door, though," Addi reiterated. "He definitely didn't want anyone to know he was leaving. I don't see why he would have done that if he wasn't up to something suspicious."

"You're sure it wasn't Emmeline?" Leo asked.

"Does Emmeline have long, black hair?"

Leo shook his head. "Not the last time I saw it. Did you see her face?"

"Nope. Emmerson pretty much just got straight into the taxi and then it left."

Leo lowered his voice as Sawyer shimmied by with a collection of costume items and started handing them out to the chorus. "You didn't hear anything?"

"I was on the opposite side of the street, and the wind was blowing too loudly anyway."

Leo shrugged. "I wouldn't look into it. Emmeline and Emmerson have been in business in this city for decades; they know a hell of a lot of people around here. It sounds like he was just catching up with someone."

"It definitely seemed like something shifty," Addi pressed. "He really snuck out like he didn't want anyone to see him."

Leo waved it off. "Sounds like pretty typical showman Halloway behaviour to me. They could make breathing air look sneaky. I know someone's just died, but that doesn't mean we have to now treat everyone's coffee dates as suspicious activity, you know."

Addi bit her lip dubiously. Maybe Leo was happy shrugging it off as in-character for the owner, but she wasn't going to give her trust to Emmerson that easily.

Leo glanced down at the navy couch.

Addi followed his gaze and opened her mouth to farewell Leo before Quinn spotted them talking, but then decided against it. Why should she give up her friendship with Leo? "Look, I guess we don't have to talk if you're worried Quinn's going to see and get mad at you for it," she began to gush, "but this morning was so weird and I'm sorry I couldn't stick up for you and I really need a friend right now and..."

"Whoa, take a breath," Leo stopped her. "I'm the one who should be sorry. Lying like that and making you have to choose whether to lie or tell the truth was really shitty of me. You did the right thing, I respect you for that."

Addi gave a small, empty laugh. "Thanks. At least that's one less person who hates me now."

"Hey, just like you said to Quinn earlier, this will all blow over in a few days and people will forget what was said," Leo tried to comfort her.

"Yeah, I kind of regret saying that. It is completely different now it's happening to me. This isn't just some dumb rumour at school. It's a murder. People actually think that I had something to do with..." Addi couldn't even bring herself to say it. She felt tears of frustration starting to prick her eyes and willed them away. She didn't want Leo to have to comfort her. "I've been here for what, two weeks?" she tried to mask dabbing at her eyes as itching her face. "No one's going to be on my side. It was just so mean of Quinn to throw me under the bus like that when I didn't even do anything."

"I know you might not be able to understand it, and I'm not trying to defend the things she said, but Kyle was ganging up on me and Quinn and she couldn't see another way out so she accused you to protect us. Kind of like survival instinct. There's no way she believes you actually had anything to do with it."

"I don't care what she thinks," Addi snapped. "She did this to me all because I wouldn't side with her and take part in some stupid, high-school revenge. The fact that she told everyone about my age... she doesn't understand. She grew up with parents that literally paid for her to go to university. Meanwhile my families probably only kept me as long as they did for the tax benefits." Addi didn't care how much Leo tried to reason. She didn't ever want to forgive Quinn.

"Honestly, I think the best thing you could do right now is just keep your head down and act like you don't care," Leo suggested. "Emmerson and Freddy are untrustworthy in general; that's not really news. Be careful there. There are a lot of people in this place that you don't want to be getting on the bad side of. Keep to yourself for now and be careful who you trust."

Sawyer flounced over, glancing behind him at Jen going over her new moves. "I hate to break up this tea party but it's time to get your tush back on stage."

"Sorry," Addi immediately hurried out of the way.

"Have fun down there," Leo called after her.

Addi simply grimaced.

The music started, then faltered. She heard Sawyer calling out for someone to fix it as she left the stage, feeling a little lighter now that she had patched things up with Leo. It wasn't until she entered the clanging and steam of the kitchen that she realised he still hadn't mentioned where, in fact, he had been the night that Grayson died.

Ralph swayed back and forth behind the silver bench, tossing vegetables around in a massive frypan and checking on countless chicken drumsticks in the oven. "Did you see them all? Just getting carrots in here is like a circus. A bloody circus! All I wanted was some carrots!"

Logan afforded him a laughing smile as he chopped herbs at the bench. Danika had her back turned, whipping up bulk amounts of cream with giant beaters.

"These people, they all bought their tickets to see us, Logan. They wanna see us!" Ralph chortled crazily, hitting Logan on the arm in humour. "Oh, good morning, Channel Ten. Hello there, Channel Seven and Eight. I'm ready for my interview, Channel Two." Ralph wiggled his tea towel above his head and moved across the floor as if waltzing, pretending he was famous. "They'll be liiiining up for my autograph, I tell you. Liiiining up. Ha! Won't they, young Adelaide? You tell them I'm in here if they ask!"

"I'll let 'em know," Addi sung back without even looking at him.

"Maybe I should hire you as my PR person. You might like it better than this job – Logan, did you hear that? She might like it better than this job!" Ralph chortled.

"Publicist," Addi corrected him before speeding out of the kitchen.

"Yeah," she heard Logan chuckle before she left, responding to Ralph obediently. "Who wouldn't, hey?"

"Nooo idea, them waitresses..." Ralph's voice faded as Addi entered the performance hall again. The music jolted, started and stopping again in staccato beats.

"No, no, just stop! *What* is going on here? You're all getting in each other's way and holding back, it's like watching toddlers trying to dance," Sawyer glared around at the faces on stage. Everyone was standing in awkward formation, as they had been suddenly stopped between movements. "Chorus, what's happening?"

There was a stretched silence before Quinn's former understudy stepped forward. "To be honest, in light of what happened I don't think that everyone feels comfortable performing with certain people here." She shot a pointed look at Leo.

"Wow," Quinn interjected from her spot on the couch. "Now I really don't care that you got demoted."

Sawyer surveyed the understudy. "You do realise the implications behind what you're saying?"

She held a defensive stance. "Perhaps you didn't hear what's been happening for the past few days."

"You're part of a team. How are we supposed to deliver an amazing performance when we're not working together?" Sawyer posed.

"They know something," another girl piped up, also nodding at Addi on the floor.

Quinn's eye roll could have hit the ceiling. "Oh god, what is this, Attack of the Chorus Girls: The Sequel?"

Sawyer scowled. "You can't prove that. Until the police find out what happened, we don't know anything. Anyone who is making assumptions, buying into rumours and spreading lies should feel ashamed."

"I agree with Kyle. Why can't you just tell us where you were, Leo?" Jen prodded faux-sweetly.

Leo gritted his teeth. "I really can't believe you're doing this, Jen."

"Jen, I know it's hard for you but could you try not to be daft?" Quinn added. "You know Leo wouldn't place a finger on anyone."

As they bickered, dropping Addi's name into the argument periodically, Addi saw Emmerson flit back into the room, place his hat back on the stand and head towards Freddy, who was counting notes at the till inside the bar. She walked over quietly and ducked behind the bar on the other side so they wouldn't notice her. She began to rinse glasses and stack them in the dishwasher.

"What was the deal with that new chick and Grayson, anyway?" Jen demanded from the stage. "Were they hooking up?"

"What does this high school gossip have to do with dancing?" Sawyer bellowed.

The performers on stage shrunk in on themselves. Jen threw a last reproachful look to Quinn and Leo before stepping back too.

"Anyone?" Sawyer glared around at them pointedly. They all kept quiet. "Good answer. If you don't mind, let's have less of this nonsense and more of what you're actually being paid to do. From the beginning! The next person who makes a mistake will be swapped out for a shift in the kitchen with Ralph."

The music started up again. Sawyer turned away from the stage and came up to lean on the bar, reaching for a bottle of gin. Addi handed him a clean tumbler.

"Ah, some days I have to remind myself multiple times that I once dreamt of this," Sawyer unscrewed the bottle cap and poured generously. "I feel like I'm teaching pre-schoolers."

Addi laughed. "I'm sure they'll get over it soon and start gossiping about something else," she lied, more to herself than Sawyer.

Sawyer raised the glass to his lips and took a big gulp, smacking his lips together. "One would hope. Is there any lime back there?"

Addi cut a wedge on the chopping board on the bench and dropped it in his glass for him.

"The idea that Quinn or Leo... I mean, it's just ridiculous," Sawyer continued.

"Tell me about it. I guess this is what happens when people are worried, though. They just jump to any conclusion that's offered up and cling on to that because, I don't know..." Addi drifted off, glancing at Freddy and Emmerson to her side. They were having a low conversation. "Blaming someone tricks them into a sense of closure."

Sawyer inclined his head at her. "That's very astute. But honestly, Leo? He wouldn't hurt a fly. They don't know him at all." Sawyer gulped down the rest of his drink and poured himself just shy of a shot. "Don't worry about Quinn too much, honey," he consoled her. "She goes off like a firecracker at me for God knows what every second day." He winked and threw back the clear liquor. "Ah, that should be enough to help me forget that I should be in a company right now, but instead I'm spending my twilight years babysitting this lot."

As Sawyer bustled away, Addi heard Emmerson murmuring to Freddy. "...she's here."

Addi didn't look behind her, but she heard Freddy close the till sharply before responding, "I guess you can't keep running anymore."

Emmerson bristled. "Watch your mouth, Frederick." He strode away.

Freddy turned, noticing Addi's presence, and the pair locked eyes, alone behind the bar. Addi tried to shift her expression into one of cool relaxation, suddenly extremely aware that her manager had overheard her age being cast into suspicion earlier that day.

"I expect we'll be busy this evening, sweetheart, so I'll keep you in the kitchen today."

There was a silent beat of mutual appreciation for dodging the elephant in the bar, during which Addi breathed a sigh of relief. Apparently her underage runaway status was safe in her manager's ambiguous hands — for now. "No problem, boss."

"Run along," Freddy waved his tattooed arm.

In her haste to hurry away from that particular slice of guilt and potential for serious trouble, she almost collided into Summer.

"Well, if it isn't my favourite customer."

Addi breathed in the dancer's musky perfume as she searched for a clever response. "I'd say you've got a few people with that title."

A smile twinged on Summer's lips, quickly replaced with a frown. "How are you doing, Addi? This morning was a hot bloody mess, wasn't it?"

Addi laughed. It felt good after the day she'd had. "I couldn't say it better myself. That was... so embarrassing," she admitted, beginning to blush.

Summer put a warm hand on her shoulder. "Hey, I honestly think you held up pretty well under that level of bitchiness. Quinn's a tough one to battle with for your first rodeo, yet here you stand."

Summer let her hand drop.

Addi noticed its absence perhaps more than she should have. "Still breathing," she joked.

"Speaking of breathing," Summer reached into the navy lace bra peeking out beneath a loose tank top to retrieve a hand-rolled cigarette, "I was just about to head out for a bit of chill, if you catch my drift."

Ah, not just a cigarette, Addi corrected herself, thankful to have realised before her naivety in the world of substances could come through to Summer. She studied the joint for a few seconds, trying to memorise it for future reference.

Summer tucked the weed back into her bra. "Seems like you could use a breather too if you'd like to join."

"Really?" Addi blurted before thinking. In high school, beautiful girls like Summer had never wanted to be her friend. "I mean, of course. You're right; I really do need to get out of here."

Summer grinned. "I thought as much."

The dancer grabbed Addi's hand and pulled her down the hall and out the front door, down those concrete steps that where a mere week or two earlier her life had changed forever. Back out on the sidewalks leading past the city's old terrace houses was still disorienting to Addi, but Summer confidently led them down the streets and skinny lanes until they reached a small park of manicured green grass, shrubs and benches, contrasting starkly with the concrete world around it. The pair trod across the grass until they found a patch away from the mums with children and office workers on lunch breaks dotted throughout the greenery and sat down.

Addi stared ahead at the view of the city skyline, towering buildings stretching up into the air. "Wow."

Summer lit the joint and took her first breath in. "It's one of my favourite spots around here. Sometimes you just need some grass under your butt and to breathe air that doesn't smell like Freddy's cigars, you know?"

She passed the joint to Addi, who took it uncertainly.

Summer didn't miss the hint. "First time?"

Addi blushed. "I seem to be having all my firsts here."

"It's easy. Just try to hold the smoke in here." The dancer softly tapped her fingers on Addi's chest, sending a jolt through Addi's body.

Addi drew the joint to her lips and sucked in, slightly more prepared for the hit of smoke after her first encounter with Quinn's cigarette. She tried her best to breathe it into her chest as Summer had instructed and held it in for a few counts before gladly letting it furl out of her.

Addi grinned as she passed it back to Summer. "That was much better than my first attempt at smoking."

Summer laid back on her elbows, letting her head drop back as she exhaled smoke. "Everything in life is practice."

Keen to keep impressing Summer, Addi accepted the joint again and took another puff. "Just like your dancing, huh? Do you ever get used to it? Being that... intimate with strangers, I mean."

Summer grinned. "I'll let you know if I ever do."

Addi coughed on another puff. "I could never show myself like that to people. I think it's really brave."

"It's not yourself, though. I think that's the only way I *can* do it. I'm showing them Jayda, not me; she's just a fictional character I made up. Being vulnerable with yourself is a whole other kettle of fish. You don't do it in this industry if you want to survive."

Addi passed the joint back to the dancer. "Yeah, I'm learning that the hard way. I should never have told Quinn my age."

Summer frowned. "No, Quinn should never have told everyone else something you confided in her. I was talking about worker-to-client relationships. The people you work with here *should* always have your back. That's what it's like with us girls upstairs. That's another thing you gotta survive in this industry. I don't know what happened to Grayson here," she knocked some ash away from the end of the burning joint, whittling it down as the conversation went on, "but it's changed something. I mean, duh; but beyond the obvious. The energy's shifted. They've started attacking each other. We cop enough shit from customers and the outside world for the work we do, we shouldn't be turning on each other." The dancer brushed some hair off her shoulder, and Addi couldn't help but stare at her dark caramel skin under the sun. "I hate all this drama. I just want to lie here in this park for a week."

"That sounds like a good idea," Addi agreed slowly, letting herself lie back on the grass. The weed was already going to her head. Lying there next to Summer under the sunshine with the majestic city harbour in the background, it was growing more difficult for her to remember what she had been so stressed about a mere hour ago.

"You're good to stay though, right? Like Freddy didn't get you into trouble or something, did he?" Summer asked.

"He just kicked me off bar duty for now, which is fine by me. It was awkward. I don't know what's going to happen but I really can't lose this job. This place. I don't know where I would go if he fired me."

"He didn't, though. He could have straight away but if you still have a job I think that's a pretty good sign," Summer reasoned.

Addi felt the sun warming her through her shirt and smiled lazily. "Yeah, that's so true."

Summer pulled some grass out of her thick head of curls. "It's out there now. Sometimes we waste so much time stressing about things outside of our control, you know. All that time spent worrying isn't going to change what happens. I think you may just have to ride this one out, Addi, and deal with whatever comes up as it comes. No point stressing about things you can't control."

Addi giggled.

Summer propped herself up on an elbow to face her. "What is it?"

Addi turned on her side to face her. "You're right. I'm just having a hard time right now remembering why I was so..." her brain hazily searched for the word, "wound up over things."

Summer started laughing with her. "Yeah, that's the weed talking now."

Addi placed her hand on her belly. It felt good to be laughing at nothing. "You're so different from Quinn or Leo. Quinn attacked me. Leo's advice was basically to stop trusting people." She turned to look at the dancer again, who was basking in the sun with a contented smile on her red-painted lips. "Thanks for getting me out of there, Summer."

"Any time." Summer reached out a hand and tucked a curl behind Addi's ear.

Without realising, Addi pulled back. Her body seemed to be moving before her mind could catch up to it.

Summer drew her hand away, a crinkle of hurt between her eyebrows. "What's wrong, Addi?"

"I..." Addi started. She sat up, brushing grass off her and avoiding Summer's gaze as she clumsily got to her feet. "I should get back and get ready for work. Sorry, I just... sorry," she finished pathetically, turning and walking across the grass out of the park.

She hit the tar pathway in a daze, staring around slowly to try and locate the buildings they had passed on the way to the park to help her find her way back. Her brain felt like it was lagging behind by about a minute, but she saw a café sign she recognised and began meandering her way back, accidentally bumping into a passer-by, distracted, as she went.

What are you so scared of?, she chastised herself. She wanted Summer, didn't she? There was no denying what she felt when she was even standing in her vicinity. Yet one week ago, she'd had a crush on Grayson; a boy. Before him, she'd never come close to having anything with any guy at her high school. She'd always put that down to her general awkwardness and lack of physical desirability, but was it actually because she herself wasn't as interested in boys as she thought? She needed to lie down before work — there were far too many thoughts rattling around inside her mind.

Studying a street sign for far too long, she turned down a lane lined with council garbage bins, a scrawny ginger cat darting across the road and squeezing between the bars of an iron fence into the small front courtyard of one of the terrace houses. She'd meant what she said — Summer *was* different. If she was being honest with herself, between Grayson, Quinn, Freddy, Emmerson and the foster parents she'd just run away from, she didn't know who she could trust. She'd had a good feeling about being friends with Quinn and look what had happened. She'd had a so-called "family" that in the end she only wanted to escape. Apparently, she couldn't even trust her own feelings anymore.

As the House came further into view, Addi noticed a cop car parked against the curb a few metres away. Her high started to fizzle immediately as she felt the familiar flutter of nervousness. She made her way down the side street to the courtyard so she could enter through the back, and hopefully dodge the officer, to take a shower, brush her teeth, douse herself in any perfume she could find lying around in the dormitory and get rid of any lingering smell of the weed.

She knew she should have been more concerned with the police presence, but she couldn't stop replaying that blip of time in the park in her mind. Her triumph at finding her way back to House of Nightshade in her sluggish state was dulled considerably by the sinking feeling that Summer was probably never going to try anything with her again.

Chapter Eight

*"There is nothing more deceptive than an obvious fact." — Arthur
Conan Doyle*

T*oxicology report reveals illicit drugs were involved in House of
Nightshade murder*

*The report reveals substances in the victim's body the night he was
killed.*

*Weeks after the body of Grayson Reid was discovered in his room at
House of Nightshade by the venue's cleaner, coroners have now produced
a toxicology report confirming a high level of the drug ketamine — a
dissociative anaesthetic — in the victim's system.*

*"My team and I are taking this finding extremely seriously. It's
imperative that we discover whether the boy happened to take illicit
drugs of his own accord that night or if he was coerced into doing so. Due
to the, ahem, nature of work that employees undertake at the venue,
both options are equally likely. If it's the latter, that combined with
the wound to his head shows us very clearly that someone planned this
murder with strong intent to kill the young man," says lead detective,
Officer Knight.*

*While that question remains to be answered, detectives are hoping
that this new finding will enable them to create a more concrete picture
of the events that took place that night.*

The Homicide Squad have commenced a search of the premises.

•

Addi followed Leo's pacing with her eyes as she set tables; one side of the room to the other, barely stopping. His face was more pale than usual. Sawyer glanced over to the lead performer every now and then with trepidation as he plotted out choreography and flicked through song options. Addi began to feel slightly irritated by the disjointed sound of the director playing a track for 20 seconds then deciding it wasn't a good fit and skipping to the next one. Quinn's forehead and chest glistened with beads of sweat as she tested moves with her injured ankle, wincing periodically but continuing to push through.

Kyle, dressed in old gym clothes with a bag hanging over one shoulder, blundered by Addi. "Your friend looks worried. Interesting timing, wouldn't you agree?" He gave his signature smirk.

Addi squinted at the clock behind the bar, still feeling the effect of the joint in the park. The minutes since the detectives had turned up with their search warrant dragged by.

"Damn. Surely there'll be lots to find, right?" Addi had whispered to Ivy once the officers had been escorted upstairs by Emmerson.

"Not as much as you would think," Ivy had whispered back. "The exotic dancers generally get party favours from their customers who sneak them in, plus they're gorgeous — they know they can mostly get drugs for free if they go out in the city. They don't really ever *need* to buy them."

"And the performers?"

"From what I've heard over the years, I think the girls might keep some stuff in boxes of tampons in the dressing room, if they have it. You didn't hear that from me, though."

Addi had mimed zipping her lips. "Let's hope they've run out, then."

Now, Addi could definitely feel some tension in the air, all of the staff knowing that there were detectives on the floor above their heads, searching through all of their personal belongings. Even though she knew she had nothing to hide, owning hardly anything of her own for them to search through, Addi couldn't help but feel a little nervous.

Her imagination was just about to start jumping to ridiculous possibilities (wherein someone was framing her for the murder and the police happened to find the murder weapon underneath her bed) when the return of Officer Knight and his team was announced by the rumble of their heavy boots clunking on the staircase.

Face stern, Emmerson led them into the performance hall and surveyed the scene. He spoke a few words to the officers before turning to Kyle.

Officer Knight jerked his head and two of his team began making their way through the chairs and tables. Addi's stomach dropped as they reached Leo, whose face had turned ashen.

Sawyer's music halted, and Quinn froze mid-step.

Leo nodded, lips pressed into a firm line, and turned around to follow the officers out.

"Leo!" Quinn shouted, limping after him.

Addi and Sawyer both lunged towards Quinn and each placed one of her arms around their shoulders for support. In her state, Quinn didn't even object to the help from Addi. The three of them trailed after the last of the detective squad and stopped at the top of the stairs. The police car with Leo in the back was already pulling out into the flow of traffic, drivers screeching to a halt at the sight of a law enforcer's vehicle to virtuously let it merge.

They watched the car go until it was swallowed whole by the notorious city traffic.

●

Addi would have laughed had the circumstances been less undesirable. Sawyer and Quinn perched on chairs in the exact same position, one leg propped over the other, arms crossed until the need for a drag of their cigarette arose, surveying the rehearsal with a frown.

Sawyer was forlorn. "Both lead performers out. Both! Look at them up there. They're like a pack of confused sheep."

He reached for consolation in the form of a bottle of amber liquid from the bar.

Quinn pointed her cigarette at Jen. "She's totally butchering your choreography. Also, I've heard her singing in the shower before and trust me, you don't want to give her anything with high notes. I will never understand why the hell you gave her my spot. Why? Why did you give her my spot?"

"Well, you know..." Sawyer pushed his thick-rimmed glasses further up the ridge of his nose. "She was a better fit for the long-term."

"Whatever. Give me that." Quinn swiped Sawyer's liquor.

Addi wondered what Leo was doing at this very moment. She pictured him in a dingy room, sitting across the table from an officer just like in a television show. Something irked her even more than thinking back to a few hours ago when he had been led out of the House by the detectives, though: the fact that when she tried to reassure herself that surely good, reasonable Leo, the only person in this place who had really made an effort on her first day to be her friend, didn't have anything to do with murdering Grayson, her stomach gurgled with uncertainty. Emmerson had assured them that Leo was simply being taken to the police station for questioning, but every passing tick of the clock made Addi more nervous that the police were finding something to hold Leo there.

Night had well and truly blanketed the city when they heard the front door of the house open with a squeal. Leo trailed into the room (with noticeable shadows under his eyes but the colour returned to his cheeks) to elated whoops from Quinn, who, with nothing better to do aside from pass loud judgements about Jen's dancing and sip liquor, had fallen into an afternoon drunken stupor. She wrapped him up in a hug from her chair and began to slur about the injustice of the police and how much she loved him. Addi felt her shoulders relax a little at the sight of Leo back at the House, and even Sawyer went to greet the performer with the first smile Addi had seen him don all day.

Leo grinned as he pulled away from Quinn when Addi approached. "Hey, Addi." They hugged briefly. Over his shoulder, Addi could see Jen monitoring Leo's return as she blocked out moves.

Sawyer patted Leo on the shoulder. "Good to have you back."

"Excuse me, director," Jen called haughtily. "That wouldn't be you playing favourites over there, would it?"

"Ah, duh, and for good reason!" Quinn rebutted quickly.

Sawyer scowled at Jen. "Excuse me." He strode onto the stage and pulled Jen aside to give her a talking to.

"Sawyer's been tearing his hair out all day with both of us gone," Quinn told Leo. "No wonder he's tense. Anyway, what the hell happened over there? Tell us all of it, right now. We await with eager participation."

Leo laughed. "*An*ticipation, I think you mean, and oof, girl, you smell like half the contents of the bar." He waved a hand in front of his face. "Well, they found my stash of ketamine, and I was the only one with it so they arrested me for questioning based on the toxicology report. They basically just grilled me about that night again, asking if I'd given it to Grayson or forced it on him and if I'd noticed any missing."

"They think he stole it?" Addi asked.

Leo turned to her. "It's a possibility. I don't keep track of it on nights out, though, so I really wasn't sure. I told them the truth and then they gave me a fine for possession and let me go. I mean, it's such a common drug; Grayson could have got it from anyone. I think it was pretty clear that I didn't have much to do with the guy, so I certainly didn't peer pressure him into taking anything. Do you guys want food? I'm starving, let's order takeaway..."

Sawyer returned to oversee rehearsals, appearing remarkably happier now that at least one of his star performers was back in action. Leo leant his head on Quinn's as they perused menus on her phone. It was subtle, but Addi felt like the way Leo had cut the conversation and was now avoiding her gaze as he focussed on Quinn was a clear message that he didn't want to talk about what he was still hiding from the night that Grayson had been murdered.

As Quinn laughed loudly, capturing attention from the few staff who were also spending their night off milling around the communal area. Addi turned on her heel and marched out of the performance hall. She really wasn't in the mood to hang around a loud, drunk Quinn after what the performer had done to her. She grabbed a meal from under the heat lights in the kitchen, where two other dancers were examining what to eat, and strode outside, plonking herself down at an old, dusty slat table.

The swelling drone of the motorcycle reached her ears before entering the bleak city courtyard. In a protective black jacket and jeans, face obscured behind a jet-black helmet, the figure was almost foreboding; of course the stature gave way that it was merely her manager.

The shiny silver and red of the bike glinted even in the dim light emanating from an old, rusted lightbulb, moths fluttering around it as if in a tizzy. The engine spluttered to a halt as Freddy cut it and swung his leg off, making way for the city background noise of post-dusk commuter traffic and wailing sirens to mix back in with the rehearsal music from the hall and the clanging and sizzling from the kitchen. He lifted the seat and retrieved a half-eaten sandwich wrapped in deli paper.

"Miss Addilyn," Freddy acknowledged her, pulling off his helmet and tousling the brunette locks underneath to coax it back from helmet hair. "What are you doing out here in the dark by yourself?"

Addi pushed the food to one side in her mouth so she could respond. "Just had to get a moment of peace from all of that." She jerked her head towards the House.

Freddy chuckled. "You are preaching to the choir." He motioned to his parked vehicle. He set his helmet on the dirty wooden table beside her plate and sat down on the edge of a garden bed, crossing his ankle over his knee.

A moment of peace, and yet he sits down to join, Addi inwardly rolled her eyes. "Where have you come back from?" is what she actually asked aloud.

In response, Freddy pulled out a fresh cigar and a lighter, inhaled the vice and sighed in relief before taking a bite of his sandwich. "Had to pick up the necessities, of course."

"Of course," Addi afforded him.

"There's this great sandwich place near here. Then I headed over to the bridge and around the harbour. I used to be over that way all the time when I was in school; it was in the city. Depending on how much my parents were fighting that week sometimes I'd hang out around there after school. One year I remember they were in a really bad phase, fighting so incessantly I couldn't even get my homework done at home. I think mum even threatened to hire a private detective on dad at one point," Freddy chuckled, "one might say she's always had a penchant for melodrama and it drives my dad up the wall. Safe to say I practically lived on those streets during that time, writing my essays in cafes. I hardly went home. Now I spend all my time here and it's a lucky day if I see the sun." Freddy scratched at some stubble that was forming along his jawline. "You probably won't understand it now, but when you're older it can be gratifying in a strange way to revisit those places you went through hard times in. You can appreciate how much you've grown out of them."

Addi shuffled food around her plate absentmindedly. "I don't know that I'd ever want to go back to those places."

"Look who's decided to turn up. You're late, mate; the cops've gone home!"

Addi jumped slightly as the mad chef entered the courtyard from the kitchen behind her, having forgotten for a moment that they weren't the only ones in the vicinity.

"Welcome back to your kingdom, sire. Ha! If I had your tricycle, I wouldn't have bothered coming back to this place, oh no. I would have just kept on riding in the opposite direction. Can't be a smart one, can he, young Adelaide? Still hiding, hiding out here in the dark." Ralph disappeared into the storeroom.

Addi turned back to Freddy, swallowed her food and asked as if they hadn't been interrupted by Ralph's nonsensical rambling, "Just a solo adventure, then?"

"Yeah, just me and the bike. Anyway, have there been any, ah, updates while I've been out?"

Addi figured he would spot the little smudge of red lipstick near his jaw soon enough. She placed her knife and fork down next to each other on the plate. "Leo's back from the police station, not that long ago actually."

"Ah, good." Freddy puffed on his cigar. "The show must go on."

"That is what it's all about, isn't it?" Addi quipped.

Freddy finished his sandwich in one huge mouthful. "You seem older than you are."

Addi laughed uncertainly. "Um, I'll take that as a good thing."

"You should. I wouldn't try to slip one past you."

Addi spotted a mosquito already gnawing into her exposed forearm. She slapped at it reflexively, but it had already buzzed off.

"Shall we?" Freddy balled up the now empty sandwich wrapping and gestured to the kitchen. Addi nodded, gathering her crockery, and they wandered inside.

Freddy continued behind her. "I've been managing staff for a while now and seen many people come and go. It's always interesting to notice the qualities that people possess and utilise to survive on this island."

Addi smiled along with his reality television reference, trying to push away the memory of her last foster dad who would sit in front of the T.V set all night drinking beer before his mouth would slacken and his snore would keep her awake. "So would you say I'm near the final round yet?"

Freddy gave a bark of laughter. "I think you're safe from now on."

As Addi added her plate to the stack of dirty dishes next to the sink, Logan exchanged a smirking glance with Ralph, who shook his head. Logan's eyes shot to Freddy before looking down at his work.

"Is something amusing, chefs?" Freddy asked loudly.

"Well, well, that depends, doesn't it?" Ralph added two more meals to the shelf under the heat lights for more performance girls who were coming in for dinner. "I'm not sure it's that amusing for the young snowflakes who fall victim to your..."

"Ralph!" Freddy bellowed, staring stonily at the head chef.

Ralph ignored his manager and continued dishing up. "Oh ho, I think I'm in trouble, girls, I'll be sent to the naughty corner now, ha!"

The performance girls giggled to one another. Even Addi pressed her lips together to hide a smile as Logan caught her eye.

"Stop loitering, girls!" Freddy snapped at the dancers and Addi, disappearing into the bar.

●

Kyle materialised and tapped on the kitchen bench as if he owned the place. "Addilyn!"

"What now, Kyle?" Addi sighed. With everything on her mind, Kyle's constant heckling was the last thing she had patience for anymore.

In the background, Freddy talked on the phone near Ralph's work bench, simultaneously downing an espresso and shovelling appetizers into his mouth as he listened to the person on the other end. The manager had been freezing her out since Ralph's dig two days previously, making the last twenty minutes shining cutlery for the night ahead with him working on the other side of the kitchen extremely uncomfortable.

"What are you up to?" Kyle demanded.

Addi gritted her teeth. "You can see what I'm up to, Kyle." She made a point of waving the forks in her hand in front of his face.

"Well, you can't blame me for asking when you're usually gossiping with someone," he accused her like a spiteful schoolboy.

"Oh, dear, you better go and tell on me," Addi retorted. Her stomach churned at the sight of him. It was him that had started that whole pile of accusations at breakfast to begin with — he was the reason that everyone was whispering about her. "Don't you have something better to do than hover over me?" she grumbled.

"I am a supervisor. It's my job-"

"You two, I'm sick of hearing it!" Freddy interjected, covering the mouthpiece of the phone with one hand. "Why don't you both go upstairs and help them set up tables?"

Kyle began to protest. "There's already about five people setting up upstairs."

"Just go," Freddy exhaled warily.

Addi threw a look with as much attitude as she could muster to Kyle, flung the towel she was using to wipe cutlery onto the bench and stomped upstairs, the thuds of Kyle's boots following behind her wordlessly.

"Hey," she greeted Ivy once they arrived in the private Indian-themed room. "Freddy sent us up here to help you guys set up."

"Hmm, that's strange," Ivy surveyed the activity around them as she gathered the vacuum cord together in a loop. "We're covered up here — it's pretty much done. You guys can go down to the kitchen and make sure all the cutlery is polished and everything's clean in there."

"Will do. Come get me if you need any more help," Addi said.

"Or me, I'm probably better for moving furniture," Kyle bragged.

Addi farewelled Ivy with a roll of her eyes, which Ivy knowingly returned.

Addi descended the stairs and re-entered the kitchen, still annoyed at Kyle, who ignored Ivy's request and headed back to the bar. *Where does he even get off anyway?*, she thought as she walked to the back where there was a freshly cleaned tray of cutlery. She was so over the people in this place who all thought they were better than each other, as if they were trying to win some unspoken social competition.

She reached up to the shelf above to grab one of the freshly laundered and folded tea towels and noticed something out of place. Sitting amongst the cloths and discarded salt-and-pepper shakers was the kitchen's silver meat mallet, a tea towel wrapped around its handle. *What was that doing there*, she wondered.

A phrase from the newspaper ran through her head, one that had been shoved away in a drawer in her mind with detectives and clicking pens and body bags, being from the article published the morning Grayson had been found dead.

'There was a wound on the back of his head, suspected to be from a metal object with a rounded or curved edge.'

Chapter Nine

"The easiest thing of all is to deceive one's self; for what a man wishes he generally believes to be true." — Demosthenes

Police Interview with Quinn Vandez

Officer: Miss Vandez, what were you doing last night between the hours of 10pm and 6am this morning?

Quinn: Last night was just another work night at first. I was performing when Freddy and Grayson came on-stage to move some of the props away quickly to make room for the rest of the dancers to come on. Grayson wasn't watching where he was going and next thing I knew he and the chair he was moving just barged into me and tripped me up mid-move. I'm a lead performer here, by the way, so I need to uphold a certain standard. I fell and I've twisted and bruised my ankle really badly. Freddy helped me off the stage and took me to the emergency room to get a scan straight away – we waited for, like, ever. Then he brought me home. I guess it was around midnight, the shift was over by the time I got back. I took some pain meds and went to sleep. Next thing I know someone was screaming downstairs this morning and that was when they discovered Grayson.

Officer: What happened immediately after Grayson tripped you?

Quinn: I mean, it's a bit of a blur really. I was in a lot of pain so I wasn't too focused on what was going on around me. There were lots of people gathered around, Freddy brought ice, they closed the curtains. I think Grayson was just told to go and then...

Officer: Mmm, do you remember who told him to leave?

Quinn: Ah, no... probably Freddy I guess, as he's the manager? Or maybe Sawyer, he's the director and choreographer. They would have only told him to get off the stage, though, not leave the House.

Officer: Right. How were you feeling towards Grayson at that point?

Quinn: What do you think? He had just injured me and completely embarrassed me in front of an audience, and now I don't even know when I can perform again. I was pretty annoyed at him. It was so stupid that Freddy allowed him to work here in the first place when he'd just filled the role and didn't need another staff member.

Officer: Yes, let's talk about that. Other staff members reported hearing quite a heated argument between you and Frederick last night. Do you remember any of that?

Quinn: Ugh, typical. So many gossips in this place.

Officer: What did you argue about with Freddy?

Quinn: Grayson. There was something weird going on there. As I just said, they didn't need anyone else, we'd just hired Addilyn, and then Emmerson showed up and like, *insisted* that Grayson work here. Let me tell you, it couldn't have been for his skill or personability. Of course, Freddy can't say no to his daddy. After the kid made me fall I asked Freddy to fire him, which he should have just done, but he refused to. Probably for his own personal, selfish agenda, as per usual.

Officer: What do you mean when you say Freddy was doing things for his own personal agenda as per usual?

Quinn: Oh, you know, Freddy's always been selfish and does whatever he likes. He doesn't care if he hurts others, in my experience.

Officer: Mmm. Would you like to elaborate on that?

Quinn: Not really.

Officer: Right. Let's go back to Grayson. It has been mentioned by others that you noticeably didn't like him ever since he started.

Did you know Grayson before he began working at House of Nightshade?

Quinn: No, of course not! I'm just a really good judge of character and I could tell he was shady from the get-go.

Officer: How so?

Quinn: Just the way he acted; his demeanour. He was secretive and had that whole moody, bad boy thing he was trying to put forth. Didn't fool me, though. I know that act when I see it. He also didn't try and talk to any of us even though he was the new kid; he didn't want to get to know us. Now I think about it, actually, it was almost as if he knew.

Officer: Knew what?

Quinn: That he wouldn't be around here very long.

●

"Alright, hands off, I can walk for myself. I've been walking all these years, haven't I? Never needed a hand before and don't need one now, do I?"

Addi watched from the doorway of the House as the policemen escorted the chef through the throng of media still camped out the front, holding up their hands like stop signs to try and make the crowd part. The wind swirled brown, dry leaves over the tar of the road.

"What's it like inside House of Nightshade right now?"

"Are you all still living inside?"

"Can you give us any updates on the case?"

Addi gritted her teeth, wishing the reporters would shut up and go away. Cameras continued to click and boom microphones controlled by cameramen near the back of the mass hovered above their heads.

A female reporter holding a microphone spoke to cameras near a news van to the side of the crowd. "Ralph Payne is the resident Head Chef at House of Nightshade and has worked with the business for over a decade. He has just been taken in for questioning after new evidence was uncovered by a staff member in the very kitchen he manages."

Ralph was led into the backseat of the police car parked by the curb. The officers hopped in and the car started to crawl through the swarm of photographers, who ran after it down the street, their cameras clicking in a frenzy.

Freddy touched Addi's shoulder and drew her back into the hallways as the police car disappeared. He closed the door with a loud thud and clicked all the locks, closing them in from the prying press who circled outside like seagulls searching for tidbits.

Addi looked up at Freddy sheepishly.

"You did the right thing," Freddy reassured her, looking seriously at the floor a little over her shoulder.

"I don't know what to think," Addi responded truthfully.

"Nor do we all, sweetheart."

Thinking about having just watched Ralph disappear in a police car, Addi couldn't say that she felt bad per se — not after all the things he had said to her and the way he behaved in general. She didn't know that she would have turned someone in just by discovering that meat mallet, but if anyone had to be arrested, she was glad it was insane, rude Ralph, who enjoyed watching other people's misery, instead of herself or Leo. Was she a bad person for not feeling bad?

Freddy mistook Addi's silence and smiled sympathetically. "He's just going to be interviewed at the police station," he reminded her gently. "It will surely take them a few days to test the evidence and return it with any concrete proof. We don't know what the outcome will be, but if he's not guilty he'll come right back, and he had a chance to go and talk the ears off someone different for a change."

Addi gave an appeasing smile. "That's true."

They had just begun to walk back down the hall when Freddy stopped abruptly. He turned to face her and reached out to put a hand on her shoulder. Addi looked down at it, confused. "Are you okay, though, Addilyn?" he asked her seriously.

Addi noticed the dark shadows that stubbornly remained under his eyes. He looked paler than she remembered from when she had first met him. "I... yes, of course. Why?" she responded, a little bemused.

Freddy started to walk again slowly. "Okay, good. You're new here and I can't help but think we haven't made the, ah, greatest impression."

"It's been... eventful," Addi responded.

"That's one way of putting it," Freddy inclined his head, drawing a cigar out and lighting it as they approached the performance hall. "Now you've found that piece of evidence, you're even more wrapped up in it. You've just started working and all this tragedy happens, and then you're accused of killing the boy. It must be almost too much to take in."

"Yeah, I guess it's been a lot." Addi thought of what Leo had told her about the way Freddy treated Quinn, and her eyes narrowed. "You didn't seem to have much to say at that breakfast, though."

"Pardon?"

"When Kyle was accusing Quinn, Leo and I. You would have known that was wrong, I'm sure, but you didn't tell Kyle to stop."

Freddy looked at her. "I... well, what could any of us say? We're all new to this situation. I manage venues, I don't solve murders."

Addi raised her eyebrows. "Right." She could feel him studying her out of the corner of her eye, but didn't afford him her gaze. He hadn't really addressed her point.

"I'm sorry if you felt unsupported dealing with those comments from the others at breakfast," Freddy subtly turned her complaint back on her, "however it appears you've been dealing with the situation quite well."

...Absolving me of any responsibility, Addi finished Freddy's sentiment in her head.

"Yeah, well, I'm not exactly unfamiliar with adversity in my life, I guess. One minute it was Quinn, the next it was Leo, then me. I'm sure there'll be a brand new suspect that they'll all be attacking soon."

Freddy surveyed her. "You've got us all figured out, haven't you? I can tell you that with the drama and the, ah, personalities," he accentuated the word delicately, "in this place, you're on the money. Yes, that's a very mature way to look at it."

'Yeah, well, secrets can't hide forever," she directed at Freddy with a measured expression. "The truth of what happened will come out eventually."

"Mm. You're right, sweetheart. I wouldn't go looking for any more clues, though, if I were you. Now that the officers have that piece of evidence, just let them do their job. Now, we don't have long before the guests start showing up. I might get you to help me at the door with ticketing tonight, actually. Is that okay?" He didn't stop to hear her response. "Excuse me, I have to sort out this newly imposed staffing conundrum, seeing as our head chef is now detained. Meet me there in twenty minutes." He pushed the door to the performance hall open and made a beeline for the kitchen.

Addi could sense eyes on her. She followed the feeling to see Quinn and Leo sitting near the stage, Leo chatting to Quinn as he waited for the rest of the chorus to rehearse a number. As soon as Addi made eye contact, Leo waved her over frantically. She hovered for a second, not wanting to go near Quinn, but then shrugged — she shouldn't have to not talk to Leo because of her. She weaved through the chairs, tables and squishy couches.

"Okay, Detective Addi, what the hell did you find? What was that?" Leo blurted out.

Quinn pretended to study her nails, but Addi saw her glance up quizzically.

Addi explained how she had discovered the meat mallet hidden suspiciously on the shelf in the kitchen and made the connection to the murder weapon described in the article, so went to alert Freddy who had called the police.

"Oh, damn," Leo responded. "This whole murder case was kind of unreal before, wasn't it? Now you've actually found a piece of evidence it feels a lot more serious. *Ralph*, though? It doesn't make sense."

"Yeah, I know," Addi whispered. "He's been taken in, but only because they found the mallet and, well, he's the boss of the kitchen I suppose, and with his mental condition and everything...." she trailed off, "I mean, who knows?"

"And it was just sitting there on the shelf?" Quinn interrupted.

Addi faltered for a second, surprised Quinn had actually addressed her. "Pretty much. On the shelf above where we dry the cutlery, next to the tea towels."

"Why would it be there, next to something that all you waitstaff are constantly using, instead of its usual place?" Leo posed.

"Then again, Ralph *is* totally loco," Quinn reasoned, inserting herself into the conversation.

Addi pondered aloud. "It's like Leo said, though. What would Ralph have against Grayson? What was in it for him?"

"Money?" Quinn proposed.

"From who?"

"How would I know?" Quinn replied indignantly. "I know they keep saying that it was someone here who did it, but it could very well have been someone outside the House who wanted to get rid of him. They could have been paying someone on the inside to do their dirty work. It could be any random who had a grudge against him."

"You know Quinn, I didn't think of that before," Addi admitted. "That it could be someone outside the House, I mean."

"Yeah, neither," Leo said. "Geez, that's scary. We get so sucked into this place sometimes we forget there's an outside world."

"There is?" Quinn quipped.

"Plus, Ralph is in debt," Leo added.

"Really?"

Leo nodded. "Yup. He tried to go out on his own, you know, run his own restaurant. He put all his family's savings into it, pretty much everything he had to his name, and then it totally flopped."

"Ralph has a family?" Addi asked.

"Had," Leo corrected her wryly. "I think losing all his wife's savings broke that relationship."

"Along with his mind," Addi added.

"How did you know that?" Quinn asked Leo.

"Oh, ah, I think Sawyer was talking about it a while ago."

Quinn rolled her eyes. "Typical gossip."

On their way to the stage, a few performers eyed Addi warily and whispered to each other with smirks.

"Whoever it was, I just want the truth to come out soon. I'm sick of people talking about me," Addi muttered.

Leo elbowed Quinn gently.

"Uh, yeah, Addi," Quinn cleared her throat. "I just wanted to say..." she glanced to Leo, who nodded encouragingly. Quinn sighed and started talking very quickly. "I wanted to say sorry or whatever for outing you in public like that and telling everyone your secret, but I was just trying to protect me and Leo."

"I'll take it, " Addi responded, knowing that was the best she was going to get. She was beyond tired of spending energy being mad at Quinn.

"I don't apologise often so you should count yourself lucky," Quinn added.

Leo groaned. "*Quinn.*"

Quinn flicked her hair. "What? It's true."

"Leo," Sawyer called. "Less gab, more tap. Come on."

Leo jumped back onto the stage. "Duty's calling. Well, I for one am glad you ladies are talking again now. It makes organising my social schedule much easier." He winked. "See ya later, Addi."

Sawyer and the performers all disappeared backstage to get ready as the sky outside darkened. Yellow lampposts on the street outside flickered on and shouts and shrieks of laughter signalled the excitement of a weekend night in the city.

Addi almost collided with Freddy at the bottom of the stairs after she came down to start her shift, hair smoothed down as much as was possible for her unruly curls and adjusting her bowtie so it didn't make her feel as if she was choking.

"Ah, just the girl I was looking for. Come." He led her brusquely down the hall and pushed open the front door.

Addi reached his side. "Is the line normally this long?"

"Nope," Freddy smiled calmly ahead at the waiting people who stretched all the way down the uneven pathway and around the corner of the block.

Donning puffy fur coats and smart suit jackets, the patrons clasped tickets in their hands as they chatted amongst their groups and took drags of cigarettes, smoke curling up and disappearing into the night sky. A few cameramen were pacing back and forth on the curb, capturing finely-dressed figures, filming the line and holding out microphones for comments. A group of about five people near the door were unsubtly trying to conceal a bottle of sparkling as they passed it along to one another, each person crouching down in an attempt to hide as they took a swig.

"Should we be saying something about that?" Addi pointed, definitely thinking they should.

"Nah," Freddy waved a hand, "It's all part of the fun. Alright, let's open the door."

Addi dug the end of the clipboard that contained a list of names into her hip and clicked her pen. Freddy shifted the stands at the bottom of the stairs that were holding up loops of thick, burgundy-coloured rope so that they were no longer closing off the entrance and ascended to push open the front door. Addi went to stand on the bottom step.

Excitedly, the line of people perked up and began eagerly jostling forward. Addi crossed off name after name as she took tickets from gloved hands and was given swift smiles before the guests flounced up the stairs and stepped over the front mat with expectant looks of glee. Freddy stood just inside the doorframe, helping men and women shrug out of coats with his polite, hospitality smile plastered on, throwing the coats at a poor waiter next to him whose duty it was to rush back and forth to hang them up in the adjoining room. Freddy would then gesture grandly down the hall with a sweep of his arm, where candles on every available surface lit the way like a landing strip right to the open entrance to the performance hall, from which upbeat swing jazz floated out. Addi could see Kyle's blonde head and smarmy smile waiting to welcome them with a packed tray of tipples.

The line moved fast, everyone crowding into the performance hall, filling tables and double-parking drinks. The vast room was bursting at the seams; Freddy and Emmerson had decided to move all the exotic dancers in there for the night to minimise the amount of people that would trudge upstairs and see Grayson's former bedroom taped off.

"Phew," Freddy exhaled as he ushered the last people through, the waiter nearby treading on the hem of someone's large overcoat as he whisked it away into the adjoining room. "Nice work. Now," he drew a cigar and lighter from his pocket, lit it and puffed on it therapeutically, "we're about to have a lot of fun in the kitchen tonight." He grimaced, beckoned her inside and hastened down the hall.

Addi hurried to keep up with the strides of his long legs.

"The chefs will be under a lot of stress with a man down, so if anyone asks you to help with anything, just say yes. We'll all need to step up tonight." Freddy checked his watch. "Hold that thought."

How Freddy managed to slip through the crowd so agilely, Addi had no idea; guests were crammed together near the entrance to the hall as they waited for drinks. As she squeezed her way through with great difficulty, Addi saw Kyle's pink face, sweat glistening on his forehead as he and a few other waitstaff behind the bar struggled to meet the demand. She clung to the walls, trying to move out of everyone's way, as the lights dimmed.

"Ladies and gentlemen," came Freddy's smooth voice through the speakers, "welcome to House of Nightshade and thank you for joining us tonight. Please make your way to your seats for the beginning of tonight's performance. Your drink orders will be delivered to your table."

Everyone who was still standing accelerated to find a couch or table, dispersing from the back of the room.

"Please turn your phones to silent and do not take photos of the performance. House of Nightshade is an experience to immerse yourself in. Sit back, relax. We hope you enjoy the show."

The lights transitioned completely to black, the candles on tables causing the whole room to flicker. Hushed quiet was broken only by a few soft whispers of anticipation as everyone stared at the thick, navy curtain hiding the stage from view. A violin trembled ominously. After ten seconds, the curtain slowly rose, revealing a faded, antique velvet lounge with claw feet. Addi could see a figure in the dark sitting on the couch, legs stretched out across its width.

"*I was five and he was six...*"

The voice resounded deeply through the room and the violins continued to reverberate. The lights on stage slowly turned on, illuminating Quinn on the sofa. Her hair was piled messily atop her head and she was wearing a long, navy split dress, half of the skirt spilling over the side of the couch and pooling on the floor, revealing her bare legs. While she still couldn't dance, the performer had managed to convince Sawyer to give her a solo that didn't require too much physical activity, after which she had gleefully alerted Jen that her time in the spotlight was running out.

"*He wore black and I wore white...*" she started to stand up, swinging her legs slowly off the couch and gracefully coming to a stand.

Addi was broken from her trance as Freddy tapped her on the shoulder. "Let's go," he whispered, jerking his head to signal her to follow him around the back of the room and down the side to the kitchen. It probably wouldn't have made a difference if they'd gone straight through the room; everyone was transfixed on Quinn.

"*Bang bang,*" Quinn sang as she walked closer to the front of the stage, staring off into the distance. "*He shot me down...*"

Freddy paused a moment with his hand on the kitchen door and turned his head to watch Quinn, almost as if he was trying to resist but couldn't. The atmosphere in the room was palpable, the patrons eyes hooked on Quinn as she looked around the room, singing slowly and dramatically. Finally, her eyes landed on Addi and Freddy at the door. Looking directly at Freddy, who stood unmoving, she sang, "*...My baby shot me down.*"

●

"Pass me that one. No, not that. *That* one."

After the staff had pushed the last of the jovial, drunken guests out the door for the night, shut off the music and turned the lights back on, a few of the performers, dancers and wait staff were blowing off steam and resting their blistered feet in one of House of Nightshade's upstairs rooms.

Sawyer, who had now swapped his bejewelled showtime dress for a garish, red silk gown obviously plucked out of a second-hand store ("Let me slip into something more comfortable," he had announced in response to the suggestion of after-work tipples), snapped his fingers at a poor off-duty chorus member who had gotten stuck in the task of costume manager for an after-hours, tipsy performance from the choreographer himself. The chorus boy searched through a pile of vintage dresses and wigs, holding up various options only for Sawyer to wave them away in diva-like fashion as he gulped down wine.

"More bubbles?" Leo held up a bottle of prosecco.

Addi, curled up in a corner of a couch, was already feeling the light-headed buzz from her last glass. "I shouldn't."

"But you will," Quinn grinned at Addi mischievously and held out her glass for Leo to pour from the armchair she'd procured for herself, a bag of peas on her ankle.

"Fine, top me up," Addi caved. She couldn't deny that she was enjoying being back in Quinn's good books. "Maybe I'll get drunk enough that I'll forget seeing Sawyer's current performance."

Quinn snorted into her bubbles. "One can only hope."

Jen, who was stretching on the floor with a few of the other dancers across the room, held up her glass and wiggled it at Leo. "I'll have some more too, thanks Leo."

Leo barely glanced at her as he lifted a carton of coconut water to his lips. "Get it yourself, then."

"Ah, yes," Sawyer suddenly announced.

The performer sitting amongst Sawyer's strewn costumes had apparently struck gold with a voluminous black wig which the director promptly snatched out of his hands, performatively bent forward to position on his head then flipped back up, faux plastic hair bouncing around his face. The boy took his opportunity and scurried out of the room.

Sawyer clutched a wine bottle as if it was a microphone. "Ladies and gentle ones, this is a little ditty I like to call 'The Cher'. *I don't need your sympathy...*" he began belting out one of the pop star's popular hits.

Addi's eyes wandered over to Summer, who was lying near Jen across the laps of two other exotic dancers who had swapped the lingerie for Ugg boots and silky robes blowing out smoke from a thin joint before passing it around. Addi knew Summer would be able to feel her stare, but the dancer was choosing to avoid her gaze completely. For how much she was noticing her at that moment, Addi may as well have been another piece of Emmeline's eclectic antique furniture. Wallowing, she downed some more bubbles.

Leo nudged her. "Who are you staring at there, hm?"

Addi blushed. "No one..."

Leo waggled his eyebrows. "Could it be that my gaydar detects a hint of lusting after a certain attractive lady lying on that couch? As your Gay Best Friend you absolutely have to fill me in. I'm already booking our wagon in Mardi Gras parade next year."

Addi flapped her hands. "Sh, sh. Maybe, I don't know... Leo, I don't know what I feel. I mean, maybe I do. Ugh, but even if I *do* like Summer I totally messed everything up the other day and now she's absolutely never going to even look at me again. How did you know you were...?"

Leo smirked. "Destined for a life of boy problems? It wasn't a question for me. I was never interested in your species. Objectively, I can see that boobs are *nice*. They look, I don't know," he searched for a compliment, "Soft? Like little cushions."

It was Addi's turn to snort. "You flatter us, sir."

Leo winked. "Anyway, all my crushes in high school were guys. In terms of knowing my identity, it was easy for me — the hard part was being accepted in high school. I just never got that spark from the ladies. Not interested. Not at all about what you've got going on."

Addi moaned. "See, why can't it be that easy to know?"

Leo propped his chin on his fist. "Don't worry about it so much, seriously. Sexuality is fluid. It's a scale. It's not black and white. You can be bisexual, pansexual, whatever. You like who you like. Maybe it doesn't have to be so complicated. Besides, we're young. We don't *have* to know. My advice is to just focus on how you feel about the person and forget the rest. So, what happened between you two?"

"I royally screwed up any chance I have with her," Addi rested her head back on the seat. It felt so good to be talking to Leo about everything with Summer. She couldn't believe she'd been so caught up with everything going on she hadn't thought to come to Leo before. "We had a moment in the park, but I guess I got scared and ran away."

"Uh oh," Leo pressed his lips together in sympathy. "Classic confused adolescent behaviour. I think you just need to explain to Summer that you weren't running away from *her*."

Addi stared through her bubble haze at the dancer. "I wish I could. I think she's literally pretending I don't exist right now. Maybe I should try messaging her when we go to bed-"

"No," Leo cut in.

Addi frowned. "Why?"

"Oh, Addi," Leo gave a large mock sigh. "Still so much to learn. Whether you meant to or not — don't give me that look, I know you didn't mean to — you've obviously hurt her feelings and embarrassed her. Give her some time to cool off first. Then when she starts at least acknowledging your existence you can slowly build it up again. She needs to gain the power back, let her come to you first."

"Wow. I wouldn't have thought of that. You should have a column in one of those magazines. How did you become such an expert?"

Leo raised his glass to her in thanks. "Living and working with this amount of women has given me unique and real-world insight into their ways, so much so that I've learnt to dissect and even speak the dialect. Fascinating stuff."

On a futon next to Summer and her friends, the waiter who had spotted Addi outside Grayson's room was entwined with another exotic dancer, pulling back in between kisses to stare in awe at her, not believing his luck. Early morning breeze wafted generously in through the French doors onto the balcony that had been flung open and through the room, relieving them all from the build-up of smoke, sweat and cheap perfume that cloaked the House long after the guests were gone. Beyond Sawyer's off-key Cher impression and the old record player softly circling Ella Fitzgerald looped the constant city backdrop of cars, drunken shouts and the occasional siren.

Freddy slunk into the room and made for a deep red armchair in the corner. Jen perked up expectantly and flounced over to him. "What did you think of my dance with Leo tonight, Freddy?" she attempted to sit on his lap.

Freddy moved her off, sneaking a glance at Quinn before getting distracted with Sawyer's one-man show. "I wasn't really paying attention to the performance," he lied.

Jen pouted. "Where did you just get back from? Have you been with a girl tonight?"

A smirk swam in Freddy's eyes. "She was of the female persuasion, yes."

Scorned, Jen scuttled away.

"Hey, look!" Summer had moved over to stand in front of the French doors to cool off further. "I think Ralph is back, there's a cop car down there. Shit, I hope they don't come in here." She surveyed Sawyer in his wig and her friends with the joint and giggled before turning to keep watch again. "Phew, they're pulling away. False alarm everybody."

"Oi," Addi heard the mad chef call from the street, "Are you lot having a welcome party for me up there? You just can't survive without me, can you? Alright, alright, stop begging, I'll drop by then!"

"Oh god," Addi emerged from her content cloud of boozy bubbles and shot upright in her seat, spilling some of her prosecco on the gold-dotted navy carpet. "He can't come in here, he's going to be so mad at me for getting him taken to the station."

Leo immediately jumped into consoling mode. "It's a murder investigation, we're all getting questioned. There's no reason for him to be mad at you specifically."

"Reason? We're talking about Ralph here!" Addi's voice raised an octave.

Quinn laughed. "That's so true. He ain't gonna be happy."

Leo turned to her sternly. "Quinn-delin, I love you, but for once in your life can you please support my pep talks?"

Quinn downed the rest of her glass and shifted to face Addi. "Okay, okay, let's get serious. Number one, I think we should order some nuggets. Number two, Jesus Addi — you need to get some lady balls. First you're whinging about Kyle, then me, then that rando guy down the hall, and now you're scared of old Screw Loose coming up here. You gotta be like the lion and stand up to people. You did something pretty badass running away from your foster home and getting a job here, underage nonetheless-"

"It amazes me that you seem to wait exclusively until the entirety of House of Nightshade is assembled in a room until you bring that up," Leo snorted into his glass.

Addi giggled. "I feel triggered."

Quinn breezed on. "And you've started living your own damn life. You learnt how to stick it to Kyle when he's being an asshole, which is 24/7. Where's that chick? She's cool. Speaking of chicken, who wants nuggets?"

"Damn," Addi turned to Leo, who simply cocked his head at Quinn in bemused wonder. "That was a bit of a slap in the face, wasn't it?"

Leo patted her hand. "You know what Quinn's like when she's drunk..."

Addi pulled her hand away and pressed her lips together with determination. "No, you know what Leo? She's right. I did come here and it *was* pretty badass. Why should I be scared of one person?"

"I'm back, baby!" Ralph strode into the room, still dressed in the chef whites he was taken away in. "Did you miss me? I didn't miss any of you lot for one second, oh no, those were the most peaceful hours of my life being away from this mess, weren't they? Even the cop shop isn't as bad as this place. I had me some fun down there, those lads didn't know what they'd gotten themselves into with me. Ha!" Eyes sparkling despite the late hour and having spent the last few hours being questioned, Ralph approached Sawyer. "Oh boy, what do we have here? Cher's here to serenade me!"

Sawyer ditched the bottle and shimmied over to his colleague, lifting a hairy leg out from under his gown and wrapping it around the chef's waist. "Care for a dance, sugar?"

"I thought you'd never ask!" Ralph threw his head back as he cackled.

"Avert your eyes, children," Freddy's dulcet tone came from the corner.

As Ralph's eyes gleefully swept the room, basking in the laughter, he spotted Leo and Quinn before resting on Addi.

"Here she is," he pointed at Addi. "Chief Detective Adderall. Don't you like me, Adelaide? You tried to get me locked up. Ha!

I knew she didn't like me. Big, bad Ralph with his big, bad schnitzel-maker."

Addi looked to Quinn, who imitated a snarling lion at her in response. "Ralph, I didn't try to get you arrested when I…" she began as calmly as possible.

"I think it might be time for bed, everyone," Freddy interjected before she could get any more words out, standing up. "Chef, it was bad enough trying to do service without you tonight — I don't need you tired or hungover tomorrow. Clean this up, everyone."

There was a collective rumble as Sawyer pulled off his wig and the staff gathered empty bottles. The exotic dancer pulled the waiter by the hand, no doubt into another one of the empty upstairs rooms, and Quinn moved to lounge on the doorframe, lighting a cigarette.

Addi went to lift the needle off the record player and Freddy approached her. "I didn't mean to cut you off back there but I thought I'd save you the hassle of having to deal with Ralph — at least for tonight."

Addi recalled their earlier conversation. "Yes, I did notice you standing up for me this time. Good job." She gave him a mock thumbs up.

Freddy chuckled. "Sleep well, miss Addilyn. It's been a big day for you." His eyes drifted above her head to Quinn and he paced over towards the attractive lead performer.

Jen watched Freddy huffily, narrowing her eyes, then went to intercept Sawyer, who was struggling in his state to fold his wardrobe options.

"Shall we retire, madam?" Leo paused on his way to the door and convivially held an arm out for Addi.

"We shall, good sir," she accepted.

Leo had barely left after tucking Addi in when someone pounced on top of her.

"What the...?! Quinn, what are you doing? I'm trying to sleep." Addi tried and failed to shove the voluptuous dancer off.

"Addi," Quinn hissed, breath reeking of alcohol and cigarettes. "I was just talking to Freddy back there and heard something weird. Well, I'm pretty sure I did, anyway."

Addi rubbed her eyes and propped herself up on her elbows. Now lying back in a horizontal position, the wine had left her with that spinning feeling in her head as if she was on a boat. "What did you hear?"

"Shut up!" one of the girls in the dorm called to them.

Quinn ignored the request and lowered her voice. "So it was just me and Freddy and Chorus Girl Seventy Five and Sawyer across the room. I wasn't really paying attention but then there was a gap in our conversation and I swear I heard Chorus say to Sawyer 'I know what you did that night.'"

"'I know what you did that night'?" Addi repeated.

"I'm pretty positive that's what she said."

Addi stared off into the shadowy darkness of the room. "I guess I hadn't even thought about Sawyer having any connection to him before, but I suppose Grayson was the reason that his performance was messed up that night in front of those critics. Do you really think he could...?"

Addi didn't finish the question. She could see Quinn's frown even in the dimness.

"I mean, *I* was so mad at Grayson and all he did was trip me up. The guy did literally blow Sawyer's future career prospects to smithereens. But I just can't picture Sawyer having anything to do with a crime. He's been my director for years."

Addi nodded. "That's what I used to think about everyone here when they discovered his body. I swear, every day I find out one more reason why I don't know people here at all."

"So what do we do now?" Quinn whispered.

Mind fuzzy, Addi didn't respond right away. Was Jen's comment about *that* night specifically? Could Sawyer *really* be hiding something? Had Quinn even overheard the conversation correctly?

"Helloooo?" Quinn poked Addi drunkenly. "Addi are you sleeping?"

"I wish I was," Addi grumbled, swatting the performer's hand away. "I was just talking to you Quinn, of course I'm not asleep. What we do now is go to bed. We don't really know what they were talking about and," Addi rubbed her eyes, her head swaying, "I feel like I'm on one of those boats in the harbour right now to be honest. I guess we'll just need to keep our ears out over the next few days and see if there's any more to this. You're in a much better position to get intel from Sawyer and Chorus... I mean, Jen, than me."

Quinn took the hint and crawled off Addi's bed onto her own, discarding her clothes on the floor as she climbed under the covers. Addi rolled onto her side.

Quinn's eyes shone back at her through the dark. "I hate this feeling. Sawyer's my friend. I don't want to be suspicious of him."

"Yeah, I know what you mean," Addi murmured back, thinking of Leo.

The door of the dorm opened and closed again as a few more dancers who had been upstairs wandered to bed.

Quinn swept some hair, which had been straightened for the evening's performance, off her face. "I'm not like Leo. I don't make friends easily. I can't afford to lose them."

The performer rolled onto her other side with a mumbled goodnight. Addi shifted onto her back, staring at the shadowy ceiling while Quinn's breathing grew heavier and eventually turned into light snores. Despite wanting nothing more than to fall asleep mere minutes ago, she now felt wide awake.

Chapter Ten

"Without the errors, wrong turns and blind alleys, without the doubling back and misdirection and fumbling and chance discoveries, there was not one bit of joy in walking the labyrinth." — William Least Heat-Moon

Police interview with Sawyer Hawkins

Sawyer: Hel-lo, officer. That's a nice uniform you've got there.

Officer: Yes, um, thank you. What is your position at House of Nightshade?

Sawyer: Director, Choreographer, Emcee and Drag Queen. Keeper of Keys and Grounds.

Officer: Keeper of...what?

Sawyer: My good man, surely you read *Harry Potter*. No? Alright then, reference missed.

Officer: Moving on. How long have you been with House of Nightshade?

Sawyer: For the record, too long. I'd look half as old as I do now if I didn't work here.

Officer: You look fine. Can you please take a guess at how many years?

Sawyer: Over two decades now. Don't ask me why.

Officer: You would know the ins and outs of this place pretty well, then?

Sawyer: Oh yes, more than anyone else here.

Officer: Things must have been pretty different around here back in the day.

Sawyer: You mean before you lot made your rules? I kid, of course. Yes, things were far less PC when we first opened. The Cross was the place to be, not like it is now with all these restrictions. Us queens owned these streets. Now there's lock-out laws and the nightlife in this city is slowly disappearing. I think that's the reason we're still doing as much business as we are, honestly, because people are running out of places to truly let loose. Oh, I remember those golden days all too well. Half us staff would be drunk every night. Emmerson was famous for his cocktails and shots; he'd concoct some new special recipe every week. Emmeline would sit at that piano and bang away for hours. They used to be in love back then, too, Emmerson and Emmeline. Then two decades passed and they got bored and bogged down in the numbers and responsibilities of running a business. The original crew left and new people came in, and it's just not the same as when it was new and exciting in the beginning. We were like a family, setting up something magical together.

Officer: And things changed more when Frederick took over?

Sawyer: The energy became completely different. I mean, the man spent most of his childhood in a dark joint filled with booze and tits. That's got to do permanent damage to a kid. Mum and dad were always too busy running around here to pay him any attention. Jesus Christ, they could have at least taken him to the park on the weekend to play fetch or something. They were just so obsessed with becoming these powerful business moguls. The prominent problem was that they were absent more than anything. There was one period when Freddy was in early high school, I think, and Emmerson was just completely AWOL. Anyway, Freddy went through school and then took off to wherever it is he went. Years later, when shit hit the fan here, he came back. Hair slightly receded and a horrible attachment to those bloody cigars. He started helping with the accounts at first and then took on some of the operations. We didn't really think much of it at the time but then one day his parents packed up, said *au revoir* and left him in charge. The irony, huh? He used to skulk around the House as a kid and is still skulking around now.

Officer: And you know the staff well too, I presume?

Sawyer: Not as much as you would imagine, actually. I'm a lot older than most of them, closer to Emmerson's age than theirs. I don't really interact with a lot of the younger ones — they come and go. We always say this place is like Central station. That's typical of most hospitality venues, though, particularly if there's bad management. So I don't really bother getting to know many of them. There's also always going to be distance between staff and those who are more senior. As I direct and choreograph I can't just be "one of them" or they won't follow my instructions.

Officer: Mmm, naturally. But you do have some friends at House of Nightshade?

Sawyer: Of course.

Officer: And they are...?

Sawyer: I tend to sit with Quinn and Leo at staff meals.

Officer: Apparently Addilyn, the new girl, has also been hanging out with Quinn and Leo?

Sawyer: Either that or she's stalking them.

Officer: For the record, that last point was not a serious allegation.

Sawyer: I appreciate the closed captions.

Officer: Did you have much interaction with Grayson?

Sawyer: Barely any. Seemed like he thought he was a cut above, that one. He wasn't part of the troupe so the need to speak to him never arose and we didn't cross paths.

Officer: Until the night he died.

Sawyer: Until the night he died, yes. Of course those little gossips have already filled you in, haven't they? Although I'm one to talk, I suppose. Yes, not to take away from tragedy but last night was meant to be *my* big night. Years and years I've dreamt of leaving this god-forsaken place and having my talents recognised. Do you know how difficult it is to be in the arts? I should have just packed up and gone to Hollywood when I was young, but of course my bourgeois parents never encouraged me to pursue my artistic calling. The entertainment industry here is small at best. It's been my dream for years to work in a company and choreograph for the *real* stage, not one shovelled away in some sticky, shadowy corner while sleazebags sit upstairs getting grinded upon. Alas, as Emmerson reminds us, that's where the money is... and wouldn't he know it? Don't tell him I said that. Ah, if only I ran this joint. I'd take this show around the globe, up in lights where my troupe and I deserve to be marvelled at. Anyway, last night several noteworthy critics came to review my choreography, stage design and the like... It was my one shot. Everything was going swimmingly, we were getting along and they were enjoying my show, until that boy came rampaging across the stage with all the grace of a buffalo and bulldozed my lead performer. It was a mess. To say the least they weren't impressed. I politely suggested Grayson leave the stage and that was the last time I saw him. I had to use the understudy and, bless her fishnet stockings, she's not the lead for a reason. I believe any future career prospects of mine left the building when the critics did... but of course, you know, I understand it was a mistake. I mean, who would hold that much of a grudge against a teenage boy?

●

Sunlight streamed through the blinds when Addi groggily awoke the next morning, signalling that it was pressing midday. She reached out to her bedside table, desperately searching for a water bottle to remedy the dryness of her mouth and queasiness in her stomach.

Not dissimilar to the day before, there seemed to be a flurry of activity going on around her. She looked beside her to Quinn's bed but it was empty. All the girls who remained in the dormitory were smoothing their covers and shoving piles of clothes, magazines and dirty laundry under the beds out of view — even Quinn's discarded clothes from the night before were out of sight. Wondering why everyone was suddenly in a cleaning frenzy, Addi got up, pulled on some baggy jeans and her striped T-shirt — now more carefree than ever about appearing undressed in the company of her dormmates — and wandered downstairs, rubbing the gunk out of her eyes and ignoring the way the girls in her dormitory skirted around her. Her stomach churned as she sniffed the toast and freshly-cooked eggs and bacon that was being served, as usual, in the performance hall.

Thinking she might be able to stomach some toast at least, Addi walked through the open doors to see a woman that she had only seen once before. A woman that she had seen with Emmerson.

It wasn't the woman from the taxi.

"In France, we had warm croissants and coffee every morning on *le balcon.*"

Perched at one of the smaller tables with one leg crossed over the other and an orange headscarf tied around her wild, steel grey hair, Emmeline was just as grand as she had appeared in the black and white photo from the newspaper. A long, floral shawl draped over her skinny frame and a bunch of thick bracelets clinked together as she raised a tiny espresso cup to painted red lips.

Freddy, sitting opposite her in a charcoal knit jumper, gave an exasperated chuckle. "I can't help that it's raining, Mum."

"No need to be smart, *mon cheri.*"

Everyone else having breakfast in the room was oddly quiet, like at school when the principal was nearby. Addi spotted Quinn,

Leo, Ivy and Sawyer sinking back on a set of couches around a low table near the front of the stage, as if they were hoping to stay inconspicuous. Addi headed as quietly as possible to the breakfast bain-marie and quickly loaded up a plate. As she went to sit with the others, she stole a glance at Emmeline, who spied her. Quickly, Addi ducked her head down, not wanting to draw attention to herself, but it was already too late.

"Bonjour," Emmeline waved at her, bracelets clanging. "Who is this?"

"This is our newest waitress, Addilyn," Freddy answered.

Emmeline pushed her chair back, gracefully drew her shawl around her and swanned over to Addi. "I love your curls," she shook her hand daintily, then reached up and lightly lifted up a few strands as if inspecting them.

"Um, thanks," Addi laughed lightly and absentmindedly patted them down. "They can be a bit hard to tame."

Emmeline gestured at her own unruly hair. "This I know. Some things in life are not meant to be tamed." She grandly swept her own hair from her face.

Addi found it off-putting how she talked in a clearly cultivated posh accent, as if descended from royalty .

"Where did you come from?"

Addi blushed a little under Emmeline's forthright scrutiny. "All around the suburbs. I was a foster kid so I moved from place to place."

"Oh," the mogul assembled her expression into something appropriately pitying, "Well, we're glad to have you as part of the House of Nightshade family. Have you ever danced?"

"Have I ever...? No, not really. None of my foster parents ever wanted to pay for me to do extra-curricular activities."

Emmeline tutted. "What a waste." She reached out and grabbed Addi's forearm, lifting it up from her side and tilting her head to examine Addi's waist. "You are so petite; the body of a dancer," she declared, pronouncing the last word with an *ah* sound.

Freddy gulped his coffee resignedly, obviously accustomed to his mother's blatancy.

Emmeline turned to her son. "Perhaps she is in the wrong department, Frederick?"

"The stage can barely hold the performers we have at the moment, mother. Besides, she's a good waitress. I'd like to keep her there." He raised his cup to Addi.

Addi hovered with her breakfast, unsure of what she was supposed to do or say.

Emmeline studied her for a couple seconds more. "There's an idea. We could do a piece with the waitstaff." She resumed her seat.

Addi took that to mean she was dismissed and rushed off to join the others before Emmeline could say anything else.

"Sawyer, join me," Emmeline called to their vicinity. "I've had the most brilliant idea."

"Please don't let that happen," Addi appealed through a mouthful of dry toast.

"Oh, heavens." Sawyer robotically turned on a smile and reluctantly dragged himself to Emmeline and Freddy's table.

Leo crossed his legs. "It's going to be one of *those* days."

Quinn snorted. "You say that nearly every day."

"Every day it's true," Leo responded sagely.

Addi felt a wave of nausea in response to the food and set her toast back down. "Do you guys know why she's back?"

Leo shrugged. "Someone dies in your business; I guess the holiday's over."

"Fair point. I wonder where Emmerson is?" Addi searched the hall but there was no sign of him.

Emmeline's voice drifted across the room. "What do you mean you don't think it's a good idea? The point I'm trying to make is that we need to give them another reason to look at us other than the fact that a boy died here. Oh, I should have come back sooner."

Around them, other staff members were inhaling their meals and fleeing as soon as they could.

"You're here now," Freddy reminded his mum gently. "That's what's important."

"I know, but the press! The police! The scandal! I shouldn't have left you and your father to deal with it all alone."

"We've handled it just fine," Freddy responded gruffly.

Sawyer's eyebrows shot up to his hairline.

Emmeline lent a pitying smile and patted Freddy's cheek. "*Mon cheri*, we all have our strengths. I'm used to putting out fires. Where's your notebook?" she demanded of Sawyer. "We need to plan a new performance."

Sawyer gaped at her. "What do you think my job is?"

Emmeline blundered on. "If I cannot have a croissant," she pronounced the pastry with a French accent, "someone fetch me a croque monsieur from the deli."

Sawyer raised an eyebrow suggestively. "A *what* monsieur?"

"Croque," Emmeline repeated, sliding the French 'r' purposefully. "Croque monsieur. It's a French sandwich."

Sawyer waggled his eyebrows. "Wouldn't mind me a French monsieur."

Addi exchanged a look with Quinn, who pressed her lips together in understanding, their conversation the previous night about the director obviously playing on both of their minds.

"Hurricane Emmeline has well and truly arrived," Ivy quipped as she got up to take her plate away.

Addi made sure her supervisor was out of earshot of the table before facing Leo and Quinn. "I was thinking about this whole thing with the mallet when Ralph came back last night and how I found it right there in the kitchen, where half of us in this place work almost every day. It got me thinking about what else might be right in front of us that we missed. There's one place that we haven't even thought to look yet but would surely hold some sort of clue."

"Where's that?" Quinn queried.

"Grayson's old room." Addi turned her head to check no one was near them who might be listening. "I mean, it's right there. Makes sense to check it out."

"I'll be real, the thought of going into some dead guy's room is not my idea of a good time," Quinn tossed her hair, "but it does make sense to have a look ourselves. It's not like the police seem to be making headway and I am bloody over these bitches in here walking around thinking we had something to do with it."

"Exactly," Addi affirmed.

"We could check it out this morning? I'd rather get it over and done with," Quinn suggested. "Everyone's running out of here because of Emmeline, no one will be hanging around to spot us — it's perfect. Leo, you in?"

"I do love snooping but I have an appointment," Leo collected his breakfast dishes and stood. "You kids have fun and I expect a full report as soon as I get back."

Quinn shrugged. "Then there were two."

Addi attempted nibbling on some more toast. "A mission for us ladies."

"Girl power," Quinn nodded approvingly. "I like it. So, we'll need the key to get in."

"Potentially a problem," Addi pointed out.

Quinn tapped the side of her head. "Not if you used to hook up with the guy who ran this place and know where they're kept. At least that relationship was useful for one thing."

Addi snorted. "Speaking of Freddy, we'll have to make sure none of the Halloways spot us."

The two friends peered over again at Freddy and Emmeline, who was being brushed off by an irritated Sawyer as he made a run for it ("No! No, I'm not creating a new performance with zero notice this morning, Emmeline, I'm busy. You'll just have to wreak havoc with my choreography some other time.")

"Emmeline will no doubt entertain herself rearranging the business, but how do we make sure Freddy and Emmerson are distracted?"

Addi cocked her head to the side, recalling a certain conversation she'd had the previous night over the bubbles that were leaving her feeling off her food that morning. Despite what Leo had advised, this could be the perfect excuse. "I have an idea."

●

Later that morning, three women from the three different departments of House of Nightshade descended the stairs together.

"Thanks so much for helping us," Addi gushed.

Summer regarded Addi for a fleeting second before pursing her lips and addressing Quinn. "Happy to help you, Quinny. I guess you could say I'm used to keeping business under wraps. Thanks for the party favours." She lightly shook the small, clear bag Quinn had passed to her earlier before hiding it in her cleavage.

Addi tried her best not to look too overtly. At least it had worked; Summer had been forced to acknowledge her existence once again.

The dancer shimmied off into the performance hall to work her magic on her bosses, arm grazing Addi's as she passed and sending a small shiver through Addi's body.

"Are you sure that'll be okay with Leo that we took from his stash?" Addi turned to Quinn uncertainly.

Quinn waved a hand. "He probably wouldn't even notice if we didn't say anything, but I'm sure he'll be fine with it. He owes us anyway for not being here while we travel into the depths of some dead guy's room. If not I can always blackmail him with that Niagara Falls I spotted, if you know what I mean," Quinn snorted.

Addi blank-faced the dancer, not caring to lie. "I really don't."

Quinn ruffled her hair. "You can't stay young and innocent in this place for long, can you? It's slang for Viagra."

Addi's eyes widened. "What's he got that for?"

Quinn waggled her eyebrows. "What else? Don't worry, I'm sure his reproductive organ health is just fine. Some young people just use it for a bit of a... boost."

Addi grimaced. "Quinn, can we never talk about Leo's reproductive organs again, please?"

Quinn mimed zipping her lips. "I'll grab the key — you wait here."

Quinn disappeared to put her knowledge gained from her time with Freddy and her long tenure at the House to good use. Addi ducked into the performance hall to check on the distraction; Freddy leant on a chair, throwing his head back in laughter at something that Summer was saying as she tucked a strand of hair behind her ear. In typical hawklike fashion, Kyle lurked near his manager, setting tumblers out on the tables and staring over at the exotic dancer, calculating how he was going to inject himself into the conversation.

A tap on her arm pulled her gaze away from Summer, and Quinn held up a bunch of silver keys to signal her success. The pair rushed down the hall and up the creaky, wooden stairs with its patterned carpet lining the middle. Quinn shoved the keys into her pocket and held a hand over them to help conceal the bulge as a dancer passed in the opposite direction. The pair shared a polite greeting with their co-worker. Once she had passed, Quinn eyed Addi and they couldn't help but giggle at their sleuthing.

"This is kind of exhilarating," Addi breathed.

They slowed as they reached the boys' floor. Goose bumps popped up along Addi's arms in the quiet of the hallway. They edged closer to the room where the police tape across the door was beginning to droop and curl in on itself.

Quinn peered back down the hallway to check that no one was coming. She sorted through the keys, trying a few similar silver ones. "It definitely should be one of these, hang on..." The door clicked as Quinn found the right key, but the lead performer hesitated.

"What is it?" Addi asked.

Quinn's voice grew slightly higher. "You know, I think I am a bit of a superstitious person after all... this is creeping me out. He literally *died* in here. I mean, it's perfectly rational to not want to go in. It's bad juju."

"This isn't exactly my idea of a good time either," Addi nodded in agreeance. "But it's now or never and if going in here gives us something to help clear us of suspicion or some sort of clue to figure out what happened to him then it's worth it."

Quinn took a step back. "I can't do it Addi, I don't want to-"

"Nope, no way are you leaving me to go in here alone," Addi pulled her friend's arm. "What happened to girl power? Don't you remember the speech you gave me last night?"

Quinn rolled her eyes. "Actually I don't, I was really drunk."

"Lion, Quinn. That's what you told me to be. We don't have much time; I'm going in."

Sounding braver than she felt, Addi pushed the door open and stepped over the faded police tape. Quinn followed closely behind her with an unconvinced whimper.

The room was nearly bare; it was evident that someone hadn't been there long enough to settle in and get comfortable. Addi shivered in the cold and Quinn scrunched her nose at the musty, stale air. The covers were dragging on the floor on one side and bunched at the end of the bed, as if someone had been thrashing around in their sleep. Grayson's small travel bag was open in the corner, clothes spilling out of it carelessly. Seeing the space now with hardly anything left behind by its previous occupant, Addi felt a pang of sadness for Grayson and the little that remained of his life.

The memory of him felt like a character from a movie. A recollection that she had been trying to push away flooded back into her mind; the last time she had talked to him and how excited she had been at the prospect of going out in the city with him. She had been trying not to think about it too much, to focus instead on getting to the bottom of what happened. Now, however, being in his old room, the conversations and glances at each other were all she could think of. It was like he had known that something was going to happen. He had even told her to stay away. What was it he had known that no one else did?

There was a soft thud. Quinn was on her knees on the floorboards next to Grayson's bag, rummaging through the few black and white T-shirts and grey skinny jeans he had brought with him. In her hand she held a thick, yellow envelope.

Addi crouched down next to her. The word 'takings' was scrawled on the front, dated only a few days before Addi, and therefore Grayson, had arrived at the house. Inside was a thick bundle of cash.

"That's Freddy's handwriting," Quinn pointed out.

Addi gulped. "Jesus. So he stole from them."

Quinn reached into the bag and fished the last few things out — earphones, deodorant, a vape and slouchy beanie — then tipped the whole bag upside down and shook it.

Addi ran her hand through what lay on the floor. "Nothing else," she confirmed.

Quinn tapped the envelope. "Still, that's not fivers in there. He got a decent whack." She shoved the clothes and envelope back into his bag.

Addi knelt to check under the bed. There was nothing there, however a piece of paper that had floated down underneath the bedside table caught her eye. She reached over to take it, holding it up in front of her face so she could read. It was a page torn out of the lifestyle section of the local paper. There was a section for new-release movies, events that you could take your family to on the weekend and, down the right-hand side of the page, a break-out box with a write-up on House of Nightshade. Emmerson and Emmeline's portrait sat at the bottom of the piece, and handwritten underneath that in blue pen was a phone number.

Quinn approached Addi and peered over her shoulder. "What's that?"

"A write-up on the House," Addi answered, flipping it over to see a half-page advertisement on the back. "And someone's phone number. I wonder who..."

Before she could finish her thought, footsteps sounded nearby, perhaps in the hallway below.

"We should probably get back," Quinn suggested. "I don't really think there's much else and I'm not hanging around here longer than we have to." Her eyes did a final sweep around the scant room.

Addi folded the torn newspaper page and pocketed it before following Quinn out.

When they got to the bottom of the stairs, a group of dancers in leotards, hair pulled back into tight buns, were rushing into the performance hall.

"There you are!" one of them called when she spotted Quinn. "Come on, we have to go and rehearse some new number that Emmeline's come up with and she wants you in it."

"Well, duh, I am the lead," Quinn responded to the girl, tying her hair up. She turned to Addi and quickly passed her the keys, muttering "top drawer in the corner" before she was pulled by the performance troupe down the hall.

After slinking into the empty office, with its outdated PC on a ginormous, mahogany desk piled with enough papers to give anyone anxiety, and depositing the keys, Addi rushed upstairs to pull on her uniform and made her way to the kitchen to start her shift.

Emmeline pointed as she entered as if accusing someone across a courtroom. "You! The one who should have been a dancer."

Bemoaning the fact that she didn't think to enter the kitchen through the back door, Addi dragged her feet over to the unbridled owner.

Emmeline, Emmerson and Freddy appeared as if they were in the middle of a stand-off. Freddy and Emmerson both had their arms folded and wore frowns, in contrast to the performance crew who were dressed up in puffy skirts or pants and colourful vests as they did a final run-through of an upbeat number. A disgruntled Ivy entered from the hallway, a folded up screen under one arm and a candelabra in her other hand — it must have been her that Addi and Quinn had heard going upstairs. She stopped near the management huddle, setting the screen down on the floor and resting the candelabra on the nearest table.

"Good start, dear," Emmeline waved an arm absent-mindedly at Ivy. "I think we still need more, though. "

Addi could see Ivy battling with her own preference for rule following, but in the end let out a sigh before traipsing back out to heed Emmeline's wishes.

Emmeline gestured to Addi. "Come over here."

Addi felt her stomach churn — had she and Quinn been spotted? She desperately tried to rack her brains for a possible excuse for entering a crime scene. As she walked tentatively forward, Emmeline leant towards Freddy and murmured close to his ear. She was close enough to hear him reply, "Her name is Addilyn."

Emmeline turned to Addi with a smile. "Addilyn, perfect timing."

Emmerson simply surveyed his wife crossly.

"I'm sure Addilyn should be helping set up, mum," Freddy suggested.

"Oh, there'll be plenty of people for that. Stand up tall, dear," Emmeline commanded Addi.

Addi straightened her back as much as she could.

Emmeline reached out and pushed on the top of her shoulders. "Relax them back and down. There you go. Does that feel better?"

"Um, yeah," Addi appeased her. *I would feel more relaxed if you weren't hovering over me.*

Freddy shook his head at his mother with a mixed expression of exasperation and admiration while Addi stood there like a stiff mannequin. "What's the plan, mother? You're going to teach our waitstaff to dance in an hour?"

"Of course not, *mon cheri*. It takes years to hone style." Emmeline let the sarcasm roll over her. "You're smart, aren't you, Addilyn?"

"I like to think so," Addi offered, wishing she could leave this odd family disagreement.

"There you go. I'm sure our waitstaff have seen enough performances while working here that they could pick up some basic moves. You need to believe in people more, *mon cheri*."

"I actually haven't been here that long," Addi offered hopefully, mortified at the thought of having to add dancing to her work tasks.

Addi could tell Emmerson was trying to not roll his eyes. He cleared his throat instead. "Be reasonable, darling. We don't have much time until tonight's performance. You don't want our show to look like a mess, do you? You know that's the first thing they'll publish in the reviews."

Emmeline threw her hands up in the air. "Reasonable? You can't just keep churning out the same type of performance night after night. It's boring!"

Emmerson raised his voice. "You know you do this every time you come back, don't you? And you never learn! You cannot just waltz in here and interfere with your outlandish ideas when we already pay a director who knows what he's doing. I mean really, Emmeline, if you want to try and teach the waitstaff how to dance why don't you just call in the zoo animals? That's not refined or creative, my dear; it's messy."

Freddy turned to Addi as his parents began to bicker, decibel-level rising steadily. "A piece of advice: don't go into business with your family. Why don't you head to the kitchen..."

"Addilyn, come here!" Emmeline cut through. "Ivy, you too," she commanded as Ivy returned with more props for the stage. "Where are the rest of the waitstaff? Gather everyone here now."

"Oh, here we go," Emmerson grumbled, apparently giving up. "No one listens to me, do they? What do I know? I only own half this goddamn business. Right. Seeing as no one cares about my opinion, I may as well not even be here." He strode from the room, tapping his walking cane sporadically against the ground as he did so.

"Fine, I'll just stay here and deal with this, then?" Freddy called after his father.

Emmeline patted Freddy's cheek. "Don't worry, *mon cheri*, I'm on top of it."

The front doorbell buzzed.

"Why don't you go and get that?" Emmeline suggested.

"Okay, mother, I guess I'll have to trust you," he said with a small smile before strolling off down the hall, the smell of his cigars hanging around in the air after he had exited.

Addi, Ivy and the other waitstaff gathered at the front of the stage while the performance crew were stopped above them. Quinn tapped her foot impatiently.

"*Typical*," Leo mouthed to Addi.

Emmeline began explaining her new plan, pacing as she attempted to illustrate it. "What I'm picturing is the dancers up on stage, and then in the finale we have the waitstaff drop everything and mirror what they're doing up there. Except a simplified version, obviously. I just think something to get the audience down here really engaged..."

"So what are you saying, we're not *engaging* enough?" Quinn fired at Emmeline.

Emmeline pursed her lips. "Quinn, I see you haven't changed one iota since I was last here. No, that is not what I said. This really isn't about you at all."

Quinn continued brashly. "Do you know how insulting it is pouring so much time and energy into rehearsals here and then having management turn around and decide on a whim that they're going to pass over stage time to completely untrained, incapable dish pigs?"

Ivy's eyebrows shot up to her hair. "Dish pigs? Why, thank you."

Jen stepped forward behind Quinn. "As much as I despise agreeing with her, Quinn has a point. My stage time has already been cut because Little Miss Diva here couldn't possibly stand not being in the spotlight for one more week and bullied Sawyer into giving her a solo with a bad ankle so she could loll around on the couch in front of her adoring fans-"

Emmeline snapped her fingers. "Get to the point, Jennifer."

Quinn smirked. "She's just really obsessed with me, Emmeline, that's why she can't stop talking about me."

A trill of mirth swept through the performance crew.

Jen gritted her teeth. "You can't just cut our performance. We work so hard every day on these routines."

"Plus," Leo piped up. "I don't really think people will be happy about paying to see waitstaff dancing at the level of some primary school disco. No offense, guys."

"I wholeheartedly agree," Ivy nodded. "Can we just get back to our jobs?"

Emmeline clapped her hands. "No you cannot. End of discussion. We are wasting precious time."

"Sawyer?" Quinn appealed desperately.

Sawyer leaned on the edge of a table, arms folded and lips pouted. "My hands are tied here, people." He looked to Emmeline in surrender. "Fine, let's show the waitstaff the final number and see if we can make something out of this."

Both the performers and waitstaff gave a collective groan and reluctantly shuffled to assemble themselves. Emmeline gave a smug "Hmph" of triumph.

Ivy tapped Addi on the shoulder. "Look, that officer is back."

Addi turned. Freddy had invited Officer Knight to the bar area and was pouring him a glass of water.

"Come on, let's find out what he's saying," Addi whispered to Ivy.

"Addi," Ivy eyed the two men with caution. "We're not meant to hear that. Besides, they'll see us."

Addi gestured around. "With all this going on? Come on, we'll hide behind those chairs. Wasn't it you who once told me if they wanted a private conversation they should have it somewhere else?" Addi nudged the supervisor, grinning.

Ivy's eyes sparked. "Well, how am I supposed to argue with myself?"

While everyone else concentrated on the dance number being demonstrated to them on stage, the two girls floated towards the back of the room to eavesdrop. They dropped to the ground and crouched behind the tables closest to them as they drew closer to where Freddy and the officer were standing.

"...couldn't hold him without valid grounds, of course, but we're still investigating. We want to seek a professional opinion. Has he ever been medically diagnosed with anything to your knowledge?"

"No," Freddy answered. "Ralph would never go to a doctor, not even for an injury. He's great at what he does in the kitchen, so as long as he doesn't interact with the customers we'll keep him around. Definitely something missing there socially."

"I'll agree with you there," the officer nodded. "Mental instability does throw a spanner in the works of cases. More paperwork for us to look into it; more difficult to rule them out. One more question, if you don't mind. To your knowledge does the chef ever have fits of rage or emotional outbursts?"

"He gets angry, yes. He'll go off at staff and say upsetting things. Honestly, I would have to describe his emotions as unpredictable at best."

"Thank you." Officer Knight flipped his notebook closed. "We'll try and get an opinion from a psychiatrist and go from there, but it'll take some time. Red tape, you know."

"Of course," Freddy returned.

"It's not looking good for him, though. A drugged dinner, hidden potential murder weapon and a mentally unstable chef — as we say, the evidence points true. Well," there was the sound of someone being clapped on the back, "I have to get back to the station. Thanks for your time."

"Anything I can do, Officer," Freddy offered.

Their footfalls retreated.

Ivy locked eyes with Addi. "He was spiked in our kitchen?"

"Poor Grayson," Addi whispered, diverting from Ivy's gaze to stare at the floor. She could picture it now — Grayson eating his meal none-the-wiser, starting to not feel well, retiring to his room. The sheets had been twisted when she and Quinn searched the room; had Grayson been writhing around in agony? She tried to think about something else to stop her mind from going around in circles. "No wonder he accidentally ran into Quinn on stage," she recalled. "He must have been feeling out of it."

"Oh, yeah. I completely forgot about that," Ivy said sadly. "That's horrible. Do you think it was really Ralph, though, as they're saying? I've never seen him care about anyone in this place. Why would he kill a teenager he didn't even know?"

"I agree. I think it *looks* like him," Addi replied slowly.

"Makes you wonder—"

What exactly it was making Ivy wonder, Addi never found out.

"Girls! *What* are you two doing down there?" Emmeline stood above them with her hands on her hips, her wildly curly hair around her face making her a formidable figure.

The waitstaff had ceased attempting to learn the dance and were staring at Addi and Ivy crouched behind the furniture.

Ivy jumped upright as if she'd been jolted. "Sorry, Emmeline," she apologised promptly, cheeks turning red.

"We thought we saw something," Addi muttered in a pathetic excuse, rising slowly.

"I think I see something also." Emmeline dramatically pretended to peer into the distance with a hand over her eye as if looking out to sea. "It's tomorrow's poor review in the paper because we weren't rehearsed enough. Now, chop, chop," she clicked her fingers impatiently, bracelets jingling. "Time to make a show."

It wasn't until later, when all the waitstaff were running around in a last-minute frenzy to set up because they'd wasted too much time trying (and failing) to learn Emmeline's choreography, that Addi remembered the folded newspaper article she'd found in Grayson's room. It was still inside her pocket. She glanced at the bar. No one was there — not even Kyle — all too busy preparing tables, folding napkins or polishing cutlery.

Addi ducked behind the bar and headed to the bench where the till was, surrounded by numerous faded receipts and wine-bottle caps. She picked up the old-fashioned phone, with its rotary dial and dirty gold earpiece flecked with black spots of rust, and pulled the dial clockwise. She held her breath as it rang, glancing up to ensure no one was watching.

The line picked up on the other end.

"Hello?" The gruff voice of Emmerson was easily recognisable, even obscured through the phone line.

Addi hung up abruptly, the handset landing with an antique clang.

Chapter Eleven

"There is so much good in the worst of us, and so much bad in the best of us, that it hardly becomes any of us to talk about the rest of us." —
Edward Wallis Hoch

Police Interview with Emmerson Halloway

Officer: Emmerson, is it?

Emmerson: Yes.

Officer: Right. Let's begin with when the victim first arrived at House of Nightshade. The staff have noted that Grayson arrived at the venue for the very first time with you.

Emmerson: Correct.

Officer: The same time that you happened to come back from... where was it, Spain?

Emmerson: France.

Officer: Ah, lovely. Your family definitely likes the life abroad. You know, because your son also... anyway. Do you know how long you'll be in Sydney?

Emmerson: Originally it was just going to be a week or two. Emmeline and I, while we spend most of our time living abroad, pop back and check in on the business every now and then. As the owners it's important to get a sense of how things are running on a daily basis. However, due to the, ah, unforeseen circumstances, I think I'll be staying until this whole thing blows over to support both my son and the business. It's obviously unfamiliar territory for all of us.

Officer: Yes, understandably. That was the reason you came back?

Emmerson: What?

Officer: Um, you just said you like to pop back and see how the business is going every now and then. Do a routine check. That was the only reason you came back? I ask because many staff have vocalised their curiosity around the timeliness of your arrival and Grayson enquiring after a job.

Emmerson: Of course they have. Yes, it was coincidental. The boy had gotten in touch perhaps a week before. Emmeline and I were discussing one of us going back anyway and it just happened to line up. I knew we needed to hire someone but didn't receive the memo that the place had been filled as I was on the flight over here when it occurred, so I thought I was going to arrive with a beneficial solution.

Officer: Right, thank you for explaining. You knew Grayson through a family connection, correct?

Emmerson: Correct.

Officer: Yes, that's back here in my notes. Poor lady. Now that you live abroad, how much involvement do you really have in House of Nightshade?

Emmerson: We still have a little involvement at a higher level. Otherwise, Frederick covers the operations and day-to-day running of the place. Living in another country our contribution is limited, which was a purposeful move on our end. It had become too much. It was our every waking minute of every day. It's difficult to cut the cord when you've raised a business for decades. Neither Emmeline or myself are getting any younger, though.

Officer: You and Emmeline don't travel back to Sydney together?

Emmerson: We often do but not every time. I'm sure you know how it can be, a man such as yourself. You spend your whole life with a certain type of woman who likes to run the show. I always say; give a forceful wife an inch and she'll nag you for a mile. "Buy this, go here, do that. Don't eat that pastry, Emmerson, it's not good for your cholesterol." It's Paris for Christ's sake, a city in which one would struggle to breathe without inhaling macarons. Sometimes a man needs to put an ocean between himself and the lady of the house.

Officer: Yes, naturally. I can sympathise — I mean not the macaron thing, but the old ball and chain, heh. Can you think of a reason why any of your staff would have wanted Grayson out of the picture?

Emmerson: Do you know why people come into our industry? They could get a job serving food or washing dishes anywhere, or join some local theatre group or do dance lessons on the weekends. They're all running away from something. House of Nightshade gives them a place to hide from their lives, to put on a new costume every day and pretend they're someone else. They're damaged souls who aren't dealing with their problems out in the real world. They think *this* is the real world. Damaged people tear others down in an attempt to regain any sort of self-worth they can possibly garner. You just watch over the next few days, Officer. You want to find your culprit? Stick around for the performance that happens when the doors are shut.

•

Leo folded his hands together on the table. "So that newspaper clipping and the envelope was all you found in his room?"

Addi sighed, clarifying for what felt like the tenth time. "Yes. There was hardly anything else there."

"And the newspaper article...?"

Addi pulled it out of her pocket. "It's just about House of Nightshade. It talks about Emmerson and Emmeline retiring and Freddy taking over."

Leo took it from her and began to read it out aloud. "Blah blah blah... *a question a lot of locals are asking is whether House of Nightshade will be the same as Frederick Halloway takes the reigns. His parents and founders of the cabaret venue, Emmerson and Emmeline*

Halloway, are minimising their involvement in the business after thirty years and intend on traveling and living overseas to enjoy the fruits of their hard-earned labour. The venue will henceforth be managed by their son Frederick, who will inherit the family enterprise as his parents slowly retire from hospitality in the near future. Will this really be the last hurrah for the business mogul couple? Only time will tell."

"See? Nothing shocking."

"Obviously Grayson was trying to find the House," Leo concluded, as they had gone over already. "And the money... did he take it or was it given to him to cover up for something else?"

"He could have also been telling the truth, though," Addi posed. "He wanted to move down to the city and had a connection to the family so that was the most logical way of finding a job."

Leo frowned. "Yeah, but they'd just hired you. It doesn't really make sense."

Quinn bit her lip, staring off at the wall as she thought.

"Honestly, I wouldn't put it past him to steal," Leo said.

"That's what I thought," Quinn agreed quickly. "Fits in with his character."

"Do you think it was just stealing, though?" Addi questioned.

Leo cocked his head. "What do you mean?"

"He's dead, right? I mean, someone murdered him."

"Yeah...?" Quinn said slowly, looking to Leo.

"And there's a wad of money in his bag. If all he did was simply steal it from the register, would someone really turn around and kill him for that?"

There was a pause as Leo and Quinn both considered what Addi had said.

Addi continued. "The motive's not big enough. If he was killed because of something to do with money there has to be more to it than the amount we found."

"Yeah, he must have been blackmailing them or something," Quinn nodded fervently, a spark in her eye. "That makes so much more sense."

"Exactly. Freddy, Emmerson and Grayson were having those private conversations before he died, and Emmerson said something about needing more time!" Addi felt like some of the fog that had been sitting on top of her brain for the last few weeks was starting to lift. Finally a piece was coming together, although she still felt like she was missing something.

"Geez," Leo shivered performatively. "You never grow up thinking that the bosses you work for might actually..." he lowered his voice to a whisper, "*kill* one of their staff members. You think it really was one of them?"

"I would not put that past Freddy at all," Quinn said.

"It's the only thing that's making sense to me right now," Addi shrugged. "Grayson came here with Emmerson, the money he had is theirs, and the newspaper clipping had Emmerson's number."

"That newspaper clipping doesn't really prove much, though," Leo whispered. "As Grayson told you, he knew the family and sought them out for work. He would have seen them again in the newspaper and then looked them up. It's not really suspicious."

"Well, yeah, that's true," Addi conceded. "The rest of it, though; it all seems to link back to Emmerson and Freddy, doesn't it? Everything does."

"But why?" Quinn whispered back. "What do they care about some rando guy?"

"What did Grayson have on them?" Leo murmured, staring seriously at the floor.

Addi tried to think back to the conversations she'd had with Grayson. "That's what I can't figure out."

"Hey, look," Leo nudged them, gazing across the room.

Addi and Quinn both glanced up to see Freddy, Emmerson and Kyle crowded around the bar, bickering.

Leo raised his eyebrows. "Trouble in paradise again."

Quinn retrieved a pack of cigarettes out of her pocket and a lighter from her bra. "Ugh, who cares?"

Other people had also stopped their conversations to stare at the three men. Addi saw Ivy nearby shake her head.

"I definitely need more coffee for this," Leo stood to fill his cup.

The shouting increased in volume, Kyle's face turning a familiar flushed pink until he flipped a tray off the counter off the bench and turned on his heel, seething. Leo paused mid-step to give the angry bar supervisor room to pass by, but instead Kyle deliberately pushed into Leo, causing the dancer to trip and drop his cup.

"What are you gawking at?" he bellowed at Leo.

"Hey, what the hell was that?" Quinn shouted.

Leo rubbed his arm, taken aback. "*Everyone* is looking at you, Kyle."

"You happy, watching all this unfold around you?" Kyle grappled to shift the focus.

"What are you talking about?" Addi defended Leo.

Kyle pointed at Leo. "I bet you're loving this, while you just sit back and hide what you three have done."

Leo blinked slowly at him again and started to laugh. "Are you crazy? I honestly have no idea what you're talking about." His tone was even, however Addi could still hear the annoyance coming through.

"Yeah, okay," Kyle glanced around at all the watching faces. "Still conveniently trying to cover up the fact that you still can't tell anyone where you were on the night that boy got..."

"Enough!"

It wasn't Leo who had yelled.

Over in the corner, Sawyer had pushed his chair back to stand and was staring Kyle down. "Leo had nothing to do with Grayson being killed."

Blush crept up Leo's cheeks. "Oh, dear." He looked apprehensively at Sawyer, trying to discreetly shake his head. "It's not worth it," he implored softly. Of course, Sawyer couldn't hear him from the other side of the room.

"Leo, what's happening?" Quinn hissed.

For the first time Addi had ever seen, Leo ignored her.

"How do you know that?" Kyle demanded.

"Because he was with me," Sawyer announced boldly.

"Right, as we all technically were whilst working. That doesn't mean that he has any more alibi than the rest—"

"He was with me all night," Sawyer cut Kyle off.

People cocked their heads at him quizzically.

"Overnight," Sawyer clarified.

Everyone still stared at him blankly.

"Jesus, you people are slow," Sawyer muttered. "Overnight, do you understand? Until the next morning."

Quinn's mouth fell open. "Oh... my god."

"Leo!" Addi accidentally exclaimed incredulously as the news clicked in her head. She turned to Quinn.

Leo put his head in his hands. "This is painful."

The murmuring started straight away. A few girls giggled.

"What's funny, huh?" Quinn shot at them, recovering herself quickly. "Are you bloody homophobes?"

Scorned, the girls shut up instantly. Someone coughed, cutting through the equally awkward and stunned silence that hung in the air.

"So, you guys..." Kyle began as if figuring out a maths equation.

"We slept together, yeah," Leo defended himself, obviously deciding to steer into the skid. "Well, that's the big secret. Are you happy now? There's my alibi," Leo affirmed. "I don't have any more time to give to this, but I think what we should all be wondering is why Kyle has been trying so hard to frame us," Leo motioned to himself, Quinn and Addi, "for murder?"

With that, the star performer waltzed from the room, not offering a second glance at the head barman he'd just put in his place. With Leo out of the vicinity, all eyes turned to Sawyer as the person of interest in the latest scandal to be revealed.

The director pushed his glasses further up the bridge of his nose to caress his wiry, steel-grey eyebrows and lifted his chin, strongly reminding Addi of a stern teacher. "If you think I'm going to indulge any childish gossip, jokes, mocking or even a hair of chatter you've got it more twisted than your pirouettes. You'd all do well to remember that it's not just the manager who's your boss around here. Besides, let's not all pretend this place isn't a cornucopia of bed-swapping. Now, as if today couldn't get any scarier, we've got our Halloween performance to rehearse. Chop chop!"

●

Addi held the flyer in one hand as she trudged a bursting rubbish bag from the kitchen to the outside bin in the courtyard:

For the spookiest spectacle you've ever seen,
We invite you to join us this Halloween
As the sun sets, the undead will rise
So join them and don your frightful disguise
Make your way through the streets if you dare
Be prepared, for no scare can compare
Magic and darkness you shall receive
At House of Nightshade this Hallow's Eve.

Emmeline careered around the corner and rumbled into the back lane in a timeworn bubble car, the vehicle literally bouncing as she swerved sharply to a halt, grey curls springing. She spied Addi, attempting to heave the splitting bag of food scraps into the stinking, overstuffed commercial bin. Logan, who was sizzling lamb backstraps on a rusted outdoor barbecue, blankly acknowledged Emmeline's expensive-linen clad figure tottering out of her car, smoke wafting all around him and encroaching into the rest of the courtyard.

Emmeline waved violently. "Addison! Come and assist me with this."

"No worries, Addison's not busy right now," Addi muttered under her breath.

Logan smirked as he rotated the pieces of meat with a pair of long, silver tongs.

What Addi replied out loud in a more helpful tone was, "Coming, Emmeline." With a grunt and a final push she managed to get the garbage bag to a point where it was half sitting atop the enormous pile, the other half sagging down the side. "Good enough." She dusted her hands off.

"Addison, just... the boot." Emmeline panted as she struggled past her and through the courtyard under the weight of a huge, open box of pumpkins, the multiple bracelets around her slim wrist jingling as she walked. Addi was impressed that she didn't trip over the long shawl and full-length skirt that swished around her high-heeled boots.

"On it. Maybe call some of the others to help?" Addi suggested.

Wind furled dead leaves across the orange, uneven bricks of the courtyard as Addi walked through the garden beds to the parked car. A crow launched from the gutter of the outhouse to land on the wooden edge of the dehydrated vegetable patch nearby.

Emmeline had stuffed her boot to the brim with knick-knacks, even piling them up on her passenger seat. Addi dived in, pulling out white sheets, eerily realistic skulls and a mammoth amount of woolly fake cobweb. She gathered up an armful and carried it back through the courtyard, smoke pluming around her.

"Save it for the smoke machine," she coughed as she passed Logan, the back of her throat tickling, and passed through the kitchen door.

"Squeeze the bag from the top down." Danika was teaching the kitchen hand how to form meringues as she guided a whizzing beater around a huge bowl. A recipe book of Halloween treats was open on the stainless silver table, now flecked with white bits of meringue mixture.

"I *am*!" the kitchen hand lied.

Ralph chortled as he mixed a blood-red cherry reduction on the stove. "Mate, I've seen pre-schoolers make better meringues than that."

The performance hall was buzzing with a flurry of activity as Addi entered. Ivy shook out deep purple and black fabrics and draped them over the tables. Rusted old candelabras were being placed on every available surface and a waiter trailed Ivy, shaking silver and gold, star-and-moon-shaped confetti across the tablecloths. Addi inwardly groaned at the effort it would take to clean it up at the end of the night — she just knew it would all wind up getting stuck in the carpet.

Freddy manned the sound deck with his usual cigar, fiddling with volume knobs to test the level of audio in different areas of the House that resulted in a soundtrack of disjointed grabs of several creepy songs.

Addi spotted Emmeline lining up pumpkins on the floor in front of the bar.

Emmerson, who stood behind the bar tying scarlet ribbons around three antique, iron keys, shook his head as he observed his wife. "That was a really important investment, was it, dear?" he called over to her grumpily. "What are we going to do with all these bloody pumpkins at the end of the night?"

Addi tried her best to look at the floor as she dumped her own armful on the ground and began to sort through it.

"What kind of Halloween event would this be without jack-o-lanterns?" Emmeline snapped. "How many knives do we have? We'll need Ralph's best ones to cut through..."

"For Christ's sake woman, why didn't you get the fake ones? We need the staff setting up. Who's going to be wasting time carving pumpkins? You don't *think* about these things."

"We'll just get the kitchen hands to do it..." Emmeline started off to the kitchen doors.

"No you don't! They're busy enough in there preparing the feast. Oh, there she goes." Emmerson gestured exasperatedly as Emmeline disappeared through the swinging doors, ignoring her husband. "You would think I'm the only voice of reason around here, wouldn't you?"

Addi, unsure if he was addressing her or not, afforded a sympathetic smile before starting to rip open the cobweb packets.

"Frederick," Emmerson started towards the sound deck, "your mother strikes again..."

Following Addi's lead, more of the waitstaff brought in decorations and costume pieces from Emmeline's car. As Addi looped cobweb material as stylishly as she could manage over tables, candle sticks and between chairs, Emmeline gathered the now-disgruntled performance troupe around the bar.

"Right, if we all start carving it shouldn't take much time at all and then you can go and get ready. Everyone grab a pumpkin and get festive!"

Sawyer scowled at Emmeline.

Addi stifled a laugh as the performers were handed various kitchen knives and sat down, rather perplexed, in front of the orange vegetables scattered across the floor.

Quinn turned the pumpkin around in her hand, searching for the best angle to insert her knife. "So do we just, like, stab its face?"

Addi snorted. "It doesn't have a face yet, Quinn. That's the point."

Leo shook his head at his own pumpkin. "I'm an artist of the stage, not the pumpkin patch. We should so not be doing this."

"Speaking of things you shouldn't be doing," Quinn began slyly, "you wanna fill us in on you and Cher over there? I need details."

Leo sighed resignedly. "I've been dreading this day. Okay, ladies, what would you like to know?"

"How long has it been happening?" Addi asked immediately.

"More importantly, is the sex good?" Quinn waggled her eyebrows.

"We've been sleeping together for a while," Leo professed. "And yes, the sex is *uh*mazing. I mean, why else would I keep going back?"

Quinn couldn't help but look impressed. "Leo, you little minx."

"You're not anything more, though?" Addi prodded, grinning.

"Strictly sex. Imagine us going out on a date? I mean, the guy's old enough to be my dad."

Quinn snorted. "That's being generous. Look at you, bagging a GILF." She swatted him playfully.

"A GILF?" Addi repeated questioningly.

Quinn guffawed. "Grandad I'd Like to—"

"Fornicate with." Leo cut in sharply to finish the sentence. "I'll have you ladies know that he's far from a grandad. Let me recite a descriptive acrostic to give you more of an idea, if I may? G stands for great in bed, R is for robust, M is for 'mmmm'..."

Addi giggled. "Leo, there is no M in Grandpa."

"Oh, true." Leo shrugged unabashedly. "Well, I don't work here because I'm a scholar. Shall I continue? D is for..."

"Okay!" Addi blocked her ears. "Thanks Leo, but this isn't a poetry slam so you can save us the misspelt details."

"I'm never going to be able to look at Sawyer the same way ever again," Quinn sighed in mirth as she finished laughing. "I am both in shock and also in awe of you." She ruffled Leo's hair.

"Well, that makes a lot more sense," Addi said. "I now understand why you couldn't really tell people your alibi."

"Exactly. It's *Sawyer*," Leo pronounced.

The group of three turned to peer at the director in question, who was now spinning across the stage as he demonstrated a move.

"Yeah, we should all be allowed to keep who we hook up with private," Quinn agreed.

Leo glared across at Jen. "The Sawyer was already out of the bag. Little Miss Nosy over there caught us coming out of Sawyer's room and she's been holding it over our heads."

Quinn lightly punched Addi's arm in understanding. "I know what you did that night," she repeated Jen's phrase.

Leo swivelled between Addi and Quinn. "What?"

"Quinn overheard Jen saying to Sawyer 'I know what you did that night," Addi filled Leo in. "We didn't know what to think of it."

"Wait a minute," Quinn interjected, frowning. "That's why she was given my role, isn't it?"

Leo nodded, grimacing awkwardly. "She was blackmailing Sawyer; she had us backed into a corner."

"That conniving little bitch! No offence Leo, but I'm glad everyone knows now so she can resume her rightful position in the back row where talentless try-hards belong."

Addi grinned across at Leo. "Peace has been restored to the kingdom at last."

●

The afternoon sky turned a hazy grey as nightfall approached. A giddiness stirred within the House as everyone rushed to put final touches on decorations throughout the many rooms for the Halloween festivities.

The delicious smell of baking pumpkin wafted from the kitchen; Emmeline had suddenly decided to use up the mountain of pumpkin flesh that had been carved out for the dinner.

"I don't know why you didn't notice this earlier. No pumpkin on a Halloween menu?!" She scolded Emmerson and Freddy.

"Ah, yes, of course we're wrong and *you* saved the day," Emmerson replied tersely, rolling his eyes at Freddy.

The result of the performance troupe carving pumpkins were extremely odd — lopsided jack-o-lanterns leading the way up the front steps of the House and placed around the halls looked as if they had been carved by primary school students.

"I'd like to see you try," Leo had defended himself when Addi giggled at his creation.

Quinn picked up some pumpkin flesh and lobbed it at Addi teasingly. She skilfully skirted around and it landed with a *splat* on the floor. Kyle didn't miss a beat in instructing her brusquely to clean it up.

Behind the bar, Kyle and Freddy tipped small vials into a large bowl of emerald-green punch. They stepped back, admiring their work, as the bowl began smouldering and artificial smoke curled out and spilled down the sides, then placed it on display at the front of the bar. Emmerson took the antique keys and disappeared into the depths of the House to hide them.

Emmeline, relishing in the pandemonium, merrily weaved her way through the chaos with a laundry basket full of items, throwing them at all the waitstaff as she passed. "Costume time! This might work with that," she said to one boy. "Here's some vampire teeth," she threw a pair to another. "Go backstage to get your face powdered white, everyone. The look we're going for is extremely dead. Here, Ivy," she pulled out a long, white gossamer dress and a black, lace veil, "Would you like to be a zombie bride?"

"Sure would," Ivy replied distractedly, eyes skimming through the hall to see what else needed to be done.

Addi noticed the veil as it passed hands. Something about it seemed familiar, but then she figured it was probably all the shawls that Emmeline wore.

"Try and get changed as quickly as you can, everyone," Ivy pleaded to the waitstaff, who were hurriedly removing their aprons and running back upstairs to change and put on make-up. "I need to brief you all on service in twenty minutes!"

Emmeline spotted Addi. "Ah, Addison. Let's see..." she rummaged through the couple of costume items leftover, "witch?" She held up a black velvet cloak and a witch's hat. "Do you have a black dress? And scary make-up, dear. Perhaps some red lippy dripping down the corner of your mouth. Get the other girls to help you."

Addi took the cape and hat and turned to walk up the stairs, nearly tripping over the power cord of the smoke machine that Freddy and Emmerson were carrying to the front door.

Addi had to admit that the waitstaff did an impressive job given the small window of time they had to get ready. Someone went backstage and brought white face powder up to the dorms, applying it to people as they changed into torn fabrics for zombies or capes and plastic teeth for vampires. Ivy slipped into the gossamer dress and threw the veil over her head before helping Addi tease her hair to be even frizzier than it already was and dust her face with black eyeshadow and red lipstick. Others simply threw a white sheet with cut-outs for their eyes,mouth and arms over their clothes and called it a day.

They leaned against benches in the kitchen as Ivy filled them in on the banquet they'd be serving and all the different Halloween-themed treats and cocktails on offer (Bloody Marys and *Mar-scream-is*). Logan, Danika and two kitchen hands scurried around at Ralph's beck and call to ready platters of canapes, topping them off with fake spiders and the cotton cobweb material. Freddy strolled in dressed in black pants, a smart white dress-shirt and black cape, its collar sticking up at the back, fittingly looking the part of a vampire.

"Run sheet," he lazily passed a piece of paper to Ivy. "We're going to start letting people in now." He swished his cape around himself as he turned and exited swiftly.

"Bloody timing," Ivy gritted her teeth, throwing the run sheet amongst the mess on the bench behind her. "Alright, most of you know the drill. There'll be props all around and smoke from the machines so take care and watch where you're going. I don't want to be taking anyone to the hospital because they accidentally lit themselves on fire by treading on a jack-o-lantern or something, okay?"

Ivy divided the team up, sending some to the bar. Addi breathed out a sigh of relief as she was directed with the rest to start taking out trays of food — she wasn't in the mood to be told off all night by Kyle.

"Oh my god," Ivy complained, fiddling around with the black veil she was wearing as Addi picked up a long, white tray of canapes and a stack of serviettes. "I can't work in this stupid thing." She pulled it off and abandoned it on one of the stainless steel benches.

The minute the doors to the kitchen swung shut behind her, Addi was enveloped in near-darkness. The only light glowed from candles, off-white wax dribbling down the rusted candelabras and congealing on tablecloths. The lights around the bar had been dimmed to the lowest possible setting. Guests dressed as witches, creepy clowns and fictional villains emerged from the smoke, clutching their tickets apprehensively as they drank in the spectacle around them. Addi jumped as a performer crept out of the shadows behind her and brushed past, dressed in an extremely torn dress with splotched brown over her entire body posing as dirt and blood. More performers in similar costumes joined her, coming down the staircase and emerging from behind the bar. Addi unconsciously found herself searching for Summer in the crowd.

The creepy music emitting from the speakers swelled. Guests giggled and bumped into one another as the performers crept into their midst, half-walking and half-dancing around them creepily, shepherding them along into the performance hall to find a seat.

Addi zigzagged around offering canapes, routinely checking behind herself for any performers lurking nearby to avoid getting a fright. A fake skeleton hung on one wall with a collection of plastic bones on random surfaces, a cluster of twig broomsticks leant against the wall in a corner and a bunch of jack-o-lanterns flickered atmospherically atop the piano. Emmeline must have dragged every spare Halloween decoration they had and put it on display, and it was all Addi could do not to trip on any of them as she navigated her way through the darkness.

Platters were cleared and bowlfuls of smoking punch drained into goblets before everyone found a seat. The low bar lights were turned off and replaced by sudden blasts of light akin to lightning. The music faded and was traded by a scream sound effect. Everyone looked around nervously to see what would happen next — even Addi hung back with her empty tray.

The curtains on stage lurched open, the sudden light startling the audience. The creature-like call and pounding of drums that signalled the beginning of *Ramalama (Bang Bang)* sounded through the speakers and the performance crew, all in the same costume of ripped clothes and bodies sponged dirt-brown and red, began an eerie, disjointed dance, descending into the audience.

Addi saw Freddy behind the sound deck, bent over the controls as he directed spotlights to follow the dancers on the ground. The song ended with all the performers rushing back onto the stage for the final beats and collapsing in a heap like a pile of dead zombies. The crowd erupted into cheering and applause as the curtain drew to a close once again.

Addi quickly dropped her empty platter in the kitchen and peeked into the bar. Kyle wasn't there, so she went and leant against the stainless steel sink in the corner, cleaning glasses and stacking them in the dishwasher so she could watch the show.

"Ladies and gentlemen," Freddy's voice rumbled through the speakers as he spoke into a microphone from the sound deck behind the audience, "we welcome you on another spook-tacular," Addi could hear the cringe in his voice as he spoke the word, "Halloween evening. Three keys have been hidden throughout House of Nightshade and it's your job to find them — you'll spot them by their red ribbons. Those in possession of a key by the end of the night will receive five free tickets to spend on any show this year. Explore the rooms and watch your back; the undead have all come out into the world of the living this Hallow's Eve. We urge you not to take any pictures or record videos, but rather immerse yourself fully in the mysteries of the night. Indulge, explore... and try not to scream." Freddy wrapped up his introduction sounding bored.

The dim lights flicked back on and the crowd began inspecting the clues in their hands, putting their heads together and pointing at the page.

"Look at them all."

Addi jumped as Emmerson spoke, not realising that he had slunk up in the dark and was standing right beside her. Emmerson didn't apologise, but merely examined the crowd alongside Addi. "Another Halloween. Each year it's bigger than before, of course. Emmeline, with all her ideas. Now..." he patted himself, searching for something, as waitstaff began bustling behind the bar and reciting drink orders.

Addi quickly began helping them pour glasses of wine, fetch beers from the cold room or scoop the bright-green, smoking punch into goblets. Meanwhile, Emmerson stood with his back to the chaos of the bar amidst the staff trying to work around him in the small space and pulled a stopper out of a bottle of brandy, pouring the amber liquid into a glass.

Emmerson tapped Addi's shoulder as she poured drinks. "Have you seen Freddy?"

"Ah, no, sorry," she replied distractedly.

A boy nearby threw Emmerson a scathing look and rolled his eyes as he was forced to reach around him for a bottle opener.

"Right," Emmerson murmured, looking around. "Right," he repeated more decisively. He stepped out of the bar, glass of brandy in hand.

"Finally," the boy sighed when Emmerson had left, stepping into the space he had been occupying and reaching for bottles of spirits to pour into glasses.

"He's so weird," Addi shook her head, helping the boy with his drinks order.

"Particularly today," the boy agreed. "Thanks for helping me do this." He carefully pulled the loaded tray off the bench and tried to balance it on his forearm to run it out to the customers. "Damn, too heavy." It shook as he coaxed it off the bench.

"I'll take some and follow you out," Addi offered quickly, picking up another tray and moving some of the load over.

The pair of them exited the bar and entered the crowd still milling around the seats in the performance hall. Addi waited for the boy to deliver all the drinks he was holding to people, then swapped trays with him and made her way back to the bar with the empty one. As she turned she bumped into one of the staff under a long, white sheet with eyeholes.

"Sorry," she muttered.

The person under the sheet didn't say anything, turning away to head for the door out of the performance hall — standing about a head taller than everyone else.

What was Freddy doing hiding under a ghost costume? Addi wondered. She watched him reach the door and then turn, looking around under the sheet. Someone else joined him, but Addi couldn't quite make them out through the haze of fog from the smoke machine and dim lighting. She navigated her way through the throng of guests and down the hall, discarding her tray on a table.

There was a sliver of light as the front door was opened. The guests and other waitstaff were all too preoccupied to notice.

Addi had to find out what Freddy was up to and follow him without being spotted. Thinking quickly, she navigated back to the kitchen with as much haste as possible through the crowds and darkness, pulled her witch's hat off and picked up the lace veil Ivy had abandoned earlier to cover her face. She pulled it over her head as she sped out the back door, through the courtyard, around the side lane and out onto the main street in front of the House.

For the first time in a while, Addi was thankful for the crowds of the city. She let herself get caught behind a group of friends that took up the entire width of the pathway dressed in costumes, some as zombies, others as barbarians and variations of animals or the classic short-skirted police women outfits from the discount store. They laughed shrilly to one another as they meandered towards their destination, taking swigs from cans of mixed drinks or bottles of beer.

Addi easily held Freddy in her sight, his stature very helpful to spot in a crowd. In the evening sky and street lights she saw that he was accompanied by none other than Emmerson. The group that she hid behind were apparently all too tipsy to notice or care that there was a stranger tagging along.

"Just this once," Addi heard Freddy say to his father. "I'm getting to the end of my tether with this."

They were funnelled into a two-person-wide file as people passed in the opposite direction. There were business people trying to speed past the merry party-goers so they would still catch their scheduled commute, people walking dogs or running by in activewear, a few younger trick-or-treaters being led around by parents and other costume-clad people heading to parties or meeting up with friends. Addi grabbed fistfuls of the long veil from the inside to stop it from dragging along the concrete and tripping her up as she got caught in the mob of people headed into the train station.

Freddy and Emmerson pulled away from the crowd towards the curb. Addi watched as Freddy stuck his hand out in the air to hail a taxi. Emmerson pushed his son's arm down, jerking his head at the train station; it was a rookie error to drive through city commuter traffic when the trains were three times as quick at that hour. The pair cut through the throng and made their way to the underground platforms.

Addi followed them down the escalator and onto a train headed toward the city, hopping on through the opposite door of the same carriage and standing back in the vestibule in order to keep an eye on them. The train stopped in the CBD, but they didn't get off. Aside from a few words murmured here and there and Emmerson brushing the shoulder of Freddy's white shirt in a quintessential father-son moment, the pair didn't seem to want to chat to each other. They merely stared out the window into the dark train tunnels and ugly steel work that surrounded the tracks as the wheels squealed painfully slowly between stops.

Just outside the city centre as the train started journeying west, they stepped off. Addi started and made her way out too, apologising as she pushed through people that had already started filing onboard. Disoriented, she whipped her head around, trying to pick the two men she was following out from the sea of people in front of her. The platform was crowded with people dressed in gothic Halloween costumes and Doc Martens. She shuffled around a big group and spotted Emmerson and Freddy already near the top of the stairs leading away from the platform. Picking up the veil that covered her again and holding it above her feet as she would a long, fancy gown, Addi took the steps two at a time to keep up with them.

A busker played the didgeridoo outside the station gates. Addi walked by him and onto what was evidently the main street. Freddy and Emmerson were waiting to cross in front of a large intersection, part of a sizable crowd who were waiting at the lights and getting buffeted by pedestrians.

Addi hung back, hovering behind a homeless man with his head bowed, holding his cap out upside-down for money. To her right, music and loud din spilt out of a three-storey pub, muscled security guards with earpieces pacing slowly back and forth on the street outside, staring after passing girls in tight clothes or revealing costumes. A small dog on her left was tied to a pole waiting for its owner, tongue hanging out as it panted excitedly at passers-by like a kid in a candy shop.

The walking signal turned green and Addi followed father and son across the road. Buses rumbled and let off exhaust as they waited at the front of the traffic queue, and a cyclist nearly ran into Addi and the people around her as he crossed over to the other side of the road. As they collectively let out jumbled noise in reaction to the near-accident, Emmerson turned his head to look behind him straight in her direction. Addi quickly flitted behind the nearest person. She had no idea how well the veil was obscuring her from view, but if they caught her following them that would be it — she would be forced to say goodbye to her life at House of Nightshade. It was a lot to gamble to follow the pair, but she felt sure that wherever they were leading her would bring her towards the answer of what happened to Grayson.

Over the curb and onto the concrete, she followed Emmerson and Freddy past the outdoor tables of a Mexican restaurant, lit by candles flickering inside coloured glass jars, and rainbow-painted wooden benches. Down a road with a few shops and eateries close to the main street, they strode by a fire station with a bowl of water for passing dogs out the front and a small bar, people sipping cocktails and swapping stories seated around tables draped with red and white chequered cloths. The businesses soon turned into terrace houses, windows giving fleeting glimpses into living rooms bathed in flickering blue light from television sets and others with housemates sipping drinks over conversation. *Were they going to visit someone's home?*

Addi pursued the two men as they turned into a skinny lane. In the quiet of the street, they were walking by a vibrantly painted garage door set in a brick house when Freddy paused mid-step and put a hand on his father's arm as he swivelled his head. Addi gasped quietly and had just enough time to duck behind some nearby bins, feeling her heart beating in her chest.

"It was probably a cat," she heard Emmerson assure his son briskly.

She exhaled as she heard them begin walking again. She waited a few more seconds before following them again onto another street similarly lined with terrace houses.

Suddenly, Emmerson and Freddy veered left off the sidewalk into what looked like a dusty car park shadowed by a magnificent oak tree. Addi whistled softly to herself as she bent her head back to take in the entire tree, its tangled boughs casting dappled light over the mulch below. Standing next to a sandstone church in front of an expansive graveyard, Addi thought the tree seemed like it was the silent keeper of the cemetery.

Freddy and Emmerson navigated their way through the sea of grey headstones, most of which were split in two from their old age. Addi trod carefully across the ground to hide between the tall roots of the colossal tree; enough to cover her if she crouched. She steadied herself on the smooth, cool bark and peered around the wide trunk.

Freddy and Emmerson had now been joined by a third person. Addi instantly recognised the lady's long, dark hair; it was the same woman she had watched Emmerson get in a taxi with.

Chapter Twelve

"What you leave behind is not what is engraved in stone monuments, but what is woven into the lives of others." — *Thucydides.*

Among the crumbling, sinking headstones, the etchings on most nearly faded and illegible, the freshly dug grave and new, dark grey tombstone stood out like a rose in a bed of thistles.

The woman cradled a bouquet of colourful flowers in her arms and what looked like a very old, dirty childhood bear that needed stitching up. She stepped prudently forward, clad in a long black dress with a black coat draped around her shoulders, and placed the flowers and small bear at the foot of the tombstone, dabbing under her eyes with a silk handkerchief.

"He is missed," Addi heard Emmerson comment gruffly, clearly as a nicety. Her stomach flipped slightly as she shifted her position to see through the small group of three to read what was etched into the tombstone, already knowing what it would be:

'*Grayson Reid, beloved son. God called me home to Heaven.*'

Addi watched the unusual meeting as they crowded around the tombstone solemnly. Freddy scratched his five-o'clock shadow uncomfortably, as if he was counting down the minutes that had to be spent at this peculiar outing. Emmerson put an arm around the woman's shoulders, patting her in an attempt to seem consoling. Addi noticed how the three of them looked like they were all matching, with their black clothes and dark hair...

She raised a hand quickly to her mouth, perhaps to stop the exclamation that she felt was about to come out of her mouth. *Of course,* she thought to herself.

She had to get back to House of Nightshade before Freddy and Emmerson travelled back themselves and realised she wasn't there — not to mention the fact that Ivy and Kyle would be wondering where she was and she would have to make up some lie. The cemetery was quiet aside from a few people walking through with their dogs who were zooming around the monuments, busily sniffing as they went.

Addi backed away slowly, keeping an eye on the small group gathered around Grayson's grave as she did. They continued their quiet tribute. As she took another backwards step a branch snapped under her foot, the sound travelling through the silence.

Addi cringed. Emmerson, Freddy and the woman all whipped their heads around. Emmerson took a few steps toward where Addi was hanging back.

"Emmeline?" he asked, peering at her as he tried to make her out in the darkness.

Not knowing what to do, Addi just shook her head, feeling the veil lightly caress her shoulders, then turned and walked speedily out of the graveyard. She didn't hear anyone coming after her. When she reached the gravel of the carpark in front of the church, she stepped out onto the street path and made a run for it, tearing the veil off and bundling it up underneath her arm.

Back on the main street she waited at the crossing, glancing behind herself every five seconds and tapping her foot impatiently. The little red man blinked at her teasingly. She couldn't wait anymore and risk Emmerson and Freddy catching up with her. She elbowed her way through the crowd and, in a small break of traffic as the oncoming cars trailed behind a slow bus, she darted across the huge intersection, a car coming the opposite direction beeping at her as it hit the brakes.

The pub pumped out music as she proceeded to the train station. *"This train will stop at..."* she heard the smooth, electronic voice of the announcer that accompanied a train that had just pulled in. Rushing and ducking between people, she careened down the stairs and managed to jump into the carriage of the departing train back through the city a few seconds before the doors closed, breathing out a sigh of relief.

When she had almost reached the House, Addi was about to cross the road a few terraces away when she stopped in her tracks. Standing sentinel at the front of the steps under the light was none other than Kyle.

"Shit," Addi muttered under her breath.

A pedestrian behind her bumped into her as she stopped abruptly, throwing her a dirty look as he sidestepped. Addi swerved as fast as she could and headed around the corner and up the side street so she could enter the House through the back. Was Kyle standing there of his own agenda, or had Emmerson and Freddy called him and asked him to keep watch? Addi had a strong feeling she knew which one it was.

The back gate to the courtyard creaked as she pushed it open. She trod over the bricks through the flowerbeds and, thinking quickly, into the large storeroom out the back, leaving the bundled veil there and picking up two bottles of wine before she headed back through the kitchen.

Ivy looked both relieved and annoyed as she spotted her walking back through the flaps. "Addi, where have you been?"

Addi held up the bottles, one in each hand. "I just ducked out to get these. Kyle had me running drinks."

Ivy's hair was falling out of its ponytail and frizzing around the front of her face. "You do look a bit flushed. I swear I've been losing everyone tonight with all the rooms in darkness and everyone in costumes. I haven't seen Freddy *or* Emmerson for about an hour, have they been in the bar at all?"

Addi shook her head, trying her best to appear sincere. "Haven't seen them."

"Typical. No wonder you got pulled into the bar then, those two were supposed to be helping out Kyle. Okay, time to get these entrees out. Front left corner first, then snake around. Guys, come on," Ivy called to the other wait staff who were munching on leftover canapes and polishing cutlery.

They rushed over to the bench where the entrées of blood-red soup in small, shallow dishes were waiting under the heat lights. Addi stacked three plates on her hands and forearm and pushed the kitchen door open with her foot, the other waiters following behind her.

People traipsed down the stairs, performers dressed as zombies jerkily descending and jumping out at guests as they walked. The guests laughed nervously or gave small shrieks as they sped down the stairs away from them. Addi scanned all the people walking down the stairs for a sign of Leo or Quinn but, as Ivy had pointed out, it was almost impossible with the costumes and flurry of movement.

In the meantime, Ivy had recruited Emmeline, who was carrying a half-full glass of champagne in one hand. They exchanged a few sentences, Ivy shrugging. Emmeline scanned the room then threw her spare hand up in frustration and swanned into the kitchen, Ivy following behind.

As she hurried back to grab more entrees, Addi saw Freddy slink into the performance hall, adjusting his vampire cape around his collar and glancing around. Addi kept her head down.

"...see you've already started on the champagne." Emmerson was also back, standing in the kitchen in front of the cutlery tray near the door to the courtyard. He made towards the chef's bench and grabbed a leftover piece of bread, tearing off a chunk. Emmeline fluttered around him like a mosquito as he strode around the kitchen trying to shrug her off.

"The staff haven't been able to find either of you for about an hour. I honestly just sometimes wonder what you do..."

"More than you, I would hazard a guess, my dear. How many glasses have you had tonight?"

Addi heard the dark, Halloween-themed music starting up in the performance hall — Freddy was obviously back behind the sound deck. She waited by the heated bench for more entrées as the kitchen hand pulsed a huge pot of soup. Danika rolled her eyes at Emmerson and Emmeline as she picked the leaves off herb stalks for garnishing. Addi bit her lip. Emmerson had obviously figured out that it *hadn't* been Emmeline who he thought he had seen at the cemetery.

Emmeline pointed her index finger at her husband. "Don't you lecture me. I have been having important conversations..."

"Important?" Emmerson barked a laugh. "Is that what you call gossiping with your snobby, housewife girlfriends?"

"It's called hospitality!" Emmeline smacked a hand down on the stainless steel bench. "Need I remind you that's been sorely missing from this place while we've been gone? And you would do well to encourage our son to do a little more hosting. I swear, since I came back all you two have been doing is running off and hiding during service. Without our customers we don't have a business."

"If you have a problem with the way Frederick runs things, don't whinge to me. Go and talk to your son." Emmerson gestured out into the performance hall. "Heaven forbid you should ever have a stern word with your much-loved *mon cheri*. No, let me always be the bad guy."

"I am not whinging, Emmerson. I am stating a fact that we both know to be true. I'm simply saying that he needs to be doing more to engage with guests..."

"This sounds like an excellent conversation you could be having with *Fred-er-ick*," Emmerson enunciated his son's name to emphasise his point. "Why don't you run along and find him?" Emmerson dismissed his wife, dodging around her with his hunk of bread and walking back out into the courtyard, chewing.

"Emmerson!" Emmeline gaped after him. "Yes, great, go off and disappear again! Oh, you know what ladies," Emmeline swept around to face Addi and Danika, her arms flapping to her side, "this is what happens when we leave men in charge. Disaster." She grabbed her champagne glass off the bench, took a generous gulp and walked over to study the soup. "Hm. It's a bit boring, can you add a little something else? Some croutons or something." She wiggled her fingers over the nearest bowl.

"Oh ho!" Ralph turned around from the stove, ladle in hand. "Would you like to do my job for me, then, Madame? Guess I should just pack up and go home then. Not like this is my kitchen or anything."

"Of course you can go home, Ralph. It's up to you whether you'd like to remain employed," Emmeline snapped. She shook her head in a moment of recovery and attempted futilely to pat her hair down. "Now, where is Frederick?" With that, she waltzed out.

"There was already bread," Danika muttered, exasperated, as the kitchen door swung closed.

The guests chatted jovially over the music as they slurped on soup, bowls emptied in a matter of minutes. Addi and the other waitstaff buzzed around the tables clearing piles of dishes away. The kitchen filled with the smell of the barbecued meat that Logan had been cooking outside earlier as they took the lids off the warmers. One of the kitchen hands lined up heavy, white plates on the bench and spooned a small mountain of mashed potato onto each one, the potato landing with a *splat*. Logan and Danika added greens, baked pumpkin and meat, Ralph finishing the plates off with a jus and wiping the edges spotless. The hot plates almost burnt the waiters' arms and hands as they walked them out to tables as fast as possible.

"I'll help take staff meals," Addi volunteered as they finished dropping the main course to all the guests in the performance hall. She needed to find Quinn and Leo.

"Great," Ivy nodded distractedly. "Okay, you lot all go and eat outside quickly," she told the rest of the waitstaff who were lolling around the kitchen, "and get the bar staff too. Where is Kyle? Why is everyone going missing tonight?"

The performers were busy reapplying thick make-up or fake blood when Addi entered backstage.

"Addi!"

Addi jumped as someone touched her arm, but it was just Leo, still dressed as a zombie from the dance at the beginning of the night with his typical coconut water in hand.

He helped her steady the plates. "Oops. My costume obviously works then."

"Where's Quinn?"

"Well, hello to you too. Did you see our dance? Pretty awesome, huh? I wasn't really sure we were going to pull it off, actually, it was really technical..."

Addi cut him off. "Leo, where's Quinn?"

"Gee, what's up with you? She's over there at the make-up table." Leo pointed grudgingly.

"Sorry, I just really need to tell you guys something."

She palmed off the meals to the nearest three performers and dragged Leo by the wrist over to Quinn.

"Oh, hey Addi," Quinn greeted her cheerfully as she swept across her cheekbone with bronzer to make her face appear more hollow and zombie-like. "We bloody killed it out there, didn't we? I really suit this dead look." She patted her matted hair and pursed her lips, admiring herself. She stopped and noticed Addi's foreboding look. "You don't think I look good?"

"It's not that. I think... I mean, I just went..." Addi glanced around. Nearby, two of the performance girls were throwing her uneasy looks. "We can't talk here, we have to go somewhere private."

Leo and Quinn looked at one another, raising their eyebrows.

Quinn sighed. "Alright, but we literally only have like, five minutes, before we have to go on again."

A bunch of other waiters came in carrying staff meals. The performers flocked to them like seagulls, closing in on the promise of sustenance. No one saw Addi, Leo and Quinn slip away.

"Much better," Addi said as they slunk into a small room near the front hallway that was used only for storing crockery and candlesticks. The chiming of cutlery on plates, creepy background music and chatter from the main performance hall subsided as Addi partially closed the heavy door.

"What's going on?" Leo demanded. "If we're missing out on food, this better be important."

"It is. Earlier tonight, I noticed Freddy sneak out disguised under a sheet as a ghost..." Addi began, continuing to recount how she had followed Freddy and Emmerson all the way to the graveyard where they had met the lady with the dark hair and gathered around Grayson's grave, and how they had seen her and thought she was Emmeline.

"Why the secrecy though?" Quinn talked as she tried to make sense of it all. "That strange lady must be Grayson's mum. If she and Emmerson are friends, why would Freddy and Emmerson be sneaking around and trying to hide..."

"Oh." Leo grabbed Addi's arm and turned to her, his eyes widening in realisation. Addi nodded at him slowly. "Oh my god, *no*."

"Yep, that's exactly what I think," Addi replied. "I mean, I never saw it before, but they all have dark hair, and Grayson was a bit unusual and moody, just like—"

"Freddy," Quinn finished, staring at Addi in near disbelief. "I even said that myself once, that Grayson reminded me of him! How could I have been so stupid?"

"So they're... *brothers*?" Leo summed up.

"That's what I reckon," Addi nodded fervently. "Well, half-brothers I guess. That lady is — was — Grayson's mum, and Emmerson is Grayson's dad."

"Okay," Quinn began slowly as Leo blew out a stream of air. "They're one big, messed-up family. Shit, this is crazy. So with the money..."

"I reckon you were right, Quinn," Addi said. "Grayson must have been blackmailing Emmerson. Wanting a pay-back for him and his mum after all those years with nothing in housing commission, while Emmerson lived it up around the world. How much would you bet that poor Emmeline has no idea that her husband has a second son with another woman?"

"There's the leverage," Leo nodded excitedly. "I bet Freddy didn't know either. That's why he was so angry after Emmerson arrived with Grayson. Emmerson must have told him what was going on and asked him to keep it from Emmeline."

Quinn scoffed. "Ooh, mummy's boy Freddy would not have liked that."

"Their secret conversations make a lot more sense now," Addi noted. "Maybe the envelope of money in his room was like a down payment or something. That could have been Emmerson and Freddy just buying some time until they figured out how they were going to get rid of him."

"Why now, though?" Leo posed. "Grayson obviously knew that his dad was Emmerson, otherwise how would he have gotten the phone number? Maybe his mum even held onto it and gave it to him. He went his whole childhood not having anything to do with him — what changed?"

"The inheritance."

Addi, Leo and Quinn spun around.

Kyle leant against the doorframe, arms crossed, with that condescending smirk that Addi found infuriating painted across his face.

"How long have you been standing there?" Quinn demanded.

"Interesting conversation you're having. You know, if you don't want people to listen you should really be more careful about closing the door."

Addi narrowed her eyes at Kyle. "You followed me here. You were waiting for me on the front step."

"I wouldn't have had to if you didn't decide you could sneak out of work whenever you felt like it. Did you have a nice little trip?"

Addi ignored him. "Did Emmerson or Freddy tell you to keep watch?"

"They were concerned their staff weren't where they were supposed to be," Kyle replied promptly. "Which they were completely correct about."

Leo regarded Kyle with disdain. "So what, you're their lackey now or something? Why are you watching Addi, stalker?"

Kyle pointed belligerently at Addi. "Why is she following Emmerson and Freddy?"

Addi gritted her teeth. "I was following Emmerson and Freddy because they've been acting suspiciously and, if you really have been listening to our conversation, then you would know that we were right all along. The real question is why do *you* seem to be working with them on all of this?"

"You don't know what you're talking about," Kyle muttered, shifting his gaze away from her to the door frame around him.

"Why don't you fill us in, then?" Quinn commanded sourly. "What were you saying about an inheritance?"

Kyle couldn't help but smirk in his self-importance, being in possession of knowledge that Addi, Quinn and Leo were not. "I was answering your question. Grayson came to the House when he did because he'd read some recent article in the paper about how Emmeline and Emmerson were retiring and going to leave the family business to Freddy."

"Of course," Addi exclaimed a little louder than she intended. She turned to Leo and Quinn. "That was the newspaper clipping we found in his room."

Kyle raised his eyebrows. "You went snooping in his room?" he scoffed. "Look at the three of you, running around and poking your noses where they don't belong. You've been causing trouble since you got here," Kyle pointed at Addi, "and you just happened to find the two people in this place who also like causing drama for the sake of it to adopt you and teach you their ways."

"You are a clinical psychopath if you think people attempting to solve a murder is merely 'causing drama,'" Leo retaliated. "Tell us, Kyle, what *is* your involvement in all of this? You've been accusing myself, Quinn and Addi this whole time but you know we didn't have anything to do with it. Why are you trying to deflect suspicion from yourself?"

Kyle gulped and Addi spotted an emotion flit across his face that she'd never witnessed on the bar supervisor before; doubt. "Something happened that night. I..."

As Kyle searched for words, a memory shot through Addi's head, hazy due to being formed in the wee hours of the morning in the shadowy halls of House of Nightshade through her tired eyes. In the mayhem of the next morning she had quickly forgotten it. "Wait a minute. I heard you talking to Freddy after we'd finished working the night Grayson died. I had helped Quinn to bed and went back downstairs to get her some pain medication for her ankle. I saw you and Freddy walking down the hall. Freddy was annoyed or mad at you for something."

Kyle's face began to pale. "Good observations, but that doesn't mean anything."

"You said... oh my god. You said you'd taken care of something for him!"

Had the answer been in front of her the whole time? Had Kyle worked with Emmerson and Freddy and done their dirty work for them?

"That's it," Leo decided. "I'm calling the police. "

Quinn eyed Kyle warily, taking a step back. "You know, I really shouldn't be shocked. You've always had anger problems. I mean, you literally *shoved* Leo the other day just because you were angry after an argument."

"Let's get out of here," Leo said.

As he made to walk forward out of the room, Kyle snapped his hand on the doorframe so that his arm formed a blockage across it. "I can't let Addilyn go and tell anyone this stupid theory. I can explain..."

"Finally! Just *what* exactly is going on here?"

Addi had never been so glad to see Sawyer in her life.

Sawyer stared daggers at Quinn and Leo. "I have been looking for you two everywhere, but my sincerest apologies for interrupting your social schedule. In case you've both displaced your little brains, you're our star performers on whom rides the entire next act which is due to begin in precisely..." Sawyer pretended to consult a non-existent watch, "five minutes ago. Now hop to it," he snapped, gesturing the performers out of the room. "Kyle, what are you doing? Shouldn't you be behind the bar? Get me a gin and tonic stat — hold the tonic."

Kyle eyed the three of them without a word, gave a last pointed look at Addi and then dropped his arm from the doorframe, trudging back to the performance hall with a passing scowl at Sawyer.

"Sawyer, Kyle's going crazy, he was just blocking us from leaving..." Leo began desperately.

"Why are you still standing there? Get up on stage *now* or you lose your paycheque." Sawyer turned on his heel and stalked off, disappearing through the smoke still curling from the machines.

"Hell hath no fury like a Sawyer scorned," Quinn commented wryly.

Leo hovered, regarding Addi with extreme concern. "Or a Kyle, for that matter. What should we do now?"

Addi shooed them. "Go on, before Sawyer kills you both and we have another murder case on our hands. I'll be fine. What's Kyle going to do in front of all these people anyway? We also need to be worrying about Emmerson and Freddy," she pointed out as she followed them from the room, sounding a lot more confident than she felt. "I'll call the police."

Quinn and Leo were swallowed in a tidal wave of people heading back to their seats. Leo managed to give a half-reassuring smile before Addi lost him in the sea of costumes. She tried to get her mind back in the present — what was it she needed to be doing at that moment? She glanced down the hallway, trying to make out the front door through the smoke. Main meals were cleared, people were sitting down. *Kyle killed Grayson. Snap out of it. Think, clear your mind. Kyle was working with Emmerson and Grayson. Kyle is dangerous.*

Addi wished her head would stop racing. In fight or flight, it turned out she couldn't stop thinking long enough to figure out what to do.

Stop, she told herself sternly. *All you have to do is get to a phone and call the police.* Yes, that was it. That was all she had to do. Her phone was upstairs in the dormitory, meaning the nearest phone was in the bar. She would be protected there with all the people around, but couldn't say the same about the empty bedrooms. Just like she had out on the street following Emmerson and Freddy, she could blend in with the crowd of guests heading back to their seats in the performance hall as the lights began to dim for the next part to begin.

She joined the throng of people in their costumes making their way through the smoke hanging in the air, more raucous now they had some liquor in them. What it would feel like to simply be enjoying the Halloween celebration right now, Addi pined, rather than be stuck trying to report a murderer. *At least this is a chance to clear any suspicion of myself*, she thought in an attempt to find the silver lining.

She entered the performance hall and almost squealed. In front of the kitchen doors, staring out at the chaos around him, was none other than Officer Knight. Addi exhaled loudly. Everything was going to be okay. She made a beeline for him.

"There you are."

Kyle stepped out from the shadows near the bar and grabbed Addi's shoulder.

Addi squirmed out of his grip. "Get off me, Kyle."

In the festivities happening around them, no one paid them any attention.

"Oops, sorry," a man apologised jovially as he bumped into Kyle.

Kyle immediately let go of Addi.

"Oh hey, barman. Perfect timing!" the man roared happily, recognising Kyle's face. "I'll get a refill of rum and dry and two mojitos for the ladies." He pointed behind his shoulder to his companions.

Addi couldn't believe her luck. Internally thanking her slightly drunken saviour, she darted around them and made a break for it, skirting around the side of the hall as the last of the patrons took their seats.

"No, no," she groaned, noticing that the officer was no longer standing in front of the kitchen.

In her haste she almost collided into Sawyer, who was scurrying in the opposite direction to the sound deck at the back of the room, looking frazzled.

"Move along, honey! God, now I'm the sound engineer too, apparently. Must I do everything in this House? Where the hell is Freddy?"

"Sawyer!" Addi shouted after him over the din. "Did you see where Officer Knight went?"

"What are you talking about?" he called over his shoulder.

"Sawyer, if you see the police, tell them that Kyle killed Grayson and now he's chasing me."

"What did you say?" Sawyer paused and cupped his ear. "Honey, are you okay?"

Addi gave up; she didn't have time to hang around and let Kyle see where she was going.

The smell of baked pumpkin, cinnamon and buttered pastry hit her as she pushed the kitchen doors open. She was almost surprised to see normal service still going ahead, forgetting that not everyone was being chased through the house by a dangerous murderer.

Logan, Danika and the kitchen hand dished up pumpkin pie on the central stainless steel table, finishing the plates off with piles of fluffy, whipped cream and drizzle of cherry glaze. The waitstaff watched them assemble the desserts, poised ready to run them out the minute Leo and Quinn were clapped off stage after their final number.

Ralph leant on the side of the stainless steel bench near Logan and Danika, overseeing the operation. "Oh, surprise, it's young Adelaide! She's finally decided she's ready to work—"

"Not now, Ralph!" Addi darted behind Logan and Danika to where the knives hung on the wall and, in desperation, grabbed one. It felt odd in her hand and she didn't know the best way to hold it. The staff all stared at her with expressions of startled confusion.

"Ha!" Ralph let out a loud laugh. "And they say I'm the crazy one! Adderall's lost the plot. We've finally got to you, have we, young one?" Ralph chortled before rhyming in a sing-song voice, "*Adelaide and her big, bad knife; getting ready to cause some strife...*"

Ignoring him, Addi darted out the other door of the kitchen into the courtyard, pounding the pavement. She had no plan of what to do. It wasn't like in the books or movies. A person had gone crazy and was stalking her around the building, and her mind had only one word of advice — run. She was going to have to figure something out, though; she couldn't run from him all night. She inwardly cursed herself for not trying harder in PE class.

She followed the concrete up the side of the House, around to the front, and re-entered the venue through the front door, panting and hoping that would throw Kyle off. Now that the performance on the main stage was over, the front hall was crawling with guests as they trawled the rooms for the keys. She frantically searched the crowd for a sign of Officer Knight, but there was no sign of him. The guests pointed and laughed at Addi as she entered with the knife.

Addi felt her palm sweating around the knife. "Does anyone have their phone? I need to call the police!"

"There's a cop down there," a man donning a caveman get-up snickered, pointing at a young woman down the hall clad in a cheap police costume from a two-dollar store which probably had the word 'sexy' written somewhere on the flimsy plastic packaging she bought it in.

A young woman drunkenly swaggered towards Addi, breathing prosecco on her. "Hey, cool fake knife."

Addi flinched away from the stranger. "It's not fake! I-I really need to borrow someone's phone. Please help me," she pleaded, but the woman was already tottering off.

The man who had inadvertently saved Addi earlier when he'd asked Kyle for drinks strolled out of one of the front rooms with his friends, whom he nudged upon seeing Addi. "Man, look, they've even hired actors for this thing. Gee, they've really gone all out this year... oh, thanks, dude!"

Kyle had arrived by the man's side with his drinks order on a tray. He stared at Addi as the drinks were claimed. "Addilyn, you can't keep running away..."

Addi squealed and lunged around Kyle and his customers while she had the chance. The floorboards creaked beneath her feet as she bounded up the grand, old staircase.

The hallway on the second floor was bathed in a yellow glow from lamps. There was always a hush over the upstairs rooms. Addi could hear glasses being set down on the table and the giggles of the dancers as they entranced whoever was sitting back on the lounges beneath them. She put a hand out on one of the door frames to steady herself, puffed from the exertion. Her legs shook slightly beneath her. Inside, dancers dressed in lacy black corsets and cat ears for Halloween gracefully pulled off their lingerie, shimmying it down to their ankles as they entertained patrons dressed in their Halloween costumes. Addi scanned the room for Summer. She was the only one up here who would listen to her right now.

A familiar thudding sounded on the stairs.

Addi careered down the navy blue runner to the least frequented rooms at the very end of the hallway. She was in luck: both were empty, furniture sitting still in the darkness, eerily silent compared to the entertainment occurring down the hall. She flew through the door of the room on her left, which hosted a vintage screen in the corner. She inched herself behind it, its cream covering flaking slightly between chestnut wooden borders, and drew it back into place around herself.

She crouched and tried to quiet her breathing. There were now visible streaks of sweat on the knife handle where she'd been clutching it tightly in her hand. What was she thinking? She had no idea how to use a knife. She certainly had no idea how to defend herself. Kyle was twice her size. *I'll know what to do if the time comes*, Addi tried to convince herself. This was just a precaution. She tried to suck in a big breath of air to regain her breath. Hopefully the fact that she had a knife would be enough to frighten him.

There was a scrape of furniture from down the hall, followed by a girl's voice. "What are you doing, Kyle?"

Addi could just picture him pushing aside a chair or a screen, craning his neck to see if she was hiding behind it. "Shit," she breathed to herself, feeling a familiar anxious nausea entering her stomach. She heard the heavy stomp of his feet in his thick work boots as he moved to another room, drawing closer and closer, until finally he reached the room where she hid.

"Come out, Addilyn. We need to have a talk."

Addi remained still. It was just Kyle, she told herself — the bar supervisor Kyle doing his usual act of trying to be important and powerful. There were others just down the hall. She could handle this. She took in a deep breath and stepped out from behind the screen. "Talk then."

Beads of sweat dotted Kyle's forehead, chest visibly falling up and down from the running, pink face starkly contrasted with his almost bleached-blonde hair and eyebrows. "Because you wouldn't listen. It's all too late now. The police think... but they've got it wrong." His hands balled up into fists at his sides. "I shouldn't have done it, it was stupid, but how could I have known what would happen?"

"The police have got what wrong, Kyle?" Addi whispered tentatively. "What shouldn't you have done?"

"The night Grayson died, I slipped something into his dinner."

Chapter Thirteen

"More important than finding the truth is finding the reason why one needs to lie."
— *Mystqx Skye*

Police Interview with Ralph Payne

Officer: You seem quite jittery.

Ralph: I've been locked up in here all day, haven't I, officer? You'd know that though. No need to tell you that, oh no, you're a man with a clue! Well, several clues, that's your job, clues for Mr. Cluedo...

Officer: Right. Let's proceed, shall we? I take it you know why we've brought you in for questioning?

Ralph: Think I killed the young one, don't you? Think you've caught me, think you've nabbed me, oh yes, you've done your day's work and you'll go home and have a nice meal cooked for you and that cash liiining your pocket, liiining your pocket. You'll be put up on that wall, won't you, Officer?

Officer: You are suspected of having involvement in the murder of Grayson Reid. This is extremely serious, do you understand that?

Ralph: Oh yes, Mr. Cluedo. Very serious game here. It was Mr. Ralph, in the kitchen. Ha! Get it? Meanwhile Colonel Mustard was upstairs in the living room, with the candlesticks. Ha! So many candlesticks on every bloody surface.

Officer: So are you saying it was, erm, Mr. Ralph?

Ralph: Oh, aren't you so smart, Mr. Cluedo? Think you're sooo smart, sooo clever. In fact, what would I have to do with the young one? Didn't even *know* the young one, did I? Didn't even *talk* to the young one, did I? But oh no, if you say so then it must have been me.

Officer: A meat mallet was found in your kitchen in an unusual spot, with the handle wrapped in a tea towel. What can you tell me about that?

Ralph: I can play your game, Mr. Cluedo.

Officer: This is not a game, Ralph. Someone is dead.

Ralph: What about Miss Scarlett? Did you talk to Miss Scarlett? She must have been quite scarlet after her little tumble! Ha!

Officer: Are you referring to Quinn Vandez?

Ralph: And what about Mrs Peacock, oh Mrs. Peacock, pish-posh, pastries and tea, fancy Mrs. Peacock. You know who she'd kill, you know who'd she kill? She could use a candlestick. Let's see, who else?

Officer: Ralph, please, can we get back to the—

Ralph: You simply cannot forget Reverend Green! Surely not! Ah, the trickery. A fool would believe, wouldn't they? But then they are all fools in that joint.

Officer: For the record, we are now stopping this interview here for today.

Ralph: And Professor White and Mrs. Plum...

Officer: It's Professor Plum and Mrs. White, actually. Let's wrap up here, shall we? We might get you to have a conversation with another type of professional.

Ralph: A slip of the hand, that's all. Just a sprinkle.

Officer: Pardon?

Ralph: Only a second it took and then they were off. Almost missed it myself.

Officer: What are you talking about? Who was off?

Ralph: Which one, Mr. Cluedo, which one? In the kitchen with the poison.

•

"You... what?" Addi gave a puzzled, hollow laugh as Kyle's words sunk in. "What do you mean?"

"I mean I drugged him," Kyle yelled at her in frustration.

Addi took a step back. "Do you mean...? You *poisoned* Grayson?"

Kyle shook his head quickly. "No, I said drugged. I just drugged him."

"Oh," Addi replied, her voice faint, "just drugged him, did you? Is that all?"

Kyle scowled at her.

Trying to process the information, Addi hadn't purposefully meant it to sound mocking. "You have about one minute to explain."

"The night he died, I... well, I roofied him. I put it in his soup before he had his dinner break."

Addi was immediately transported to that night in the kitchen, slurping the very same soup with Grayson as they flirted and butterflies in her tummy at the prospect of something happening with him. "Kyle... *why?*" She was thankful that he maintained the large distance from each other in the room, still unsure about what he was admitting to.

"He wasn't a nice person..." Kyle began.

"Neither are you but we don't all go around trying to drug you!" Addi yelled shrilly.

Kyle gritted his teeth. "Do you want me to explain this to you or not?"

Addi pursed her lips but remained silent.

Kyle continued. "He was a bad person, even though he might have had you duped. I found out what he was up to early on when I walked in on a fight between Freddy and Emmerson soon after the boy got here. I'd overheard too much; they had to tell me the rest of what was going on. Years and years ago, Emmerson had an affair with another woman and it resulted in Grayson."

"And Emmerson just left them both with no support whatsoever," Addi recalled from a conversation with Grayson.

"That's right," Kyle nodded. "He never wanted to know Grayson. He didn't want Emmeline to ever find out about the affair, and regularly seeing or supporting a secret love child, well, she would have noticed something. Anyway, Emmerson didn't really have to think about it for 18 years until Grayson contacted him. He'd read about the inheritance promised to Freddy in a newspaper article and said that money from the business belonged to himself and his mum."

"He was abandoned his entire life by his parent, who, meanwhile, had his own family and was living it up overseas," Addi pointed out testily. "He did have every right to that money."

Kyle sighed. "Addilyn, he threatened to *hurt* Freddy unless the inheritance was redirected into his name. He told Emmerson on the phone that he would be coming here and wouldn't leave until he got what he wanted. Emmerson didn't fully take him seriously until Grayson did indeed show up in the city. He told Emmerson, 'If you can pretend one of your sons doesn't exist, then I guess you'll be okay with your other son not existing either.'"

Addi bit her lip. "Well, he was probably bluffing..."

Kyle interrupted her. "Would you have taken your chances if it was your family?"

Addi stayed silent. How could she understand that, when she didn't even know what it was like to have her own family?

Kyle continued. "So, I knew that was happening. The inheritance, the business — that's their whole life. On top of that, if Emmerson signed it over he would have to explain everything to Emmeline. He'd not only have lost the business and their income but also his wife. There was a lot at stake. They gave Grayson a little bit of cash to buy themselves some time. Then Grayson stupidly yelled at me that night in the kitchen."

"*You* started that," Addi reminded him.

Kyle cut over the top of her. "Don't lecture me! I was so mad. How dare he come here and blackmail our bosses and then parade around as if he was innocent, threatening everything we all work so hard for? I try my best every damn night to do a good job for this business. He thought he was so much better than everyone else."

Addi had to raise her eyebrows at the hypocrisy. "You couldn't stand not ruling it over everyone, you mean."

Kyle clenched his fists but pressed on. "I wanted to do something to help Emmerson and Freddy, and that kid deserved it after how he spoke back to me, so I drugged him to teach him a lesson. I just took a bit from Leo's stash; he always blabs about it so I knew where he hid it in the dorm. It would have just lasted the night. I only meant to teach him a lesson and put him back in his place a bit."

"Oh, Jesus, Kyle," Addi surveyed him with a mixture of pity and revilement, thinking back to that night. "No wonder Grayson tripped up Quinn, he must have been totally zonked out. This isn't going to look good for you. No one cares what your reasons are. You can't go around *drugging* people, that's a serious offence! And a bunch of us saw you smashing that bag of ice with the meat mallet."

Kyle held his hands up and, for the first time Addi had ever seen, looked like he was pleading. "That's all I did though, I swear. The meat mallet... someone planted that. Someone is trying to frame me. If I had killed him with it, why would I have left the weapon right there in the kitchen? I'm not stupid."

Addi bit her lip. "How can I believe you after you tried to frame me, Quinn and Leo *and* drugged Grayson?"

"Addilyn..." Kyle began, but he was interrupted by the heavy pounding of several people racing down the hall and into the room.

"Don't move!"

Officer Knight entered the room, now accompanied by a second, younger officer, who walked straight over to Kyle and pulled his hands behind his back, handcuffing him.

Sawyer followed right behind them, with Freddy and Emmerson bringing up the rear.

At the sight of Addi, the director let out a loud exhale and placed a hand over his heart. "Oh, Addilyn! For the life of me I couldn't hear what you were saying except for something about Kyle and then you ran off looking all crazy. I realised you must have been in some sort of trouble so I found the officers as quickly as I could. Thank goodness you're okay."

Sawyer kept a distance from her with his hands outstretched. It was then that Addi remembered the knife she was holding by her side and hurried to put it down on a pouffe.

She gave him a smile. "Thanks for helping me, Sawyer."

"Are you okay?" Sawyer asked her carefully. "Did he try to hurt you?"

"What?" Addi asked distractedly as she watched the officer begin to push Kyle out the door.

"It wasn't me, I swear. Someone's setting me up. Addilyn will tell you, she knows what really happened. Tell them, Addilyn, please!" Kyle called desperately as he was forced out of the room and down the hallway.

Emmerson watched after him with a stern expression, then clapped Officer Knight on the back. Freddy stared off after Kyle contemplatively, taking a cigar out of his pocket and lighting it.

Officer Knight addressed Addi. "Miss, we'll need to get your statement about the events of this evening."

"Can't it wait, officer?" Sawyer interjected like a concerned parent. "At least let the poor girl have a cup of tea or something, she's just been chased through this place by a murderer for Christ's sake!"

Freddy cleared his throat. "Good idea, Sawyer. Addilyn, you must be quite shaken."

"No, I feel fine enough to make my statement now," Addi rebutted. She felt frustrated that Freddy was sitting there telling her how she should feel. Of course it suited him to delay her talking to the police.

Sawyer put an arm on her shoulder. "No need to be brave, honey."

"Yes, good idea," Officer Knight interjected. "How about we all go and get tea and then we can…"

"I don't want tea!" Addi found herself shrieking. She felt like Quinn as everyone stopped fussing and stared at her. "If you're arresting Kyle, then you need to be arresting them, too." She pointed at Freddy and Emmerson.

Emmerson's expression grew, if possible, even more stony.

Officer Knight looked at her gently. "Now, now, you've just been through a shock. Someone who you thought was your colleague, your teammate, turned out to be a murderer and put you in danger. It's perfectly normal to feel as if everyone else around you is therefore out to get you when we experience betrayal from someone we're close to. We can arrange for some counselling services…"

"I don't need counselling," Addi cut in again. "I'm not traumatised, I wasn't even close to Kyle. You've taken the wrong person."

Freddy eyed Addi wearily and moved to place a hand on her arm. "Sweetheart, stop with the theatrics. You know me, don't you? We're friends; we have a lot in common. I think you know deep down it's a ridiculous idea that myself or my father would be behind any of this. You need to see you've become a bit too caught up in the drama and take a step away."

Addi stared back at the manager's imploring gaze, remembering all the conversations they'd shared where he'd opened up to her and the ones she'd overheard without him meaning her to. The times he'd been happy to get along with her and the times he hadn't — playing manager friend in front of his mum, ignoring her when Ralph made one simple comment, checking in on her sweetly then in the same sentence putting her down and advising her to stay away from the case. She recalled how quickly he had jumped to talking about the instability of Ralph, one of the longest-standing employees at the House, when Officer Knight came knocking with his theory, and how easily he had just watched Kyle, his supposed right-hand man, being taken away without a single protest.

She looked down at his arm that was placed on hers, seeing the tattooed colon inside his wrist. She recalled what Freddy had told her behind the bar about why he'd gotten it. *A reminder that you have the power to add more to the story — and knowing when it's right to do so.*

Addi shook off his hand, looking away from his gaze as she pressed her lips together defiantly. "No. I know what I'm talking about. Grayson is — was — Emmerson's son. He came here to blackmail them for their money so they killed him."

Freddy turned to Officer Knight. "Yes, I think it's best to get her some counselling assistance as soon as possible. She is clearly distressed and coming up with unbelievable stories that make no sense."

Addi tried to make her case again. "I'm telling you, Grayson was blackmailing and threatening Emmerson and Freddy and now he's dead. That's not a coincidence. He has money in his room."

Officer Knight turned back to her, looking unsure. "An accusation like this needs serious evidence to back it up. Money in an employee's room from his employer is nothing unusual. Besides, how do you know there was money in his room? Did you violate a crime scene?"

"I... no, I was in there before he died," Addi lied. "We were friends. I told you that in my interview."

"Right," Officer Knight narrowed his eyes, unconvinced. If he hadn't believed her about Freddy and Emmerson earlier, he definitely didn't now that he also suspected her of breaching a crime scene. "Look, Miss," he sighed, "the chef gave us the statement we needed and our evidence just came back from the lab. The mallet had Kyle's fingerprints on it. Ralph told us he saw Kyle slip something into the boy's dinner in the kitchen. It all points to him."

Addi protested. "A couple of days ago didn't you think the evidence all pointed to Ralph? Yes, Kyle roofied him, but he told me the whole story before and he seemed really truthful when he told me he's convinced that someone's framing him–"

"This is preposterous," Emmerson declared loudly. "If Kyle had simply drugged the boy, why wouldn't he have told the police earlier?"

Addi was beside herself trying to make the officer see the truth. "Because it would make him look guilty!"

"You know, I think that cup of tea is a great idea," the officer cut in. "Let's go down to the kitchen, I could use a cuppa for the road." He turned to Addi. "I appreciate your opinion but we need to have substantial claims here. " His voice was firm. Addi sensed not to push it much further at that moment so as not to risk being labelled completely insane.

Looking relieved to be helping in some way as his earlier suggestion of tea was taken up, Sawyer led the group from the room. As they trod down the hallway runner through the ambient candle light, decorations lining the walls, Addi thought it seemed quite ironic now; the House dressed in its spooky charade while someone was arrested inside and murderers walked through its halls.

"Nice costume, bro!" one of the guests called to Officer Knight as he passed in the opposite direction.

The waitstaff gawked at Addi as she filed into the kitchen with management and the detective. Sawyer excused himself to oversee the final number of the night and fluttered back to the sound deck in a tizzy.

"What are you all staring at?" Freddy barked.

The waitstaff turned away immediately to stack away piles of dessert plates and polished cutlery, throwing utensils into the cutlery drawers with a clang.

"Ivy, can you put on some tea?"

"Did I just see Kyle getting *arrested*?" Ivy replied, wide-eyed.

Ralph sat on the stainless steel bench in the corner, legs swinging as he surveyed the commotion of the kitchen gleefully. "You got him, Mr. Cluedo. In the kitchen with the poison!"

"Stop being melodramatic, Ralph. Tea for everyone, please, Ivy." Freddy pinched the bridge of his nose with his forefinger and thumb. "I need something a bit stronger." He disappeared to the bar.

Music resonated through the doors as Ivy poured steaming water into cups. Addi watched as the tea bags inflated with the heat and rose with the water. She wished she could just go to sleep and forget everything to do with Grayson.

While Officer Knight talked seriously to Emmerson in a corner, Quinn and Leo burst into the kitchen, foreheads and chests glistening with sweat from the show.

"Addi," Leo rushed to put an arm around her. "Sawyer just told us you were in here with the police. What happened after we left? Are you okay?"

"They arrested Kyle," Addi told them.

"Well, thank god," Quinn exhaled. "Doesn't that mean this whole mess is over now?"

"Yeah..."

Leo furrowed his brow. "What's wrong, Addi?"

"I just," she bit her lip, "I'm not sure now. Kyle reckons he's being set up. He told me that he roofied Grayson that night but he didn't kill him. I really don't feel like he was the one who murdered him."

"I bet I'd tell any lie I could if I was about to be arrested," Quinn pointed out. "Addi, he's a horrible person. We can't trust anything he says."

"I know, but... something isn't right. I feel as if we're still missing some of the story."

Officer Knight appeared at her side. "Addilyn, I'll take your statement now. Come with me."

"Where are you taking her?"

"Miss Vandez, isn't it?" The detective turned to Quinn. "I just need a statement about this evening from your friend here."

"We were cornered by Kyle tonight, too, actually. I think we should both be there with Addi to confirm what happened. Three witnesses are better than one, right?" Quinn arched an eyebrow.

Officer Knight patted around his pockets for his notepad and pen. "Of course. Follow me, then."

Addi, Quinn and Leo trailed the detective to a separate room, while the guests continued to drink and party the night away in the performance hall. Between the three of them they recounted what had happened that night, from Addi following Freddy and Emmerson to the graveyard, to the conclusion they had arrived at, to Kyle finding them and chasing after Addi.

"Kyle seemed genuinely afraid, though, Officer," Addi implored as they wrapped up. "I know we don't have much in the way of evidence about Freddy and Emmerson but it was them."

"Look..." Officer Knight scratched the side of his head with his pen, "people visiting a grave isn't what you would call suspicious activity; in fact, it's a normal part of the grieving process. There's no evidence I can draw from that. Also, we're not here to investigate how many affairs Emmerson has had," the detective opened his palms apologetically. "We're here to solve a murder. We go off physical evidence, and all our evidence is pointing to Kyle." With that, he left the room.

"Well I would say that went swimmingly, wouldn't you?" Leo commented drolly.

"Why do none of them listen?" Addi bemoaned, stomping from the room.

"'Coz they've found an easy answer and they can't be bothered to dig deeper beyond that," Quinn grumbled, following Addi out with Leo next to her. "What we don't have, which we need, is a solid piece of evidence that Emmerson and Freddy had something to do with it. All we have is a newspaper clipping, an envelope of money and our retelling of the times Addi followed them, which could also be seen as very stalkerish."

"I prefer investigative," Addi countered.

They pushed the swinging doors to the kitchen open and entered. The spectators were all there among the rest of the staff; Freddy sipped amber liquid from a tumbler, Ralph cleaned benches and Emmerson shook hands with Officer Knight before he hastily slipped around Addi, Quinn and Leo, gave a wave and headed back to the police station.

Emmeline flounced into the kitchen, clutching her champagne glass which was now stained around the rim with her red lipstick. In the other hand she held up the black, lace veil that Addi had donned earlier on her journey to the cemetery. "Ivy, would you like to inform me as to why you dumped my veil in the storeroom? I got this in a vintage boutique in France, you know."

As Ivy began to protest, that's when it hit Addi. She had thought there was something familiar about it when she'd first seen the black lace veil, and when Emmerson had spotted her in the graveyard he had thought it was Emmeline.

She now remembered where she recognised it from. There had been a lady sitting at a table in the performance hall wearing that exact same veil the night Grayson was killed.

Addi stared at Emmeline. She felt like she had found what had been lost since Grayson died; a feeling that had been building so high she felt like she might explode. The missing piece, finally clunking into place. She tried to make a sound but nothing came out.

Emmeline raised a finely-pencilled eyebrow at her. "What exactly has happened to you? Have you forgotten how to pick up plates? Dancers in the kitchen and waitresses who've suddenly become immobile. Honestly!" She swept out of the kitchen into the courtyard, veil and champagne still in hand.

Leo clicked his fingers in front of Addi's face. "Hello. Earth to Addi."

"Emmeline," Addi managed.

Quinn eyed Leo. "Yes," she began slowly, "Well done, that is her name. Why are you self-combusting?"

"That veil," Addi pointed. "I saw a woman wearing that exact veil here at the House the night Grayson was killed. It was *her*!"

For the umpteenth time that night, Addi started running, feeling like she was in a dream as she sprinted out the kitchen door to follow Emmeline. She had to know the truth. She had spent too much time and energy trying to solve what happened to Grayson to not find out for herself once and for all.

"Wait, what?" Quinn and Leo were hot on her heels.

To think mere minutes ago she had been so terrified of Kyle that she had run from him with a knife for self-defence. It now seemed laughable. Of course she had been so focussed on the men — who had traditionally been the ones to treat her poorly — that she had unknowingly completely written off the potential that it was a woman.

They didn't have to run far. Under the dim, yellow glow of the outdoor lights, Emmeline was pulling a few weeds out of the raised vegetable patches. The three halted, leaving a solid distance between themselves and the formidable woman in front of them.

Emmeline looked up. "You three again. Have you decided to take a holiday for yourselves? If you don't get back to work I'm going to deduct tonight's pay. Addison, you waitstaff really should pay more mind to these vegetables. I'm the owner of this business but what, suddenly I'm the gardener too? No one—"

Addi stepped forward. "It's Addilyn, actually. My name is Addilyn." She took a deep breath. She was no longer shaking. She had Quinn and Leo right behind her. "I think you should pay more mind to the fact that we know what you did to Grayson."

Emmeline abandoned the weeds and stood straight, pursing her lips. "What exactly would that be?"

Addi nodded at the veil that Emmeline had placed on the wooden edge of the garden bed. "I knew I recognised that from somewhere when I saw it earlier. You were here that night, sitting in the audience under that veil. No one else knew you were back in the country. It's the perfect alibi."

Emmeline narrowed her eyes but didn't speak.

Addi swallowed under Emmeline's gaze, but she wouldn't back down. She couldn't — not after everything they had figured out and now Kyle wrongfully arrested. Not without at least trying to get justice for the boy who, despite having known him for the shortest time, had actually understood her. "You murdered Grayson, didn't you?"

Emmeline placed her hands on her hips as she surveyed her three employees. "You think I didn't know about my husband's affair? Just like dear Emmerson, you underestimate me, Addilyn. You wait until you get married. We know when our husbands are hiding something from us. I knew about Grayson when he was just a newborn, and even back then I predicted that child would come back to bite us one day. Someone had to look out for our family and the legacy that we've built. My private detective has been keeping tabs on the boy for years. I knew full well when he decided to come here and threaten *mon cheri garcon*. Of course I was on the next flight here. My boy," Emmeline wistfully picked up her champagne glass and took a large gulp, "Well, you three are just children yourselves. You have no idea how strong a mother's love truly is until you have your own child."

Addi fidgeted.

Emmeline continued. "My poor Frederick. Emmerson never treated him fairly as he grew up. He was too hard on him. You think Emmerson listened to me when I told him to treat the boy with some love? Freddy was always sensitive and his father can't understand it. Then they grow up and go out in the world and you have no idea what they're really doing, how they're treating themselves or what they're going through inside. I know how my Frederick suffers — the psychologists and the prescriptions. I think, should I have done more? Was this my fault? Should I have taken him and left my husband? But look at what I have built." She gestured around her. "You think this came from Emmerson's brain? House of Nightshade is my second child. Look at the decorations in the rooms. It's me everywhere, but do you think people remember that? Of course not, they all look to Emmerson and Freddy. I'm just the wife. I gave this business everything. If I had chosen to leave I wouldn't have been left with anything. Perhaps not even custody of my own son. So I chose to stay, and at the end of the day I need to accept how my decision played a part in my baby growing up to suffer. Don't you think for one second I was going to let any other threat waltz in and hurt *mon cheri garcon*."

It was Addi's turn to narrow her eyes. "Just like Grayson and his mum were left with nothing."

"Yes, exactly. You think it sounds hypocritical, of course; you're naive. It's human nature. Immature minds such as yourselves and the imbeciles that flounce across my stage every night waste their time fighting with their own," she gestured to Addi, Quinn and Leo. "Meanwhile mature humans fight *for* their own. It's tribal. It was me and Freddy, or the woman who had had an affair with my husband and the result of a relationship that shouldn't have happened to begin with."

Quinn brushed her hair away from her face as she cut in. "So let's get this story straight — Freddy, Emmerson and Kyle aren't actually to blame for Grayson's death?"

Emmeline's nostrils flared. "Of course they're to blame! And aren't you, too? Was it not your pills in the soup?" She pointed her glass vigorously at Leo, champagne sloshing out of the rim and down the side. "Was it not you and Sawyer who yelled him off to his room alone when he was in a drugged state?" The glass swept across to Quinn. "And was it not because he was defending *you*," the glass finally landed on Addi, "That pitted Kyle against him in the first place? You think anyone in this House paid any mind to his whereabouts that night except you pathetically swooning at his door?"

Addi suddenly realised it had been Emmeline in Grayson's room that she had heard that night. Had Grayson just been killed mere seconds before she knocked on the door? She felt bile rising up in her throat.

Emmeline continued. "Nonetheless, I've said it before and I'll say it again. Disaster is what happens when we leave the men in charge. Is there anything more typical than a wife cleaning up after her husband's mess? Between the top three men in this business — unfortunately including my son — all they had managed to do was roofie the boy. I simply found the obvious solution; finish the job and plant false evidence. We are all guilty in some way or another."

Leo stood stunned and motionless. Quinn stared at Emmeline with her mouth gaping open and placed a protective hand on Addi's forearm, pulling her closer, away from the murderer.

"False evidence?" Leo repeated.

"Ah. The meat mallet," Quinn pieced it together.

Addi recalled how it had been sitting there strangely out of place when she discovered it on the shelf in the kitchen. "Kyle smashed the ice with it that night. He was the last one to touch it."

Leo narrowed his eyes at his boss. "How did you manage to sneak into the kitchen without anyone seeing?"

Emmeline placed the glass, with its red-stained rim, next to the veil. Addi suddenly remembered the conversation she had had with Freddy in the very same courtyard when he had returned from the city with an identical red lipstick smudge on his jaw. At the time, she had assumed it had been from some random woman that he had hooked up with. "Freddy," she said quietly. "He knew you were back before anyone else did, didn't he? He helped cover up for you and plant the fake evidence so you wouldn't have to risk being seen here."

The dots were all connecting now. Addi wondered how she could have missed that before. Freddy had even instructed her and Kyle to go upstairs away from the kitchen mere minutes before she'd found the mallet. As Emmeline had just pointed out, she'd been too busy bickering with her co-worker to see what was going on right in front of her face.

Emmeline folded her arms and pursed her lips without responding to the question.

Addi took that as confirmation. "We can't let an innocent person get accused for something you and your son have done."

"You're barely more than a group of teenagers without any evidence," Emmeline hissed. "No one is going to believe you and you can't prove anything."

"Prove what now? What did you and young Frederick do, eh?"

Addi, Quinn and Leo all gave a small jump and turned around to see Ralph walking out of the kitchen with a full bag of rubbish in hand. Wrapped up in Emmeline's story in the dim light of the courtyard, Addi had almost forgotten they were still standing so close to the kitchen.

"She's gone," Quinn muttered in Addi's ear.

Addi turned back around to see an empty space in the shadows where the formidable woman had stood confessing, nothing left of her except the lipstick-stained champagne glass and the back gate hanging slightly open. The sound of Emmeline's engine started up somewhere in the back lane near the courtyard before morphing into a steadier rumble that faded down the road.

"You know, I think there's something seriously wrong with that woman," Ralph spoke into the night.

"Oh Ralph," Leo clapped the deranged chef on the arm as the three filed back into the House in defeat. "For once in your life you're talking sense."

Chapter Fourteen

"Two can keep a secret if one of them is dead." — The Pierces

Barman arrested for House of Nightshade murder

House of Nightshade Bar Supervisor Kyle Howell was arrested on Halloween night for the murder of fellow employee Grayson Reid.

Detectives thought they had the culprit when they arrested House of Nightshade's Head Chef, Ralph Payne, for questioning last week. While in custody, the chef gave detectives the biggest clue in the case yet — that he had seen Mr. Howell slip something into a bowl of soup which was given to Grayson Reid that night. The victim died a few hours later.

Police had also taken a kitchen utensil for testing that matched the description of the tool used to deliver the blow to the victim's head, found in the kitchen by a staff member. It returned fingerprints belonging to Kyle Howell.

"Kyle was in charge in the bar. None of us really spent time with him or knew him that well, he was always angry and very difficult to work with. I can see why it would be him who did it. I'm still shocked, though. I just never would have thought that I'd be working and living alongside a murderer one day," says Ivy Adams, Supervisor of Food and Beverage.

The unfortunate incident has indeed left the staff of House of Nightshade quite shaken, and all eyes will be on the venue over the coming weeks to watch how it recovers from this scandal. However, if the queues that have been reaching around the corner over the last few days are anything to go by, this murder case has made House of Nightshade as intriguing as ever.

Mr. Howell will face court later this month.

•

Just like every day began at House of Nightshade, they were gathered in their morning congregation around the breakfast table. The air was filled with the smell of coffee, toast and Quinn's cigarette.

Quinn fiddled with her hair, still puffed and wild from the night before. "Did he say when he'd be coming back?"

"Nope," Leo blew on his tea. "I imagine it would take a while, though. So many papers to sign."

"I wonder if they will investigate the Halloways?" Addi speculated aloud.

"We've made a statement. They have to investigate all claims," Leo reminded her.

Quinn chimed in. "Besides, Emmerson was out the door this morning following behind his wife before anyone even knew they were leaving. Running to the airport seems pretty suspicious to me, especially after what we've told them."

"The police have made the arrest. They might just see it as the murder being 'solved'," Leo made quotation marks in the air, "Emmeline and Emmerson simply heading back to their croissant-consuming life in France... or wherever the hell they're going."

"So you'll go and visit Kyle tomorrow, right, Addi?" Quinn asked.

Addi nodded. "Yep, and I'll remember to ask him who his lawyer is like we talked about. I'll tell him that he now has four witnesses."

"Four. Yeah, great," Quinn commented wryly. "It's a damn shame the only other witness outside of us who heard Emmeline confess is Screw Loose and he's certifiably lost the plot so much that not even the cops believe a word he says anymore. I don't know what's worse — that or the fact that by telling the same story people think we're just as nuts."

Leo sighed. "We have to do what we can for Kyle. If he gets a good lawyer, a discerning jury and there's reasonable doubt against the police's case he should be able to walk free."

Addi bit her lip and swirled her orange juice around inside the crystal tumbler. "That's still a lot riding on chance. Officer Knight didn't exactly look very confident in me when I told him that Emmeline had used a candlestick; there were about ten in that room alone, he probably thought I was making it up as I went along."

Leo patted her hand. "Careful, you're starting to slip into my level of daily pessimism. He'll be back in his position as Head Asshole before you've had a chance to breathe."

"Yeah, Leo's right. It'll just take some time," Quinn added. "Then the detectives will have to go on a wild goose chase around the world after the Halloways and rue the day they ever ignored you. Also, you did succeed in one thing."

"What's that?" Addi mumbled, pushing scrambled eggs around her plate with a fork.

Quinn gave a malicious grin as she blew out smoke. "You cleared your name here, even after *I* accused you. Do you know how much authority I have in this place? That's bloody impressive."

Addi couldn't help but laugh.

"That's an achievement you should frame and put up on your wall," Leo bumped Addi with his arm playfully. "Quinn sleeps next to you; she'll hate it."

Addi laughed out loud, instantly starting to feel better.

The doors to the performance hall opened, resounding through the quieter-than-normal breakfast.

"Oh look, Mr. Manager has returned," Leo announced.

He stood there surveying the throng in smart, pinstriped pants and a large, magenta velvet coat.

"Does that turn you on now that he's your boss and you're his employee?" Quinn snickered to Leo as Sawyer spotted them and shimmied over, a binder of papers tucked under his arm.

"Good morning common peoples," Sawyer greeted them. "How does it feel to *not* be in charge of your own business today? I just wouldn't know." He grinned as he perched himself on the table, his coat magnificently draping over the edge. At the table next to them, Logan and Danika stared blankly at the new magnificent manager.

"Congrats, Sawyer," Addi laughed. "You must feel pretty on top of the world right now."

"Darling, that doesn't even begin to explain it. You know how long I've been here?"

"Since dinosaurs roamed the earth?" Quinn offered.

"Feels like it," Sawyer nodded sagely. "Watching that waste of space Frederick do absolutely bugger-all with this place. The potential we have here! I can't wait to create some new shows and makeover this tired old room," Sawyer squealed in excitement.

Leo patted him on the leg.

"Have you heard anything from Freddy?" Quinn asked.

"Not a word," Sawyer responded. "The papers were slipped under my door while I slept with the note from Emmerson and Emmeline that Freddy was heading back to the Caribbean or wherever to find some other job. No goodbyes. Typical: he never did have a backbone. Oh, who cares? Good riddance, I say. We've been cleansed of the ghost of House of Nightshade and that's something to celebrate indeed."

"Amen," Quinn agreed.

Leo smirked. "Welcome to the Era of Sawyer. Dear Lord, save us all."

"Oh, Master, Master!" Ralph called, stepping out of the kitchen and rushing towards Sawyer, sarcastically stooping before him in a deep bow. "Welcome, my Lordship, what can I bring you for breakfast? The kitchen is at your service."

Sawyer played along. "At least someone knows how to treat me. Take note, you three."

"Ha!" Ralph gave his barking laugh. "Scurried out of here this morning, the whole lotta them, didn't they? Scurried away like the rats they are. Tell you how to do this job. I'll tell you how to do this job! You'll succeed here, mister, as long as no one dies on your watch. Ha!" Ralph cackled as he made his way to the breakfast table and filled a plate for himself as a loud knock on the door sounded.

"I've got my work cut out for me, haven't I?" Sawyer sighed, swinging his legs off the table and loping down the hall to answer the door. Addi was finishing munching down her breakfast as Sawyer returned to their table, none other than Office Knight following him.

"After last night, I hoped we could perhaps go at least a few days without your shadow on our doorstep again, officer," Sawyer said grimly. "Addi, I'm afraid he's here to see you."

Officer Knight acknowledged her, Leo and Quinn with a small upturn of the corners of his mouth. "I don't mean to be back so soon, but your former manager brought something to our attention last night. It seems Addilyn here is not yet a legal adult and has run away from foster care. Is that correct, miss?"

Addi's breakfast churned in her stomach. "I... well, yes," she gulped. "I'm almost eighteen though. My families didn't treat me well."

"Yeah, we can completely vouch for that," Quinn came to Addi's defence immediately.

"Yes, and isn't there leeway if they're over the age of sixteen?" Leo chimed in.

The detective cleared his throat. "There's also the issue of the, ah, chosen establishment you're working in, Addilyn. If we find that you've been serving alcohol as part of your job here that's a very serious breach—"

"She hasn't," came a quiet voice from the table next to them. "Addi has been working in the kitchen the entire time with us, actually. We can both be witnesses for that."

Addi, Quinn, Leo and Sawyer all whipped their heads around, shocked to hear the words coming from the two people in the House who spoke the least. Danika finished speaking with a supportive smile, which Addi returned with a rush of gratitude.

"It's not the fault of the employee — they're hired at the discretion of management," Sawyer pointed out. "If you're wanting to blame anyone it's the man who sent you here. Anyway, I regret to inform you that it's really a waste of time you're here, actually, officer, since I've already begun the process of becoming Addilyn's legal guardian for the next few months until she turns eighteen."

Addi gaped at Sawyer, quickly closing her mouth and trying not to look too surprised.

Sawyer gave Addi a sly grin and continued. "Yes, we're looking into the paperwork approval. Now, as I'm sure you can appreciate, officer, it's been a long night for all my staff here and I would request that you come back with something more tangible next time although, as I've just pointed out, I fear it's all a big waste of your time. I imagine there would be just as much paperwork on your end to complete to take Addilyn here away again than what we're currently completing to have her in my guardianship in the next few weeks at most. I believe you've got plenty of work to keep you busy down at the station after last night, am I correct?" Sawyer eyed Officer Knight with a raised eyebrow.

Addi bit her lip as the detective took in their small group.

Officer Knight sighed, apparently giving in for the day. "I'll be looking for updates on your progress with the courts."

"Of course you shall receive." Sawyer convivially began waving the detective away from the table and back towards the front door. "As always, it was a pleasure."

Leo lightly punched Addi's arm. "Looks like we're truly stuck with you now, then."

Addi let out a relieved giggle. "I can't believe that just happened."

"Does that mean you're like, Addi's stepdad now, Leo?" Quinn snorted. "We've said it before and I'll say it again; one big, messed-up family."

"Sawyer," Addi felt like crying as the new manager returned to their table, "I don't know what I would have done. I can't even begin to thank you enough…"

Sawyer winked. "I'll admit this has been quite the dramatic way to kickstart my role as manager here this morning, but you know I wouldn't have it any other way. We'll have quite a lot of work to do this week to get the process started but that should have bought us some time for now." He clapped his hands. "Right, you lot," he called to the room at large. "Finish up your breakfast quickly, it's time for a staff meeting. We've got lots to do and a few new ways we'll be doing things around here. All-staff meeting!"

At once, people began downing the rest of their drinks and scraping their chairs back to drop their plates in the container at the end of the food table.

"Hey, Addi." It was Summer, who looked as beautiful as ever with her hair in a thick plait to one side and crop-top showing her pierced navel.

"Hey," Addi spluttered, having just taken a sip of orange juice.

Summer giggled. "Sorry, didn't mean to make you choke. I just wanted to say, I heard about what really happened and how you told the police it was Emmeline. Even though they didn't believe you I think you were really brave to fight for the truth."

Addi blushed. "Oh, thanks so much, Summer. I didn't... I mean, I just did what anyone would do."

"Not everyone would have done that," Summer disputed. "Anyway, I'll see you around, I guess."

"Wait, Summer," Addi blurted.

The dancer stopped walking and turned around questioningly.

Addi took a breath in, summoning her courage — if she could confront Emmeline, she could do this. She remembered the afternoon in the park lying next to the beautiful exotic dancer in the grass, the sun shining on her caramel skin and the way she'd reached out lightly to touch Addi's hair. "I was wondering if you wanted to hang out later, just the two of us?"

Summer was contemplative for a few seconds, a smile playing on her lips. "As long as you promise not to run off on me again."

Addi grinned. "Never. I think I've got things a little more figured out now."

"You can come and find me after work, then." Summer gave her a dazzling smile before heading off.

Leo and Quinn grinned malevolently at each other.

"Oooh," Quinn sung, "Addi has a cruuush."

"Addi and Summer, sitting in a tree," Leo piled on.

Addi rolled her eyes. "Please not this again. Based on my last crush, they're a lot more trouble than they're worth."

Leo chuckled.

"You've actually picked a good one this time. I approve," Quinn countered. "You can tell she likes you back."

"Plus, she's very much alive and has even managed not to blackmail anyone so far. That's a big plus in your book, right?" Leo added facetiously.

Sawyer had assumed a power pose on stage. "Okay ragamuffins, listen up!" he called for the room to fall quiet.

As they listened to Sawyer rattle off the situation to the staff, Addi surveyed everyone perched on chairs or lying back on couches as another day of business at House of Nightshade began. She felt like it was her first day all over again, but as a completely different person.

"Performers, on stage. Chefs, back in the kitchen and get those ovens pumping," Sawyer wrapped up. "Waitstaff, let's start setting up. We've got a lot to do. Music, somebody!"

Everyone scrambled to their various stations and blaring jazz music started up.

"See you later, Addi," Leo farewelled her.

Quinn was already bugging Sawyer. "Like, the *very* back. Preferably I don't want Chorus Girl Fifty Eight in my line of vision at any point throughout the night."

Sawyer ran a hand through his grey hair. "How you age me, Quinn. Of course, let me adjust my entire choreography to accommodate your absurd desire. You're going to have to learn to make friends..."

Addi grinned, heading to the swinging doors of the kitchen.

As she gathered tablecloths and cutlery from the kitchen and began setting tables, watching Quinn and Leo rehearse on stage, she remembered something that Freddy had said to her after Ralph had been arrested. "You've got us all figured out, haven't you?"

She smiled to herself. For all his wrongdoings, maybe her manager had been a little right after all.

Acknowledgements

They say it takes a village, and it would be impossible to list all the friends and family who have given me so much encouragement over the years to write this book and get it out in the world.

Firstly, the largest thank you to my talented editor, Matt Campbell, who polished this book until it shined, responding to every query down to the frantic, last-minute "Help, does 'schnitzel-maker' have a hyphen?". Yes, yes it does. I couldn't have done this without you.

Special mention to Paddy for being the first to read the messiest version of this book about two years before it was majorly updated and still telling me it was good. You're nice, different, and unusual.

To my writing buddy and kindred spirit who also happens to be my cousin Jess, thank you for the countless hours of chats, writing sessions, brainstorming, plot ideas, soundtrack song suggestions, witty one-liners, chapter edits, and endless encouragement, motivation and inspiration (sorry, I just broke the thirty-word sentence rule, but perhaps you'll excuse me for this one). I'm not sure I would have believed in myself enough to publish a book had it not been for you believing in my dream ever since I was a kid. I love you so much.

Thank you to my family for always being there for me and providing such stability and care in my life. I love you all dearly. Lastly, a special thank you to my mum. Thank you for reading to us when we were kids and instilling a love of stories. Thank you for doing the final read of this book before publication, catching mistakes and providing exceptional suggestions. Thank you for all the love and support you've given me in my life. Words will never be enough.